In the Picture

WITHDRAWN FROM STOCK
DUBLIN CITY PUBLIC LIBRARIES

Brian O'Connor
In the Picture

POOLBEG

This novel is entirely a work of fiction. The names, characters and incidents portrayed in it are the work of the author's imagination. Any resemblance to actual persons, living or dead, events or localities is entirely coincidental.

Published 2013
by Poolbeg Press Ltd.
123 Grange Hill, Baldoyle,
Dublin 13, Ireland
Email: poolbeg@poolbeg.com

© Brian O'Connor 2013

The moral right of the author has been asserted.

1

Copyright for typesetting, layout, design, ebook
© Poolbeg Press Ltd.

A catalogue record for this book is available from the British Library.

ISBN 978-1-84223-540-9

All rights reserved. No part of this publication may be reproduced or transmitted in any form or by any means, electronic or mechanical, including photography, recording, or any information storage or retrieval system, without permission in writing from the publisher. The book is sold subject to the condition that it shall not, by way of trade or otherwise, be lent, resold or otherwise circulated without the publisher's prior consent in any form of binding or cover other than that in which it is published and without a similar condition, including this condition, being imposed on the subsequent purchaser.

Printed and bound by CPI Group (UK) Ltd, Croydon, CR0 4YY

www.poolbeg.com

About the author

Brian O'Connor is the award-winning racing correspondent of *The Irish Times*. He is author of the novels *Bloodline* and *Threaten to Win*, also published by Poolbeg, as well as a number of non-fiction books. He lives in Wicklow.

Acknowledgements

Thanks to everyone on the home front and everyone at Poolbeg, especially Gaye Shortland for, yet again, pulling things out of the fire.

For Peter, Johnny, Jessica – and their mum too.

Leabharlann na Cabraí
Cabra Library
Tel: 8691414

Chapter 1

He looked uncomfortable and out of place, like a snowman on a beach. A pinstripe suit was incongruous anyway in a racing stables. But this portly figure with his battered leather satchel and tightly fitting shirt didn't look like the usual wealthy city financial type taking a morning trip to Newmarket in order to vaguely examine horses galloping. They were normally expansive and loud, not pale with retreating hair, narrow mouth and a hawkish, pointed nose. I glanced at my watch. 9.05, it said. Business hours, I reckoned, had begun.

Apart from the visitor, it was a typical working morning. Freezing cold spread the condensation from the horses' breaths around the yard, mingling with the steam rising from their sweaty backs as we removed saddles and queued to use the water sprayers. The usual irreverent and profane chatter, mixed in with an odd laugh or oath as one of our charges refused to cooperate, hooves skittering noisily on the ancient cobblestones. I lightly held Rhinestone's reins, felt his hot breath just inches from my

Leabharlanna Poibli Chathair Bhaile Átha Cliath
Dublin City Public Libraries

face and waited my turn to wash down his mucky legs: a routine performed almost daily for nearly twenty years, as familiar to me as getting up or going to bed.

"Mr Delamere?"

I turned. The visitor was standing behind Rhinestone, watching me, but very aware of the half-tonne of animal at the same time.

"You might want to move out of his line of fire," I said, glancing at the horse's back legs. "He's usually quiet, but you never know."

The short, heavy figure skipped daintily forwards, looking more incongruous than ever in such an elemental environment.

"I'm looking for Mr Luke Delamere," he said.

"You've found him."

I picked up the sprayer, tightened my grip on the reins and started washing down Rhinestone's legs. The horse moved automatically away from the cold water, making the visitor step back again.

"Luke Delamere, the artist," he persisted.

I winced at that. It was a term I found difficult to use in terms of myself. Which was ridiculous: I was an artist, in that I made my living from painting. More than that, it made sense of me, gave me purpose, challenge, satisfaction. So it only meant everything. Yet the term could make me squirm. And not just because it carried the self-regarding connotations of a term used by every lip-synching adolescent with a microphone and a craving for attention: behind it also lay a fear of believing it and maybe playing up to the artist pose, and waking up one day to find whatever talent might have been there had vanished because of that. Not particularly neurotic by nature, there were still more than enough artistic insecurities floating around to keep me from taking anything for granted.

"According to some people, yeah," I replied. "But they're probably being kind."

"Mr Luke Delamere of Foxes' Den Cottage?"

My home was a small, ancient cottage only five miles from Newmarket but remotely rural enough to make the historic centre of Britain's horseracing industry seem like a heaving mass of humanity, which it was, in a way.

"That's right," I said.

"Mr Luke Delamere, originally from St Augustine's Road in Dublin?"

I looked up. He was reading from a small notebook. His voice was determinedly neutral. I turned off the water and handed it to the next rider.

"Okay, you've got my attention."

"Is there somewhere we can talk?"

"You can follow me to this fella's box," I said, nodding to the horse. "We shouldn't be disturbed there. By the way, you have the advantage on me."

"My name is Peter Miller, solicitor, acting on behalf of a client in Ireland."

I shrugged. Usually my agent handled clients. He was good at it, exuberant and chummy, but with a nose for a deal. He certainly would have been more comfortable than I was with Peter Miller who suspiciously picked his way through bits of muck, straw and discarded tack as I led Rhinestone into his box, removed the bridle and tied him up in order to deliver a brief brushing.

I didn't have to do it. I was, strictly speaking, a guest after all. John Greening, a veteran Newmarket trainer who'd seen hundreds of staff pass through the yard in the last four decades, was unusually hot on who did what. And guests who rode out a couple of lots every second morning for free shouldn't have to indulge in such drudgery. But I'd never minded grooming horses. During the years when I was on the shop-floor myself, it was one of the few occasions when one could be alone during a bustling, busy morning. So the habit became ingrained.

"I'm sorry to be so persistent with these questions but I need to make sure you are Luke Delamere," Peter Miller continued.

"I can show you my driving licence," I said, pulling a sharp comb through Rhinestone's tangled chestnut tail.

"That won't be necessary. You're thirty-five, right? August 5th birthday?"

"That's right."

"And you were born in the Coombe Hospital in Dublin."

"The 'be' is silent," I said. "But apparently I was."

He still looked uneasy, so I stopped for a moment and did pull my driving licence out of my wallet. He momentarily looked embarrassed but checked it anyway.

"Sorry, but I have to be precise. This is a matter of some delicacy."

"Okay, who's your client?"

"Your mother."

That really did get my attention. I left Rhinestone to munch at some hay and motioned to Peter Miller to step outside. The door latches slid easily home and I folded the bridle over my arm.

"I'm afraid you really do have the wrong guy, Mr Miller. My mother died over twenty years ago."

"No, Mr Delamere. I'm talking about your birth mother."

Chapter 2

I knew I was adopted. Once it had been a big part of my life. But not any more: not for ages. There were people for whom the compulsion to find out about their biological parents was overwhelming. I wasn't one of them. There had been vague ideas once about tracking my birth parents if I ever had kids of my own, purely to find out anything genetically important that might be passed down through me. But the situation had never arisen. Girlfriends had come and gone: some serious, a couple more serious than others, yet never serious enough to make me think I was losing out by not committing to them. Single and childless, I was perfectly content to let bygones be bygones. Time wasn't meant to be turned back. Maybe that betrayed a lack of imagination on my part, or empathy, but I'd worked in racing for long enough to know that only rarely did breeding beat feeding.

Nevertheless, I couldn't have told anyone much about the short drive home after leaving Greening's. It was a good job the route had become almost automatic, leaving me to thoughts of Peter Miller and family and ignorance. All in all, not very cheerful.

Before knowing it, my cottage was in front of me. Almost 250 years old, it was really more of a small house with two floors and a stone front covered with ivy that was a nuisance to control but contributed to the warm character of the place. Years before, I'd cycled past purely by chance and fallen in love with it. Not that buying it had ever seemed realistic. But then success of a kind had come my way. And with a few quid to spend there was only one place I wanted to spend it on. Especially when I found out about the outside barn.

I walked through the house, out the back door towards what could be described as my studio. That made it sound fancier than it was. The old barn was gutted in a weekend frenzy and painted up but, apart from a few basics, it still offered the same thing it had to the farmers before me – space.

The smell of paint, white spirit, turpentine, welcomed me through the door. It was familiar and comforting, just like saddle leather and horse: one conveying the elemental, the other something more cerebral but no less real. I'd wondered before about what such different passions said about me, whether some weird yin-yang conflict existed between the physical and the creative. Better not to analyse it too much, I'd concluded. Delusions of a complicated character would be of no use in either field.

Even as a kid, I'd drawn and sketched. It always felt a natural thing to do. Even when everything was turning on its head, picking up pencils felt like a sanctuary, a place where everything could fluctuate and change too, but within a framework. There was a control there that was so desperately lacking everywhere else. And within the frame anything could happen if I wanted it to.

I wished something would happen now. A week of work was stalled. The large abstract canvas in front of me refused to give any clue about how to finish it. There were painters who believed in continuing to throw paint until something happened. I wasn't one of them. Painful experience had resulted in the idea of sudden inspiration being filed under wishful thinking. Sometimes there were tantalising moments that seemed to come from nowhere but waiting for them could mean waiting forever.

Jeremy Barnett called my style retro-chic. A decade after first meeting my agent I still wasn't sure what he meant. Somewhere in there, I suspected, was a hint of an insult but labels didn't interest me. There was good stuff and stuff that wasn't so good, and then there was stuff that was plain bad. If that sounded simplistic, then ten years as a professional painter made me even more fundamentalist: I did what I did because I liked it. The most remarkable bit was that others liked it too.

Thanks to Jeremy coming into a tiny Cambridge gallery ten years previously, demanding to meet the painter of a Norfolk fells landscape, and becoming an agent, champion and good friend, my life had changed beyond recognition. What had seemed like an impossible dream, one too ludicrous even to contemplate, suddenly became real: painting for a living, some public recognition and appreciation of what had been an intensely private and personal process, some success, some money, the satisfaction of meeting an all-consuming challenge that provided both personal and professional fulfilment.

Even the frustration of staring at a half-finished canvas couldn't prevent me from feeling grateful: back on my own patch, dealing with the tangible. And yet Peter Miller wouldn't go away. We'd spoken for only five minutes, in my car.

"Mr Delamere, I realise this is a bolt from the blue, and possibly upsetting, but I would appreciate it if you would listen to me."

"Go ahead."

"First of all, are you interested in meeting your birth mother?"

"Who is she?"

"I would prefer if you answered my question first."

"I don't know," I said. And I didn't.

"I have been instructed that I can tell you who my client – your birth mother – is. She is anxious to make contact with you."

"I'm not really anxious to make contact with her."

"That's your prerogative."

"Yes, it is."

"So, I can tell my client that you don't wish to have contact with her?"

"Yes."

He shifted uncomfortably in the seat. I suspected he was almost as uncomfortable with this situation as me. In front of us, third lot started to stream out of the yard. I rode the first two normally and then left for home, content at keeping reasonably fit and happy to keep my hand in with the big bold creatures who had dominated my life for so long. They were straightforward, most of them anyway, and I was confident in my ability to handle them; not like this.

"If you change your mind, you can contact me here," he said, handing me a business card.

"You probably think I'm being stupid, or cowardly," I said, "but this is something I've never considered. It plays no role in my life. I've no interest in digging up stuff that's irrelevant to me. You can tell this woman I bear her no grudge or resentment, if that's what's worrying her. Everything has worked out fine."

"I will pass that on," he replied. "Still, if you change your mind, you can get me on the mobile at any time."

We shook hands and that was that: except it wasn't. Working through the rest of the morning, Peter Miller and his news wouldn't stop dominating my thoughts. So much so that soon after noon, realising I was getting nowhere work-wise, I stopped completely and went back into the house for lunch. By some fortuitous telecommunications freak, my mobile phone didn't get a signal in the studio. Probably something to do with the acres of tall sycamore trees just behind it. But just yards away the phone worked perfectly well.

It beeped into life, telling me there was a message. Rooting out bread and cheese, and boiling a kettle for coffee, I listened to Jeremy Barnett's plummy tones.

"Trust you to find the one black spot in the whole of that flat desert up there," he said indulgently. Jerry lived in London and reckoned anything north of Stansted was a wasteland. "Anyway, I've got some good news for you, me broth of a boy. You're going home. Ring me back when you can."

I finished preparing my roll, took a sip of strong coffee and rang back. As usual, Jeremy answered on the first ring. Behind the offhand, rather fey exterior he presented to the world, he was a deadly serious businessman who liked to do things properly in order to make a profit. The fact he knew more about art than anyone I knew, and managed to combine that love with an ability to make money, was a rare combination I never ceased to be grateful for.

"How is Ireland's greatest living artist today?" he cooed.

"How is England's greatest wind-up artist?" I replied.

"Passable. But better since the Ormond gallery in Dublin's Fair City contacted me this morning confirming they want to put on an exhibition of your work, starting in three weeks' time."

"Well done! You're a genius," I laughed.

Even I, who knew next to nothing about galleries and the artistic establishment generally, had heard of the Ormond. Plenty well-known and established painters would cut throats to be exhibited there. I told Jeremy he was a genius – again.

"I realise most of your compatriots haven't a pot to piss in, but there must be some wealth left in that benighted isle of yours," Jeremy said. "Just tell me you have thirty-five paintings ready to go over there in a hurry."

"I reckon I can manage that, if I crack on."

"Of course it means you'll have to leave that cave and spend a few weeks in Ireland," he continued. "All that Guinness and blarney, you lucky dog."

Jeremy adopted a begorrah attitude to many things Irish, but always with affection. With a few drinks on board he was fond of recalling an adolescent crush while on holidays in Donegal – "a pale Adonis with a voice like molten gold".

In the Picture

My champion's efforts on my behalf never had any sexual motivations. Apparently he knew from the off that I was pathetically heterosexual. And so we quickly settled into an affectionately bickering and teasing relationship that I valued for itself, completely separate from business.

"By the way, that obscenity Wilkinson says he'd like to have lunch with you next time you're in London. That's okay, isn't it?" he asked.

"Damn right it's okay," I said.

James Wilkinson was a perfectly ordinary-looking man whose only known obscenity was a vast wealth that left him comfortably in the billionaire class. Jeremy treated the absurdly rich as potential targets and regarded them mostly as tasteless. I'd always found Wilkinson to be perfectly decent company, a view not completely unrelated to the fact that his purchasing power had contributed almost half my income for the previous few years. If he wanted lunch on top of the Matterhorn, it was time to start climbing. I hadn't met a serious painter yet who dismissed money as somehow artistically unworthy. That was a pose only amateurs could afford.

Jeremy called me a prole and hung up. But he would be pleased that an important client was being kept onside. And how much of a chore would it be, having a gorgeous meal at a top London restaurant? Things could indeed be a lot worse.

I finished my own much more basic lunch, checked some e-mails and returned to the task of making a maritime canvas look less self-consciously existential and more alive. It was embarrassing trying to explain how I knew when something worked. Out loud, the explanation either sounded deadly dull or incredibly fanciful. But a picture had to move in my eye. There had to be a fluidity that stepped it up from mere representation.

Jeremy reckoned it was my brush strokes. Every painter was distinguishable from the simple application of paint. Mine, apparently, were broad and delicate at the same time. I never knew if Jeremy was taking the mickey when coming out with stuff like that. To my ear it sounded bogus, but then, as my agent always said, I was only the paint-pony. No one expected me to know what I was doing.

It certainly felt like I didn't know anything about how to move this latest canvas. I always hated giving up on one, especially after spending a week on it. But bitter experience suggested this sort of block usually resolved itself into something not very good. Devoting more time to it would be throwing good money after bad. I put it in a corner devoted to the spirit-breakers and went for a walk.

The only sounds as I struck out through the trees came from pigeons and a fox shrieking in the distance. The landscape was unremarkable: flat, green and absolutely gorgeous. I never tired of it. There might not have been a spectacular mountain or roaring cliff for a hundred miles but I always looked around and thought of an iceberg: so much unseen under the surface.

Damn Peter Miller and his damn client – my mother supposedly, except she wasn't. My mother was Helen Delamere, dark-haired and vulnerable with the most wonderful green eyes that lit up with uncomplicated joy. She was the woman who made me, protected me, never doubted me, never made me feel less. Mum said I was special because she'd chosen me. And she was the woman who got cancer when I was twelve and died, shrivelled and terrified, a year later.

It would be much better if Peter Miller had stayed away. But he hadn't and this question had to be answered. Did I want to meet this woman? Did I need to? The answer to both was no. But after getting home an hour later, I took a deep breath and rang.

Chapter 3

She carried herself with a presence that far exceeded her height – no more than five-foot-four, a full half-foot shorter than mine. But she towered over me in a way that had nothing to do with bare physical size. There was a brief dispassionate moment where the habits of a lifetime took over, boiling her face down to dimensions, lines and proportions. I could have sketched that thin face that once had been beautiful very easily, full lips determinedly pointing downward, neck held up more than could be comfortable. But the eyes would be a challenge. Bright blue, watchful and defiant: a striking woman of about sixty, this Mrs Dorothy Maxwell-Williams – my mother.

"Hello," I said, standing up, and extending my hand.

I'd sat in the Dublin hotel lobby for half an hour beforehand wondering what to do, whether or not to kiss this stranger on the cheek, or embrace her, or do nothing at all. But she took my hand, shook it firmly and immediately sat down opposite.

"Would you like some tea or coffee?" I asked. "Maybe we could go somewhere quieter?"

Quite a lot of people were milling around, checking in – checking out, completely oblivious to the uncomfortable little drama being played out in front of them.

"No, here will be fine," she said in an expensively crisp Anglo-Irish accent. "You're thin."

There didn't seem much to say to that. I was thin, always had been.

"You too," I replied.

"You're a painter, I see. Are you any good?"

"I make a living."

"Rubbish. I've seen you in articles," she said. "False modesty is such a prissy virtue, I think."

There didn't seem much to say about that either. She had a tiny light mole underneath her right eye. I had the same thing underneath my left. She looked just like me around the eyes. I watched her intently, trying to find other bits that looked like me. We didn't speak for almost a minute.

"You don't say much, do you?" she said eventually.

"You're the one that wanted to meet," I replied.

"Yes. I suppose you would like to know why I gave you up?"

Suddenly I very much didn't want to know at all, didn't want to be in this situation. Too much time had passed and too much had happened. It all felt wrong. Whatever scenarios I'd played out in my head hadn't been like this. Everything felt awkward.

"Well, it's very simple really," she continued. "I got pregnant by a person who was completely unsuitable. It was a long time ago when standards were different.

16

Marriage was unthinkable. It would have been a disaster anyway. So I went away to have you."

She spoke straightforwardly, without any emotion. I knew the rest. Taken home at a couple of weeks, becoming a Delamere, growing up in Dublin, leaving, making my own way.

"Did you ever think of me?" I asked.

It sounded much too raw for these circumstances. She barely moved, stayed sitting rigidly upright in her chair, didn't flinch for a moment.

"Of course I did. But it didn't do to dwell on it. You were being looked after by a family that could look after you. And me introducing myself into that environment would have been simply upsetting for all concerned. I got on with my life. You got on with yours."

That was true. Everyone had gone on with it. But how much of that was due to the lack of an alternative? I wondered how the sixteen-year-old me would have reacted to this woman: probably not very well. The sixteen-year-old me, however, had other more pressing priorities at the time.

After Mum's death, the tensions that lay bubbling underneath the surface exploded. I had been a last resort for my parents. Years of trying to have kids had resulted in nothing but heartbreak. So they adopted. And five years later, by some miracle, Mum got pregnant with twins and even more miraculously carried them to full term.

Ben and Alex were gorgeous kids and everything was fine at first. But the biological difference between the twins and me steadily became more of an issue for our dad. Never the most demonstrative of men, he gradually became more and more distant with me. There were arguments overheard between my parents where the word *blood* kept being shouted by him. When Mum died, resentments that had been simmering tumbled out. I was different. Even the twins began to change. The grief of coping with Mum's death meant Dad clung to them even more.

It all came to a head one fateful night when I came home late from a disco. I wasn't even drunk. He was waiting in the kitchen, accusing me of defying him. My usual instinct to keep quiet deserted me and I shouted back. He hit me with real venom, the fist smashing into my cheek. But most of all I remembered him standing over me, screaming: "I can't raise someone else's fucking kid!"

I left a week later. The brother of a friend of mine was living in London and I got the ferry and the train to stay with him. Then came the tricky job of trying to make my way and survive. There were always jobs on the building sites but I was very short and light at the time so lifting bags of cement was a tough way to make a living. And then one of the lads on the sites told me I was wasting my time with a jackhammer when I was the right size to be a jockey.

I'd always loved watching the races on telly. That was unusual for a city kid. None of my pals knew or cared anything about it. But something about the animals and the colourful riders on top looked so exciting. It all seemed impossibly glamorous. Riding my bike home from school turned into an imaginary Derby, bumping over the speed-humps my Grand National.

So, sick of cement, I got a train to Newmarket and turned up out of the blue at the gates of a yard on the Bury

Road. By some fluke the trainer was leaving in his Mercedes, wound down his window and listened to a pretty lame pitch from the Irish kid. Miraculously, though, he bought it, told me to start work the following day and promised he'd teach me how to ride.

It was tough, hard work and there were bumps and grazes galore. But I loved it. Not once did the idea of riding a racehorse ever seem less than the most exciting thing to do in the world. And it wasn't difficult. So much so that after a year, apprentice forms were put in front of me and I got the chance to actually become a jockey. Over the next five years, I rode forty-two winners – never going to be a star but a good, competent rider. The only problem was a growth spurt that sent my weight rocketing. Even purging the body to exhaustion couldn't stop it. Eventually I gave into to the inevitable, stopped race-riding and faced a real world as a mature and considerably worldy-wise adult.

"You live near Newmarket, I believe," she said.

"Yes. Ever been there?"

"Just the once was enough. I prefer to sell my horses here in Ireland."

"You sell horses?"

"Yes. I breed National Hunt types. For the jumps. Have done for years."

"I used to be a jockey."

"Really? Well, that explains why you live in Newmarket," she said. "I suppose you didn't lick it off the road."

I grinned. A waiter stopped by us, wondering if we wanted to order tea or coffee. She shook her head.

"I suppose the other question you want to ask is why

I wanted to get in touch with you now."

I nodded.

"It's very simple. A few months ago I was informed I have colon cancer. It has concentrated my mind."

I nodded again and wondered what on earth to say.

"They've done some exploratory work and decided it's no dead cert that I'm for the high jump yet. In fact they seem to be quite positive. Apparently they've caught it early. But nevertheless one has to try and anticipate every eventuality."

"I'm sorry." Christ, it sounded lame. "But if they're giving you an upside, I'd cling to it."

She smiled at that. It transformed her face, opened it up, showing perfect white teeth and provoking some generous laughter lines around those eyes. I wondered how beautiful she must have been when a young woman.

"It's okay. I don't need a pep-talk," she said. "But it's kind of you."

There wasn't anything else I could think of to say.

"I wanted us to meet because there will be no point talking about it afterwards. I know you're doing well, making a success of your life. But I wanted to allow you the opportunity to know me, to speak to me, to tell me I'm the greatest cunt that's ever lived. Whatever. You deserve that. Have you questions you want answered?"

I thought about my old idle thoughts about genetics and diseases and almost blushed at the smugness of them. There was so much I wanted to ask this woman, but faced with this torrent of information nothing immediately came to mind. I paused for a few seconds.

"Who was my father?"

"His name was Hughes. Much older than me, an

auctioneer of all things, married. I knew, but he told me he loved me and that nothing else mattered. Silly of me. He died nearly twenty years ago. Nobody misses him very much."

"Did he have children of his own?"

"No, actually, he didn't. I believe his wife was as fertile as sand."

"Do you have other children?"

"I have two daughters, Alicia and Elizabeth. Married, both with children of their own. They're on holidays right now, actually. Somewhere on the continent."

There was another pause. Suddenly I wished the waiter would come back and provide some interruption, allow me gather my thoughts. Typically, there was never one around when you wanted one.

"Well, I expect you want to be getting on with things," she said, standing up, and extending her hand.

I stood and we clasped hands briefly. It seemed very formal, something I guessed she wanted.

"If you'd like to keep in touch, this is my card," she then said.

Surprised, I took it. *Mrs Dorothy Maxwell-Williams, Ardfield House, County Meath.*

"Are you going home, right now?" I asked.

"Yes. A friend drove me into town today. I have to ring her in five minutes and establish where she can pick me up."

"I could drive you – if you want."

She looked intently at me. I could feel my feet shuffling under the ferocity of that gaze.

"All right, that's kind of you," she said. "Give me a moment and I'll make my call."

* * *

The city-centre traffic was heavy but once in the suburbs we got a trouble-free run. Dorothy made small-talk with an expertise that helped dilute the awkwardness. But there was some substance too.

"Does your family know about me?" I asked.

"My husband does. My children don't," she said simply.

A few minutes later she continued.

"My husband's name is Michael. He's the money. His family owned vast chunks of Meath and north County Dublin over a century ago. It's not like that now. But we've still got a good few acres. Handy for me with my horses," she joked. "He's a good man, Michael. He took a chance marrying me. His family disapproved. I was a wanton woman after all. But he didn't care. He said he loved me and meant it. All told we've been happy."

There was another silence after that. But it wasn't particularly uncomfortable.

"Actually, Michael will quite enjoy meeting you. That is, if you want to?"

"It won't freak him out or anything?"

"No. He's a good man," she said. "He's an art trader of all things. Have you heard of him?"

"I'm afraid not. I don't know many people in the actual business. It's not my strong point."

"Not Michael's either, if truth be told. But he loves it. I've seen him cry in front of pictures. He actually admires some of your work very much indeed."

"He must have taste then," I smiled.

"Huh!" she said. "It makes a nonsense of the genetic argument though, doesn't it? You and Michael are the arty types, not me."

"Yes, but I rode horses too."

"There's an each-way bet," she said.

Granite walls tapered away from massive wrought-iron gates that towered over my car when we arrived. Dorothy produced keys and beeped the gates open. The tarmac avenue cut through paddocks where a number of horses grazed, barely raising their heads to look at us over railings that could have done with a coat of paint. I drove for almost half a mile before rounding a copse of trees. Ardfield House suddenly loomed in front of us, a huge grey three-storey pile surrounded by hedges and with the moss of ages speckled on the slate roof.

"Impressive," I said, thinking of my own little cottage at home.

"Not really – it's draughty, impractical and costs a fortune to heat," Dorothy replied.

We got out and walked towards the front door.

"Are you sure about this?" I said, stopping. "Isn't this opening a can of worms you could do without right now?"

"Nonsense," she said as she opened the door. "Michael will want to meet you. And stop with that invalid tone. I'm a long way from any kind of bed yet, never mind a box."

I grinned as I stepped inside. I was still grinning when the steel pipe slammed into my ribs. There was just a blur of form and movement out of the corner of my eye. And then pain. The cold hard black-and-white hall tiles shot up to meet me. Another blow came down on my back.

Then came what felt like a boot to the side of the head. Dorothy screamed. I tried to get up and got another boot to the head. Then, as quickly as it happened, they were gone, silently, through the front door.

It would have been lovely to just lie there, let the body try to cope in its own time. I took a deep breath and wished I hadn't. I'd broken ribs before in a fall from a horse. This didn't feel quite as bad as that, but not by much. And then I heard Dorothy again, except this time it wasn't a scream. Instead an almost primal moan came from the room to my left, much more chilling than mere terror. This was despair. It really was time to move.

Debris was scattered all over a vast drawing room. Trashed didn't do justice to the scene. That implied carelessness. But this was thorough and systematic. Nothing was left intact. Every piece of furniture was upturned and torn. Nothing still hung on the walls. Instead broken glass lay all over the floor. Mirrors and paintings were thrown around, many separated from their frames.

And in a corner, Dorothy knelt next to a body.

It was obvious he was dead. A pool of stomach-churning dark blood oozed from a skull that had been smashed, lifeless eyes stared unseeingly at the ceiling. Dorothy moaned again, her body convulsing in the agony of grief.

"Oh, Michael, what have they done to you?"

She held on to his hands in a fruitless attempt to will her own life-force into him, tears flowing down that tough, uncompromising face. I put my hands on her shoulders and kept them there, trying to will some of my own diminished strength into her. It was all I could do not to vomit. Death had always been just a concept, not a foul physical reality like this, all blood, gore and the foul stench of a man terrified out of his mind.

"Come on, Dorothy, come with me," I said, pulling slightly on her shoulders. "We have to call the police."

"No! He needs me. Please, Michael, wake up. Come back!"

"He's dead, Dorothy. He's dead."

She fought me, kicking and punching as I lifted her up and away. She was as light as a feather and the punches didn't hurt. But bending and lifting didn't do much for the rest of me. Eventually she stopped and pressed against my chest, sobbing uncontrollably. I guided her into a room across the hall. That was torn apart as well. We found a seat and Dorothy all but collapsed into it. I held her hand while dialling the police.

"Hello," I said, in a voice I didn't recognise as my own. "There's been a break-in, and a murder."

It sounded so wrong even saying it. But hearing it seemed to pierce through Dorothy's grief. She straightened her back slightly, keeping her hand in mine.

"It's his birthday next week," she said.

Present tense, I thought; grief only beginning to take its hold. I hadn't known him, barely knew her. There was no grief, just raw anger.

Chapter 4

I stood outside, watching the process of disaster taking its course. A pair of police cars had their blue lights flashing through the evening gloom, combining with an ambulance to give a surreal azure atmosphere. Unmarked police cars helped fill up the space in front of the house. Forensics officers in their bulky white suits billowed past me, apparently indifferent to the civilian presence.

"Who are you?" a voice called. "What are you doing here?"

A new figure emerged from a car and walked purposefully towards me. He was big, a light suit only barely seeming to contain his bulk.

"My name is Luke Delamere. Mrs Maxwell-Williams is my . . ." I hesitated.

"Is your what?"

"She's my mother."

"Oh, I'm sorry. But you can't stand there. This is a crime scene."

"That's okay. It's been explained to me. We were the

ones that found the body."

"Really? Wait for me a moment."

He went to another detective who I'd spoken to earlier. The pair spent a couple of minutes in deep conversation. Then he came back.

"I'm sorry about all this," he said. "Pat just filled me in on you and Mrs Maxwell-Williams."

"I'm hardly a good-luck charm, it seems."

"I don't know about that. From what I'm told, it's very lucky you were here," he said.

It was kind of him. I was grateful. There had been an absence of such kindness up to then. The police that first arrived on the scene had been polite and efficient but clearly felt their job was to get on top of a crime scene rather than provide any kind of comfort and reassurance. That was understandable enough when dealing with a murder but Dorothy seemed to become an inconvenience, another problem, one that could be parked outside in my car while the first tests were carried out.

After a couple of hours we were allowed into the kitchen which hadn't been trashed. It was a rarity. Many of the rooms on the first two floors had been torn apart. I made tea, a couple of detectives took initial statements and a police doctor offered tranquilisers to the slight woman sitting in a chair staring into an unimaginable horror.

"No," she said, shaking her head to the pills. "I have calls to make. I have to tell Alicia and Elizabeth their father is . . . They're in Italy."

One of the detectives looked at me.

"It would be better if one of you guys made those calls," I said. "They don't know me."

Dorothy recited the phone numbers and he jotted them down and went off to make the sort of call no one should have to make or receive.

The doctor then got to work on me. I took my shirt off and he poked and prodded my ribs. It wasn't fun, but not as bad as before.

"If you feel them getting worse, go to the A&E. But I suspect it's just heavy bruising," he concluded. "And your face will be fine, once the cuts and scratches heal up."

Then we were alone. I rooted out a bottle of brandy from a cupboard and poured it into our tea. Dorothy drank automatically, hardly noticing. We sat in silence with the paraphernalia of an all-too-real nightmare accumulated around us.

Helen Beasley arrived after a couple of hours. She didn't look much like a cliché housekeeper, being tall and beanpole thin. But she was someone reassuringly familiar for Dorothy.

"Oh, ma'am, I'm so sorry," she said, hugging the stricken figure in the chair.

Dorothy patted her arm and agreed to try some soup.

"Mrs Beasley, this is Luke," she said, simply. "My son."

We shook hands, incomprehension on the woman's face, mixed in with shock and concern for her employer. They started talking about Michael, the man they both knew. It felt wrong to sit listening to such painful personal memories of someone unknown to me.

I stood in the hall, out of the way of the constant stream of police moving in and out, and trying not to look into the room where the body still lay. Flashes from camera shots lit up the doorway. Maybe it was weak, even a betrayal of sorts, but I didn't want to look in there again. The only picture I had of the man was of him lying in a pool of blood with his head smashed in. And I hadn't known him. God alone knew what Dorothy was feeling.

The wide staircase stopped before splitting, with the two legs turning 180 degrees on their way to the next floor. Old teak finishes dominated, all of it grand yet comparatively understated. A massive crystal chandelier hung overhead. I couldn't help noticing cobwebs. A photo in a frame had been knocked off one of the tables close to me but remained intact. It was a black-and-white picture of Michael and Dorothy on their wedding day. She looked stunning, he understandably proud and happy. He towered over his new wife, big and broad with an uncomplicated smile, their lives ahead of them.

"Mr Delamere."

It was the big detective again.

"I don't believe I introduced myself. I'm Detective Inspector Mark Foley."

We shook hands.

"I've looked at your statement. But I like to hear things for myself. You didn't see anything about these men that might be useful?"

"Absolutely nothing, except they were wearing black. Even that was just a split-second impression. I'm sorry."

"There's no evidence of a break-in at all. You didn't see any strange vehicles?"

"No, I didn't see anything. I've never been here before."

"There's a lot of damage, but we don't know if anything has been taken. Do you think Mrs Maxwell-Williams will be able to look around and tell us if anything is missing? Nothing too detailed, just anything obvious."

"I'll ask her, but she's very upset."

"I realise that, but we have to try and establish what they've taken."

"Maybe we came in just as they were about to get to work on that," I said.

"Maybe," he said, not sounding convinced.

We stepped further to the side as some ambulance personnel entered the house, followed by a man they clearly deferred to.

"State pathologist," Mark Foley said.

An unremarkable-looking man with a moustache scuttled past us, nodding briefly at Foley.

"There's something you're not telling me, right?" I said.

He looked at me.

"How much did you see? Of the body, I mean," he asked.

"Enough," I said, the memory still making my stomach churn. "All I wanted was to get Dorothy out of there as quickly as possible."

"So you didn't examine it."

"All I could do to look, to be honest," I said.

"Can you take me through what happened between you and Mrs Maxwell-Williams today?"

"We met for the first time, in Dublin. She's my birth-mother. She wanted to meet me because she's not in the best of health right now."

"Did you plan to drive her home?"

"No. I just offered."

"Right."

"You're on the wrong track here," I said.

"What do you mean?"

"Sometimes coincidences really are coincidences."

"Not in my line of work. What's yours?"

"I paint."

"Pictures?"

"Yeah."

"The deceased was in the art business."

"Apparently so."

We stood in silence for a minute.

"What aren't you telling me?" I asked again.

Foley didn't say anything for a moment, then glanced sideways at me, his mind apparently made up.

"His fingers were broken, all of them. Smashed."

"Jesus Christ."

"And one of his kneecaps is in smithereens," he continued.

What a god-awful way to die, I thought. What a god-awful way for Dorothy to remember the man she'd spent her life with.

"Did you get a smell in there?" Foley asked

"I figured he shat himself," I said. Somehow the words seemed desperately inappropriate, blasphemous almost, in the circumstances.

"He did," the big detective said. "But did you get anything else?"

"Not really, except . . ."

"What?"

"No, it's ridiculous. I just felt there was a smell of bacon in there too."

He nodded. "You're right. Except it isn't bacon. All over his arms, even on his face, are singe marks."

"What do you mean?"

"He was burned – tortured."

Chapter 5

Dorothy reckoned nothing significant was missing, but plenty was broken. We tried to unobtrusively go round the house, picking our way through glass and police personnel still trying to unravel any forensic details that might have been left behind.

My instinct was there was unlikely to be much. There had been a ruthless efficiency to the way they'd attacked that ruled out any idea it was some random burglary by local yobs looking for a few quid. Local yobs weren't famous for torturing their victims either, or for smashing their heads in.

Apparently there was a panic button to the side of the fireplace in the drawing room, near to where the body lay. Foley didn't say it, but the impression he gave was that Michael had been trying to reach the button, an attempt that led to the torture becoming fatal.

"You live in England, don't you?" Foley had asked.

"Yes. But I'm in Dublin for a while. There's an exhibition I'm involved in."

"Good. I would like you to be available, just in case I need to ask you anything, or run something by you."

"Sure."

"What are you and your mother going to do tonight?" he asked. "I don't think it's a good idea for her to stay here."

Mrs Beasley offered to have Dorothy stay with her but the offer was gently but firmly declined. The tall woman seemed almost relieved. It was interesting to watch. There was so much mixed up in their relationship: class, accent, status. And both knew it. Yet Mrs Beasley was the one who'd come to help, and who helped her boss pack a few things in a holdall and give her a brief peck on the cheek. My enquiry about if there was any family Dorothy would like to stay with or contact was met with a slight shake of the head. She didn't want fuss.

I booked a couple of rooms in a nearby hotel. We drove there in silence, through the front gates where I noticed a couple of television cameras were pointed at the car. That would be something else to cope with. The media interest in a "Big House" kind of story like this would be significant, another good reason to get Dorothy away.

We checked in and I helped her to her room. There were still sandwiches and coffee available on room service and almost because of a need to be doing something, I ordered some.

"I'm going to take a quick shower," she announced after we had sat silently for a while.

"Right, I'll leave you to it then," I said, getting up to leave.

"There's no rush. You can stay – if you want."

As she said it, the waiter knocked on the door with a tray of food.

"You eat," Dorothy said. "I couldn't."

"You should try."

"Yes, I probably should," she said, and closed the bathroom door behind her.

My stomach was growling. Guiltily, I started eating. It was coming up to news time on the television and I turned it on, pressing the mute button as soon as the picture came up. Within a minute, a shot of the front gates of Ardfield House and a police car going in, appeared. I turned the volume up to listen to a short report about how a sixty-five-year-old man, identified locally as Michael Maxwell-Williams, had been found dead, apparently after a break-in. Tests were being carried out but the reporter quoted sources as saying the investigation was likely to be treated as murder.

It wasn't a break-in, I thought. Foley said there was no sign of a forced entry. Had Michael let them in, I wondered. Had he known them? Who could an Anglo-Irish toff know that would be capable of caving his head in? It was ridiculous.

Dorothy emerged in a dressing-gown, looking desperately fragile. I considered getting up and giving her a hug, and then cursed myself for not just doing it, for being so calculating. But I didn't know what the response would be. I didn't know this woman. What I did suspect was that any attempt to breach that stern face she presented to the world might be met with disapproval. She had enough on her hands without having to deal with such stuff.

I also suspected that sternness was only part of the

picture. There had been glimpses of a lighter side before we'd arrived in Ardfield, before her life was turned on its head. If she chose to present an aloof face to the world, then that didn't mean it was the sum of this woman. Everyone chooses a side of themselves for the world to see. It didn't mean it was the only one.

"I'm very tired," she announced.

"Of course," I replied.

She got into bed and turned off the bedside lamp. A slight glare from the street lamp outside managed to get through the curtain, allowing me to navigate my way to a cupboard. I pulled out a blanket, wound it around my shoulders and sat back in the chair. I couldn't see Dorothy but she was awake.

Chapter 6

The burly figure got straight to the point.

"Who the hell are you?" he demanded.

Dorothy and I were in the kitchen at Ardfield, staying out of the way as much as possible as the police forensic teams started to wind up their work. She dismissed any suggestion of leaving Ardfield: it would feel like desertion, she said. Michael's body had been removed during the night. At least Dorothy was spared seeing that. She just looked numb, pretending to drink coffee and staring into her memories. When her daughters and their husbands arrived, the silence was shattered.

They rushed to embrace her, clinging to the frail figure, her daughters crying in terrible grief for their dead father, all of them sharing the pain.

"I said, who are you?" he asked again.

"I'll leave Dorothy to explain," I said, starting to leave.

"Luke, please stay," the older woman said.

It was disconcerting having these four people staring warily at me.

"Luke, this is my daughter Alicia, and her husband, George Huxley."

Alicia took after her father, I noticed. Much taller than Dorothy, long greying hair resolutely left undyed, bright brown eyes, long face with a nose just too big for beauty. That would dominate any picture of her I would draw. There was little or nothing I could see of myself in her. Her husband towered over us all. Once strong, now running to fat, there was a bristling aggression to his jawline and the start of a receding hairline. He looked desperate to take command. Neither tried to shake hands or make any sort of greeting.

"And this is Elizabeth, and her husband, Myles Denning."

Elizabeth was only slightly taller than her mother. She was in her late twenties, I reckoned, a couple of years younger than her sister. Oval face, shortish brown hair, big eyes, thin also, but with stocky legs. Myles Denning was thin, average height, average weight, glasses, a good bit older than his wife, unremarkable in appearance.

"Girls, this is Luke Delamere. He is your brother."

There was silent incredulity at this new piece of information. Alicia muttered "What?" a couple of times. The others just stared. I guessed they were doing the same thing as me, trying to find resemblances, a genetic quirk to recognise. It seemed doubtful to my eye that they'd find one. We were different.

"I don't understand," George finally exclaimed.

"I knew there was something you never told us!" Alicia exploded. "What have you done, mother?"

It was time to get out. I nodded vaguely at everyone and slipped out, hearing voices rising higher with every step taken. I quickened my pace, heading towards the back of the house.

Eventually a door led outside. A small garden badly in need of some work stretched towards a big dark hedge that enclosed the green area on three sides. A path continued by the house to the left – I followed it and emerged into a square stable-yard. There were eighteen boxes, I reckoned, not all of them full. Two horses stuck their heads out to examine the new arrival. The smell of straw, muck and horse was thankfully familiar and mundane.

"Are you a guard?"

My new interrogator didn't have a fraction of George Huxley's aggression. A short, stocky man of about sixty-five, there was a smile on his round face and a spring in his step despite a slight limp.

"No. I'm Luke Delamere. I'm Dorothy's –"

"Oh, you're Mrs Maxwell-Williams' son. Helen told me about you."

"Helen?"

"Helen Beasley."

"Right, the housekeeper. She was very kind last night."

"Aye, she's good in a crisis," he said, holding out his hand to shake. "I'm Barry Lynch. I look after the horses here."

He had a northern accent, not the harsh Belfast one but more gentle, rounded, country. A wrinkled, weather-beaten face spoke of a lifetime working outdoors and he had the big, rough hands of someone not unused to hard labour.

"How many have you in?" I asked.

"A dozen," he replied. "A couple of two-year-olds, five

three-year-olds, a couple of cripples out of training and three four-year-olds we're supposed to be getting ready to put in training."

"Supposed?"

"Everything's in a bit of a tizzy here. Has been for a while. My days of riding are over, I'm afraid," he said, slapping his leg. "Arthritis is a bugger."

"I can imagine."

"Anyway, we used to have a couple of lads who used to come in and ride a few out. But they've stopped. Now I just lunge them and put them on the horse-walker every day."

"Why did they stop?"

"Why do you think?" he said, rubbing his finger together in the universal sign for money.

"Terrible about Michael," I said.

"Aye. A nice man. Some of those guards were asking if I knew anyone who might have something against him but I can't imagine that at all. It was hard to dislike him. Very easygoing, he was. It was all you could do sometimes to talk to him. He always looked like his head was in the clouds with those paintings, always in that office of his."

"Where's that?"

"In the basement. He had it converted years ago. You wouldn't see him for days sometimes he spent so much time down there."

"And Mrs Maxwell-Williams?"

"Ah, she lives out here. Always with the horses. She's bred some good ones, you know."

He listed off some famous National Hunt names that even a confirmed ex-flat jockey like me had heard of.

"Nothing is too much trouble for her when it comes to

the horses," Barry continued. "She even mucks out."

I grinned and asked if he wanted a hand.

"Can you muck out?" he asked. "I haven't the time to be going back over something if it isn't done properly."

"Let's see, shall we?"

I found a fork, encouraged the first occupant to move over into a corner and got stuck into the well-worn routine, moving the dry straw to the walls and shovelling out the wet stuff. Barry peered in after a few minutes, said nothing and went back to his own box. Exam passed, I reckoned. It felt good to do something straightforwardly physical although reminders of the circumstances were always there. The police were still clearly visible, mostly at the front. There were various checkpoints, one at the gates and another a hundred yards in front of the house. Not that they seemed to be particularly effective.

"You guys work here, then?" I heard a voice say outside.

A young man in jeans and a long leather jacket was leaning on a stable door talking to Barry.

"What was Mr Maxwell-Williams like to work for then?" he asked.

Barry glanced over the door at me, clearly uncertain about what to say or do. I walked over.

"Who are you then?" I asked.

"Terry," he replied.

"Okay, Terry. And what's your function around here?"

"What do you mean function?"

"What do you do?"

"I'm just trying to get the lie of the land," he said.

"Which paper do you work for?" I asked.

"*The Globe*," he grinned. "Bringing truth to Ireland."

I knew that the *Globe* specialised in bringing tits and scandal to Ireland, usually in as sensationalist a manner as possible. It hadn't occurred to me how good a story the death of a wealthy, posh landowner might be to the tabloids.

"How did you get past the guards?"

"There's no getting past for the *Globe*. We're the Gardaí's partner in tracking down scrotes and scoundrels." He smiled again. "And every local inspector knows it pays to keep in with the press. Good for promotion prospects, don't you know?."

"No, I don't know. But I do know that if you don't get back past that police cordon right now, I'll make whatever brass is out there jump through a hoop to get you thrown out."

"Don't be like that, man. All I want is to aid the investigation by getting information out there. Maybe even tell the family's story, sympathetically you understand."

"I understand all right. Get going."

He looked at me, shrugged and marched out of the yard, towards the side of the house. I followed just to make sure. A guard spotted him, then me, and made great play of getting Terry back to the other side of a cordon. Terry just shrugged again, clearly used to this being part of his strange job.

The mucking out took the best part of another hour. At the end my clothes didn't smell particularly fresh but the work had cleared my head. Barry gave me a lead rope and we took half a dozen of the horses out to the horse-walker, allowing them trudge around in circles to work off any freshness from being cooped up. It didn't seem to be much of an issue. They were all sound and fed, but hardly bursting with vigour, even the three four-year-olds who should have been full of the joys.

"That one, the bay with the big white nose: that's a racehorse," Barry said.

I looked at him. Tall, angular, a shell of a horse really. There was little sign of the sleek quality that characterised some of the top flat horses I'd been on. In comparison, this was an awkward, adolescent elk.

"See that knob of bone sticking out of his head, right between the eyes. That's always a sign of a good one. Never fails," Barry concluded.

"Been in the game a long time, have you?"

"Left school at fifteen. Dreamt of being a jockey. Never even got a ride. Spent a long time on the Curragh but Mrs Maxwell-Williams brought me here after I looked after one of the horses she had in training. She's been very good to me the last fifteen years. I'm very sad for her."

I nodded.

"So where did you learn about horses?" he asked.

"What makes you think I know horses?"

"Because I know horses, and I know people who can work with them. Your mother is one – you're another."

"I tried to be a jockey too, in England," I explained. "Rode a few winners but got too heavy."

It sounded so straightforward said like that: just got heavy. That hardly did justice to the pain of the daily struggle with trying to keep weight off an infuriatingly lengthening body. There were times it felt like my mind was going to bend with the strain of it. Even years later, at five-foot-ten and a comfortable eleven stone, the name Orpington could still make me queasy.

He had been a horse I'd ridden regularly at home, a slowly maturing stayer who suddenly got the hang of racing and looked thrown into the Cesarewitch off just over eight stone, a rating not reflecting his ability. The trainer had hinted he would run Orpington in the big marathon handicap and use my apprentice's claim off him. It would mean having to do 7.12. and I'd been struggling to make 8.7. But for a big race like the Cesarewitch I would try anything. And I did.

For a fortnight, I sweated, ran, hardly drank, munched on nothing more than vitamins and visited dark mental recesses I had no wish to go near ever again. But eight stone was reached just a couple of days before the race, when the trainer decided not to run. The taste of despair had been dreadful. Even a weekend spent gorging on every kind of food and drink couldn't get rid of it. Right there and then, I knew race-riding was not going to be for me. A lack of real substantive talent was enough of a problem anyway. Being the wrong shape just put a clincher on it.

"You might be able to give some of these a spin then. You look fit enough," Barry said.

There was a plea in his voice.

"I don't know what's happening yet. I mightn't even be here," I told him.

"Stick around for your mother," he said.

Even after the lengthy breathing space, voices were still being raised in the kitchen as I walked back through the door.

"But you can't *afford* not to!" Alicia shouted, overpowering everyone else.

Everyone turned to look at me.

"If you don't mind," big George said severely. "This is for family."

Dorothy looked at me, didn't say anything but there was enough in her expression to make me stay. Difficult to read she might have been but there was a desperation there that contained more than a little pleading.

"I'm simply making some tea," I said. "Anyone care to join me?"

"Get out!" Alicia shouted. "You don't belong here!"

"Alicia, please!" Elizabeth's voice was high and tremulous but her sister stopped shouting. Her husband didn't.

"Please leave here, or I'll make you leave!" George shouted, suddenly approaching menacingly.

I didn't budge, simply stepped aside and made for the kettle. He grabbed my shirt collar and the power of his grip dragged me backwards. But no one survived in a racing yard without learning a trick or two on how to handle himself. I swivelled, dropped to one knee and drove my shoulder into his plump belly. The wind gushed out of him like a pump and I pushed him back against the wall.

"Now is not the time for these kinds of dramatics," I told him quietly. "Your wife has lost her father."

His face reddened. Breathing heavily, the impulse to lash out was still intact. I hoped he wouldn't. My repertoire of defensive moves didn't extend much beyond what I'd just done. Thankfully he straightened, tried to regain his dignity and went to his wife. She didn't exactly rush to comfort him. Instead there was a slight curl of the lip I'd already seen in her mother. George looked at me. I would have to watch out for him. I'd hurt his pride. That mattered to the boorish and the bullying.

"Can we not try and get along, at least until we've buried Michael?" Myles said. His voice was surprisingly deep.

"Exactly," his wife agreed, casting me a quick look full of distrust. "Daddy would hate to see this."

A wary ceasefire continued for the rest of the day. I tried to stay out of the way, mostly in the yard, finding a grim and dusty tack room and filling time giving the equipment a much-needed polish. The family stayed inside, managing the details of death. An officer arrived around midday and delivered the coroner's report. Michael's death had been violent. The case was officially murder. His body was released for burial. In the afternoon, Mrs Beasley emerged in the yard with sandwiches for Barry and a message for me.

"Ma'am would like you to come in for tea," she said.

It sounded desperately archaic to my common ear but I was thirsty and hungry. Inside there were more sandwiches on the table but no relatives, just Dorothy.

"I'm sorry about earlier," she said.

"That's okay. The whole thing caught them on the hop. And everyone is distraught anyway. They don't need me complicating things further."

"I'm grateful for you staying. I suppose you'll want to get back to Dublin and your exhibition?"

Jerry had been on the phone a couple of times already wondering if I might indeed possibly get my arse back to where it was supposed to be. I hadn't explained where I was and why. It was too complicated. Better really to step back into the world of paint and galleries and buyers: much more reassuringly straightforward.

"I'm going to have to head back at some stage, even just to get changed," I said.

She nodded. This woman I barely knew looked desperately vulnerable despite the increasing re-emergence of that haughty tilt to her chin. Much of it I guessed was a determined effort to not let the side down. But if it helped, so much the better. The last thing Dorothy Maxwell-Williams would ever want anyone to feel towards her was pity.

"Actually one thing I hate is hotels," I continued. "I don't suppose there's any chance of a room here? I could commute in and out of town pretty easily."

She glanced sharply at me. I tried to keep my face as neutral as possible.

"That could be acceptable," she eventually said. "I'll tell Mrs Beasley to get a room ready."

Chapter 7

Jeremy Barnett glanced around the pristine white walls and down at the expensive wooden floor.

"You know, this is quite impressive," he said.

"What did you expect?" I grinned. "A shed?"

"Now, now, let's keep that Irish chippiness under control, shall we?" he sighed. "I'm simply saying this is a very nice place."

And the Ormond Gallery was very nice: down a narrow alley in the city centre and into a huge two-storey converted factory with light pouring in through a vast glass ceiling.

"I bet it makes a helluva racket when it rains," I said, looking up.

"God, you're so dreadfully practical."

Jerry was shorter than me, thinner than a whip and presented a sardonic face to the world that seemed only to encourage people into his orbit. A man of enthusiasms, nothing stirred him more than art. He'd once told me the saddest day of his life was when he concluded he had all the taste in the world, but no talent. I'd seen a few things he'd done and genuinely told him he was being too hard on himself.

"Don't be kind. It's childish, derivative rubbish," he'd snapped.

Instead he poured his passion into the business, cutting deals, spotting talent, and all the time providing endless encouragement. In such a solitary pursuit he was a real support.

"Right, let's decide where what goes where," he decided, snapping open his thick folder which provided some reassuringly old-fashioned snapshots of my pictures.

Their dimensions were as familiar to me as my own hand but Jerry had them scrawled in the margins. We spent an hour quibbling amicably about where to put them on the walls. Jerry usually got his way for the very good reason that he knew more about such stuff. I'd decided long ago to trust his judgement on most things, and it hadn't backfired yet.

"Oh, I've got a surprise for you," he piped up. "There's a journalist coming to interview you."

"When?"

"About fifteen minutes' time."

I grimaced. He knew me too well. Interviews were not my cup of tea. As a rule I tried to avoid them. They were necessary sometimes in terms of promotion and letting the public know about exhibitions. Bad experiences were rare, with reporters usually just keen to get enough copy to fill their hole in the page. Other painters I knew were expert at working the media to their advantage but the whole exercise seemed uneasily artificial, usually boiling down to two people pretending to like each other.

"So, too late to try and get out of it then," I said.

"I know my boy," Jerry grinned. "Besides, you might enjoy this one."

"I doubt it."

The café around the corner was tiny with just enough room for four tables, and a couple of more outside for those willing to brave the cool weather. The waiter brought me a coffee and I waited.

Michael's funeral was the following day. I wouldn't be going. It seemed a pointless provocation of Dorothy's children. The man was just a horrible memory to me. I would stay back, mind the fort, as I'd told Dorothy who'd simply nodded. She'd again apologised for the scene in the kitchen, said Alicia wasn't normally like that, but was under a lot of pressure. She said nothing about George.

I'd learned from Mrs Beasley and Barry that George Huxley was a businessman, although neither was sure precisely what kind of business he was involved in. The couple had one child who barely said anything, which made a contrast to his father who hardly shut up. George had made a lot of money during the boom years and loved to show off the proceeds of that with a massive house in one of Dublin's most exclusive addresses and a new luxury car every year.

The Dennings lived further down the country, I was told. His family owned land. Mrs Beasley said it in a way that didn't make one imagine Myles and Elizabeth on a tractor. It was more estate than farm. Kind of like Ardfield, I'd said, and Mrs Beasley suddenly found something important to find in the kitchen cupboards.

"Hello, are you Luke Delamere?"

I looked up at a tall figure with short dark hair and a

wide perfect smile, who was quite possibly the most beautiful woman I'd ever seen. I was aware of just staring, mouth open, and not saying or doing anything. It required a conscious effort to speak.

"Yes, that's me," I said, my voice sounding like it belonged to someone else. "Are you the journalist?"

"That's me," she said. "The journalist."

"Sorry," I said. "I didn't mean that. It's just I was miles away."

"No problem," she said, holding her hand out. "I'm Julia O'Neill."

"Can I get you anything? Coffee, tea?"

"No. I'm fine. I won't take up any more of your time than is necessary."

"No, it's okay."

"Why has it taken you so long to come to Dublin with your work?" she asked immediately, taking out a notebook and pen, and then switching her phone to audio-record.

I very much wanted to talk about something bar myself. It sounded a desperately dull subject when we could have talked about anything – like her, for instance. But she didn't look the type of woman to be charmed. Instead there was a businesslike speed to the way in which she pitched questions and scrawled little notes, every so often checking to make sure the recorder was doing its job. It was immediately obvious she knew her stuff.

"Are you an arts reporter?" I asked.

"No. I do news. This is for a column I do once a week."

"Do you paint?"

"Used to," she said, smiling slightly. "I found it hard to eat on the proceeds."

"I know how that feels."

"Oh, come on. You're doing really well."

"Yeah, but that's luck: right place, right time, right agent."

"Jeremy Barnett?"

"He's my luck."

"Can I quote you?"

"Sure, it's the truth."

She switched off the recorder, said there was enough there for a piece and started packing up. I scrambled for something to say to stop her from leaving.

"I don't suppose you knew Michael Maxwell-Williams?"

She stopped. "Awful thing to happen to anyone," she said. "Yes, I knew him. It's a small circle, the art world here in Dublin. You're always bumping into the same people. Did you know him?"

"No. But I know some of his family," I said truthfully. "What sort of man was he?"

She looked momentarily uncomfortable and straightened in her seat.

"That depends, I guess, on who you talk to," she said. "There were plenty who thought he was a great guy. But then you'd hear other things."

"Such as?"

"No. I don't know you, and it's not nice to be talking negatively about someone who isn't around to defend himself."

"Please. I'd like to know."

She looked at me intently. It was unnerving to feel the full gaze of those green eyes. Mind you, I really needed to stop staring back.

"There was never anything definite, just rumours. But there were suggestions out there that he'd sold on forged work really quickly to generate funds. Apparently his business was not going well. But when are things rosy in this business? And it's not like he was depending on it for a living."

"He had another income?"

"Well, that pad of his out in Meath has been in his family for a long time," she said. "You don't keep a pad like that going without plenty disposable cash."

"I guess not," I said. "Are you going to come to the exhibition when it opens?"

"I don't know. Am I invited?" she asked, a smile playing on her lips.

She knew all right. How couldn't she? Nearly thirty years of age, I reckoned – a woman who looked like that could hardly be unaware of the effect she provoked in men. I felt myself blush. This was ridiculous.

"Yes, you're invited," I said, standing up.

We walked outside and stood briefly.

"I'm going this way," I said, pointing left.

"It's the other way for me," she replied. "See you. And thanks."

"Don't mention it."

If my backside was in front of me, I'd have kicked it. I wasn't normally that awkward with a woman. There were no illusions about being some slick Lothario but neither was I normally some shrinking violet reduced to stammering idiocy by a nice smile. There was nothing, I guessed, but to shrug and put it down to experience.

"How'd it go?" Jerry asked when I got back. "Is she really a cracker?"

"She is that."

"I told you this one might be different. Did you click?"

"I think it's safe to say no."

"Really? Immune to that Irish charm. Who'd have thought?"

"Not you obviously."

Still, it was interesting what she'd said about Michael.

Chapter 8

Ardfield was so large and warren-like I spent an hour discovering new hallways and rooms. Everybody had left for the funeral. The place was deserted. A number of doors were open and some quick peeps had revealed spacious, high-ceilinged rooms containing valuable old furniture and an all-encompassing sense of time.

A vast upstairs drawing room was dominated by an enormous fireplace over which a portrait of an early-nineteenth-century nobleman peered down. I absentmindedly noted the unsubtle brush strokes and dubious perspective but closely examined the gilt-edged frame that looked at least as old as the painting. There was an ornate quality to it that trumped anything in the actual painting.

There wasn't anything to identify the subject, probably some long-forgotten forefather of Michael's I reckoned: a Maxwell-Williams. What would happen to the name now? Two daughters married and no son. It felt archaic to think in such terms and yet, in a family like this, such considerations would count. Probably any family. The male ego was the same no matter what the financial or historical circumstances.

I kept walking, back downstairs and down a dark hallway heading towards the back of the house. At the end was a white, thick double-glazed door whose modernity clashed with the timber atmosphere all around the rest of the house. It was locked and there was a keypad to the side. It needed a code to open. I was walking back, wondering what might need to be protected like that, when the guy turned the corner.

He was about ten metres away, tall, young, with thick stubble and a sense of bewilderment on his face that must have resembled my own. We stood, staring at each other, for what felt like forever.

Then he shouted. "Someone here!"

It took me a second to engage gear from incredulity that this was happening again, and starting to chase after him. He moved fast, towards the front door, where another figure was bolting through into the open air. I sprinted after them, not really knowing what I was going to do. A blue car was waiting a hundred yards from the house, just out of view from anyone coming down the drive. There was another man behind the wheel.

The other running figure suddenly stopped. He pulled a gun out of his jacket. It didn't seem real, this black, snub-nosed thing so familiar from TV and yet so incongruous here in reality. The man pointed his weapon and I skidded to a halt on the stones.

"Don't be a bollocks," he said, almost softly. "Fuck off back into the house."

The gun didn't waver even a fraction. Even in the

moment I thanked God he appeared to be so in control. If a frightened kid trying to prove himself the hard man was in possession of that thing, I would probably be already fighting for my life. As it was I stretched my arms out wide, transfixed by the gun, barely registering the owner bar a general impression of red hair, fair skin and freckles.

"Go on, fuck off back, and you'll be all right," he said in an accent I recognised as working-class Dublin. "And don't even think of following us."

He retreated slowly, the gun never wavering, a little grin on his face, assured in his superiority, enjoying being in charge. He climbed in and the car shot away in a blizzard of stones and dust. A pebble shot up and hit me under the eye, making me spin around in pain and anger and humiliation. The overwhelming relief at not having had a bullet put in me faded quicker than I could ever have imagined. Without even making a conscious decision to do so, I found myself behind the wheel of my car and accelerating hard off the stones and onto the smooth tarmac of the drive down to the gates.

It was a flip of the coin which way they had turned onto the road. I went right, guessing they would be heading back to Dublin. The car leapt forward and I rooted in my pocket for the phone. Trying to dial while accelerating past 100mph around a tight bend on a small country road was not an easy or advisable thing to do. The car wobbled precariously and I snatched the wheel with both hands to regain control, dropping the phone onto the floor.

I was still blindly fumbling for it with one hand, and steering with the other, when the blue car came into view as I peered over the steering wheel. Instead of hanging back and following at a distance, adrenalin got the better of sense. Closing right up, it was possible to see the first figure I'd seen in the house glance around and take in what was happening behind. They spurted away.

"I need the guards!" I shouted into the phone. "I'm chasing three men who broke into the house."

"Are you driving now?" droned a monotone voice on the other end.

"Yes, towards Dublin. We'll be hitting the motorway in a few minutes."

"Slow down and stop chasing," the voice said, tone unwavering.

"What?"

"You are a danger to yourself and others," he said. "Give me any details you have."

I babbled something about a blue car, and three men, and Ardfield House, and why was I dealing with stupid questions when these bastards were getting away?

They were too. The motorway was too obvious. Instead the driver shot right onto another small side-road and began pulling away. He knew this area, I didn't, and he hadn't a voice in his ear telling him to slow down and pull over. A few seconds later and there wasn't any choice about it.

A squad car came up behind me, lights flashing but siren silent. Instinctively I slowed down, then quickened again, thinking I could lead them up to the proper criminals. That's when the siren came on. There was nothing left but to stop.

"They're getting away!" I shouted, climbing out of the car and pointing into the distance.

The two officers got out, one carrying a baton, the

other telling me to stay calm.

"But they're getting away," I fumed.

"Put your arms on the bonnet, and shut up!" one of the police shouted.

That's when I informed them in rather industrial language of my opinion of them, and when they arrested me and took me in.

Chapter 9

"I take it you don't think much of the police, then?"

Mark Foley sauntered into the interview room with a smile on his face. I said nothing.

"Apparently only those devoid of ambition and talent, and too fond of dressing up in uniforms, join the Garda Síochána," he continued.

"All I'm saying is that instead of picking up people who're trying to do the right thing, you might consider chasing those who're actually breaking into people's houses."

I'd been in the station for five hours. The fight was gone out of me, all the indignation and frustration too.

"I'm sorry if I was abusive to your colleagues," I said.

"That's okay," Foley replied. "They tell me they aren't usually shouted at so colourfully."

"Happy to amuse them."

"Right," he continued. "I've gone to Ardfield and had a look. There's no evidence of a break-in. It might have been a bunch of gutties chancing their arm. They probably knew Mr Maxwell-Williams' funeral was today. It happens quite a lot. Opportunist stuff."

"Maybe," I said. "But they didn't seem like that."

"Meaning?"

"They knew what they were doing. When that guy pulled the gun, it looked the most natural thing in the world for him to do. His hand didn't even shake. And he was . . ."

"What?"

"He was way too confident to be some gouger chancing his arm," I said. "And even when they ran, there was no panic about it. They really seemed to know what they were about."

"You'd be surprised how sophisticated some of these house-breakers can be," Foley said. "It's like a career-choice for some of them. But I take your point. And the gun is unusual for lads just breaking and entering. The description details you've given aren't much. Is there anything else you can think of?"

"Not really. Red hair. All I really saw was the gun."

"Yes."

"Do you think they were the ones who killed Michael?"

"Who knows," Foley said. "We're continuing our investigation. It's hard to believe in coincidence but at the same time there's no reason to suggest they are definitely connected. Anyway you can go now."

"Right."

On the drive back, Jerry rang. He was back in London.

"Expected an update from you. What's happening over there?"

Without meaning to, I found myself telling him about

everything. He listened without interrupting, and at the end didn't say anything for quite a while, which for Jerry was quite an accomplishment.

"Do you want my advice?"

"Always."

"Get out of there, Luke. You don't need that kind of aggravation."

"I don't know . . ."

"Well, I do," he interrupted. "Look, I don't envy you. You've been presented with something that will make you feel shitty whatever you do. But for your own sake, you need to take several steps back. You're a grown man. You don't need this woman now. And when you did, she didn't want to know."

"That's a bit harsh. She felt she was doing the right thing – for everyone."

"Forgive me, Luke, but that sounds more than a little self-serving. As your friend, I'd hate to see you get screwed around here," he said. "And as your agent, I need your mind on what's making me cash. So can we focus on your exhibition, please, and smooching a lot of people who have lots of money?"

I pondered what he said on the drive back to Ardfield. He was right, obviously. What influence had Dorothy ever had over me? Apart from blood there was no connection whatsoever. If she hadn't made contact, each of us would have carried on with our lives, me oblivious to her presence, she continuing to ignore mine. Making something out of this made no sense logically and every instinct told me that only problems lay in wait if I didn't do what Jerry advised and retreat from this emotional vortex in a hurry.

A number of cars were outside the front door. I recognised the Mercedes that Alicia had practically pushed her mother into that morning, turning around to stare at Elizabeth in the process. There were others now, the close family members and friends gathering around to console one another. It felt wrong to intrude on that, automatically drawing attention to myself. I parked the car and quietly walked around the house towards the stables.

The half-doors were all closed, keeping the chill night air out from the horses. It was easy to unclip the top-halves and peer in. Warmth from the animals, with their rugs on their backs, gushed out. A couple were lying down, asleep, others standing, dozing. One of the four-year-olds in the corner box came over to investigate the unexpected visitor. He was bay with mostly black points, and a white nose that gave him a somewhat goofy appearance – the one Barry reckoned was a racehorse. Whatever about that he was certainly curious, sticking his head out into the cold air and nosing around my pockets in a way that suggested favouritism from Barry.

I wished I had something to give him but there was nothing except a pat on the neck. That earned a snort of disdain and a retreat back into his box. Leaning on the door I examined the big figure tearing uninterestedly at a twist of hay and wondered if he'd mind a boarder for the night. The straw was deep enough and there were spare rugs in the tack room. But it had been a hell of a day and going into the maelstrom of family emotions nearby seemed the appropriate way to wrap it up. The horse came back for one last attempt at getting something out of this strange human and I patted him on the nose. Then I closed up the door again.

There were about twenty people milling around the main drawing-room, the one where Michael had been killed. A large number of them were gathered around George who laughed loudly at one point, seemingly oblivious to the sombre atmosphere. Dorothy was out of sight somewhere.

"Thank you for today."

Elizabeth Denning stood beside me, looking over at the others. Her voice was sad and quiet.

"I'm sorry if you were upset when we first met," she continued. "Everyone was feeling very vulnerable. And Mum never mentioned anything about you. It caught us off guard. I know Mum would have liked you there today. And you probably should have been. But thank you."

Quite a brave speech in the circumstances, I thought. She was an unremarkable-looking young woman really, except for those big eyes that looked even more mournful now. Her husband I noticed standing in a corner on his own, nursing a drink, removed from the centre of attention.

"Do you have kids?" I asked her.

"Yes, a boy and a girl. Dennis and Ellen. They're staying with Myles' parents. They liked their grandad. It would have upset them to see him like that. Better to keep him alive and well in their memories. Was it awful when you found him?"

There was nothing to be gained from telling her the truth, like how I kept seeing all that blood in my dreams, and kept smelling that stench of burning flesh. What it must be like for Dorothy, God alone knew.

"It wasn't nice," I said. "But the policeman investigating the case says it was over pretty quickly."

That wasn't much, and she looked like she knew I was lying, but she nodded. We didn't say anything for a minute.

"What a welcome for you to the family," she said eventually, attempting to enliven the mood. "It must be terrible. But thank God you were with Mum when it happened. For that alone, I'm glad you're here."

It wouldn't take much to like this woman. There was a toughness there underneath the apparent meekness that contrasted with her sister's brasher personality.

Alicia was talking intently with a man in another corner of the room. He looked like he was telling her something she didn't want to hear.

"Mum, can I get you something to drink?" Elizabeth asked, turning around.

Dorothy looked desperately fragile. Even that usual defiance looked to have drained out of her, making her look much older.

"Yes, Mum, can we get you anything?" Alicia added, striding over, pointedly ignoring me and putting her arm around her mother.

"I'll have a gin, please, and not too much tonic this time," Dorothy said.

Despite everything, she looked uneasy at being coddled. Alicia practically steered her towards a drinks cabinet. Elizabeth followed, clearly used to playing second fiddle.

A number of people I'd never seen before were going to great efforts not to appear as though they were staring at the interloper. None approached, and I was in no hurry to talk to anyone.

"Luke," Dorothy called. "I'd like to introduce you to

Harry Cross. He's the family solicitor and an old family friend."

I shook hands with a thin man, about Dorothy's age, with the tired, calculating eyes of someone rarely surprised any more.

"So, you met Peter Miller then?" he said, a smile playing on his lips. "He made great play of how hard he'd worked tracking you down."

"It can hardly have been that hard," I said.

"Of course it wasn't. But he's hardly going to say it was money for old rope, now is he?"

"I guess not," I smiled.

"I'm glad you decided to meet your mother," he said, glancing at Dorothy. "She's a tough old bird, but underneath that hard exterior beats the heart of a rock."

"Oh, shush, you dreadful man!" Dorothy said.

Suddenly, George and Alicia materialised next to us.

"Alicia tells me you have some documents involving Michael's will, Harry," George announced. "Any sneak previews?"

"I hardly think this is the time or the place," Cross said.

"Okay, when would be a time and a place?" the big man smiled, although there was an edge to his voice that no one missed.

Cross looked uncomfortable. Everyone else suddenly found something interesting to look at on their shoes. George's embarrassment-quotient was all but non-existent. Dorothy broke the silence.

"There's no point putting it off longer than is necessary," she said. "Harry, can we go to your office tomorrow and we can thrash out whatever paperwork needs to be sorted? Then everybody can go home, and get back to normality."

"Of course," he said. "I'll be there at noon."

"Good. Now, if everyone would excuse me, I'm going to get ready for bed," Dorothy said.

The gathering quickly dissolved, leaving just the Huxleys and the Dennings, as well as myself. The prospect of a horse-rug, and some soft straw suddenly became even more enticing. George stared, malevolence oozing out of him, but guarded since our encounter in the kitchen. He was unlikely to get physical again here. His wife though looked like she wanted to throttle the life out of me.

"What are you still doing here?" she asked, her expensive voice echoing around the room.

"Your mum asked me to stay."

"Exactly, my mother," she said. "Her family are here now. We can look after her."

I said nothing, just stood by the fireplace, forcing myself to hold Alicia's hostile gaze. There had been enough bullies down through the years. All they needed was the merest sign of uncertainty and they pounced. Attack was usually the best form of defence. There was no way of physically going for this woman. But there was no way she was going to intimidate me either. At least I hoped not.

"Do you think it's going to be worth your while hanging around?" she continued. "Is that it? Can you smell some easy money?"

I noticed Elizabeth moving closer to her husband, clearly uncomfortable with this scene, but not jumping in to prevent it escalating either. George said nothing, but stood next to his wife in a way that made me suspect they had planned for such a scene if I showed my face again. The pair of them stood in front of me. It made me think back to just a few hours earlier when that gun was pointed at me. I almost felt nostalgia for the self-control that guy so obviously had. There might be no weapons here but it felt a lot more volatile.

"I can tell you now," Alicia said, "that you will not influence our mother against us. There is no way you will get your claws on anything that's ours."

A senior jockey I'd ridden alongside years before had advised me the best thing to do when being abused by a trainer or owner was to say nothing. Just keep your face as neutral as possible, he'd said. It had proved valuable advice through the years, and not just with owners and trainers.

Alicia moved without any warning. She strode quickly up to me and slapped my face hard. I would have loved not to move but the force of it, and the fact it was a surprise, made me step back, hand automatically touching my cheek. This was ridiculous.

Her lips quivered with temper as she stood in front of me, vehemence and anger pouring out of her. I chanced a quick glance behind at her husband who grinned nastily. Elizabeth and Myles looked shocked and embarrassed.

"Go away!" Alicia screamed. "You're not wanted!"

Jerry was right. Nothing was worth this. Whatever Dorothy and I had going on had become an irrelevance the moment Michael was killed. Now it was a side issue that threatened to dissolve her real family. Logic said it was best to get out. To hell with logic.

"Your mother had the right idea," I said quietly. "I'm going to bed. See you all tomorrow."

Chapter 10

There was a moment when I forgot where I was. My large creaky bed might have been anywhere. And then reality reasserted itself: Ardfield, families, murder. A noise had woken me up. Not the usual assortment of groans and gurgling pipes that were the sounds of this living, breathing old house. But something different. And there it was again: the sound of someone up and about downstairs.

I'd found an old hurley outside in the yard and in true paranoid fashion brought it back to put under the bed. It was probably rotten from being out in all weathers and it was a pretty flimsy weapon against a gun. But holding it helped my courage. I put on socks and tried to creep quietly downstairs. My heart beat like a jack-hammer as I padded towards the kitchen. There was definitely someone in there. I chanced a quick glimpse and Dorothy glanced up from drinking a cup of tea at the table.

"Jesus Christ," I gasped, taking a deep breath of relief.

"What's wrong?" she asked. "Why have you got that stick?"

"I thought you might have been someone else."

"Who?" Dorothy asked.

I told her what had happened the day before, but left out the gun part. Even the idea of intruders coming back however shook her. She got up to make me some tea to try and cover her anxiety.

"What did they want? Who were they?"

"I don't know. Mark Foley thinks they might be opportunists who knew everyone would be at the funeral."

"But you don't."

"I don't know," I said. "How bad was yesterday?"

"Not great obviously. But everyone was very kind, treated me like an invalid," she said, handing me the hot drink. "What did you make of Harry Cross?"

"I'd say the last pup he was sold came in a box and was wagging its tail," I smiled.

"Yes, he's a good man to have on your side, Harry. He's a good friend too. But I'm dreading going over these papers, and Michael's will. You saw what Alicia and George were like: it's going to be real succession-stakes stuff. And that's when fights start. Bad fights."

"Has Alicia always been so . . . ."

"Bitchy? Don't worry. I'm under no illusions about my family. To be fair she has her hands full with that husband. He's more than a handful, and not in the way that might be of some use to her."

I grinned. It was a good sign to hear her making jokes.

"And she was closer to Michael than she is to me. This is hitting her hard. She's actually a very dependable girl, good in many ways. Are you able to come with me today?"

"To the reading of Michael's will? I don't know if that's a good idea."

"Good or not, I would like you to be there."

I nodded. There was silence for a minute. But it wasn't uncomfortable. I asked how she felt, and she dismissively waved her hand, not wanting to talk about illness.

"What do you think of the house?" she asked.

"It's great. You can almost feel the history."

"Yes. Michael inherited it from his grandfather. Michael's own father was dissolute, a big drinker, and a big shagger. He could never have taken on the custody of this place. The old man knew it too."

"What happened to your father-in-law?"

"Blew his brains out with an old World War One Webley revolver. He was in Marrakesh at the time, probably high as a kite. He certainly wouldn't have had the courage to do it sober."

"So Michael was young when he got this place?"

"Yes, early twenties. It was unfair in many ways. Having so much responsibility so young. He didn't get a chance to be stupid and carefree, simply because his father couldn't be anything else."

"He sounds like a fine man."

"Michael? Yes, he was. He could be so much fun, and yet behind all that, he felt things very deeply. I will miss him very much."

There didn't appear to be much more to say. Death was a bastard, just as sure as it was unavoidable. The pain of my own mother's death could still stab mercilessly even more than twenty years later. All that desperate helplessness of watching a woman who had been the centre of our lives waste away. She had been brave beyond reason. Only as an adult did those telltale signs of terror and despair strike home, so much so it hurt just to remember them. But that had been her own body letting her down. How much more complicated must it be to try and cope knowing your loved one had been murdered, taken away by nothing else except malice?

"I noticed a locked door with a code-key at the other end of the house yesterday. What's that?" I asked.

"Oh, that's where Michael worked. His office, and where all his paintings are. Would you like to see it?"

We walked quietly, Dorothy occasionally touching my arm for guidance in the dark. She keyed in four numbers.

"Two – eight – zero – three, for my birthday," she explained. "No need for the year."

Fluorescent lights came on automatically, unveiling a winding staircase, at the bottom of which was a substantial open area, painted bright white with any number of pictures and prints hanging on the walls. Hundreds of others ranged like concertinas over the floor area. It was an art-lover's dream. Some of the images I recognised, others I didn't, but there were a few of them that pricked my professional interest just with the merest glance.

"This is his office," Dorothy said. "Was his office, I suppose."

It was nothing fancy, a tiny space really, with even more prints stacked against the sides. There was a large, old-fashioned computer on a desk, a battered old chair and a bulging stack of file-drawers. A bin in the corner contained a single plastic sandwich container. Idly I noticed the date was just six days before. The overall atmosphere was one of industry and purpose with a bright modernity absent from the house above.

"The police did a good job," Dorothy said. "Everything looks exactly as it was. I thought some of those clodhoppers would turn the place upside down."

"Did Michael spend a lot of time here?"

"He practically lived here. I could go the whole day without seeing him, me outside with the horses, and Michael down here, on the phone, buying and selling."

Just then the phone rang. Dorothy answered and her voice went into neutral. It was a customer from Germany making enquiries.

"I'm afraid Michael is no longer with us," she began, and I slipped out of the office.

There was a constant hum from the air-conditioner. It kept the atmosphere at a comfortable temperature, ideal for keeping the canvasses in good condition. There were a lot of impressionist prints, run-of-the-mill stuff for the mass market, ideal for keeping revenue turning over at a regular rate, I guessed. Artistic purity tended to be quickly diluted in the face of commercial reality and a master's print was more valuable currency than an unknown original any day of the week.

I flicked through the stacks, taking out ones that caught my eye. Some were unframed, just bare canvasses, recently finished. Michael liked bold colours. Quite a few I reckoned were Spanish, full of reds and blacks. It wasn't really my taste but there was no doubting the quality of a couple of them. He'd had a good eye.

"Take anything you like," Dorothy said. "Michael said his business was a bit like mine. You trust your eye and pay up, hoping to sell on at a profit later."

"And hope you get paid, right?"

"Very true. I keep forgetting you know horses."

"A long time ago."

"Not so long when you get to my age," she said. "Anyway, if anything catches your eye, just take it."

"Did Michael have any other premises?"

"No, he brought everything home and operated from here."

She sobbed suddenly, and retreated to the office, busying herself by loading a printer with paper. I found myself another rack of paintings and pretended to be interested in the contents. It was classic print stuff: Van Gogh's *Potato Eaters*, Raphael's *Portrait of a Young Man*, Matisse's *Woman with a Hat*. Typical material for a commercial art dealer to have.

"Seen enough?" Dorothy asked, composed again. "I think it might be time to try sleeping again. Sorry for waking you up."

"No, I'm glad I came down here."

"You understand it much more than I can," she said. "To me a painting is a painting is a painting. I don't understand the emotions in them that others see. Horses are easier, flesh and blood, real, if you like."

I thought of trying to explain how paint sometimes looked like it moved of its own accord in my eyes, as fluid and alive as any breathing creature. But she was right: each to their own. What I had was a blessing. There was a reason people called talent a gift: because it had nothing to do with the individual. They could make the most of it through effort and persistence but the grain of it was as arbitrary as life itself.

"How many people know the code to here?" I asked.

"Oh, I don't know. Me, Mrs Beasley obviously. The girls. It's been the same for years."

It didn't matter anyway. The material here was worth quite a bit, I guessed – but enough to kill someone, to torture them? No.

"Try and get some sleep, Luke. It's going to be a tough day."

Chapter 11

Harry Cross didn't flinch. The same couldn't be said of those sitting on the other side of the desk.

We were in his office in Dublin. Dorothy sat directly in front of Cross, her girls on either side, and their husbands next to them. I hung back, on a comfortable leather sofa clearly used for less formal meetings. This was very formal. Even me driving Dorothy into town with the others following and then trailing upstairs to the reading of the will provoked little more than mild disapproval. There was certainly no striking, unless the solicitor got in the line of fire, which couldn't be ruled out.

He'd read the documents out in a low monotone, never dramatising, even at bits of legalese that even I could grasp were dynamite in their implications. At one point, Myles stood up and walked to a window, head bowed. George appeared stunned. Dorothy I noticed sat iron-straight, her expression unreadable.

"You can't be serious," Alicia gasped as Cross stopped reading and removed his spectacles.

"I'm afraid I am," he said. "Your father owed a lot of money to a lot of people, most of all to the Revenue Commissioners."

"But how could that be?" Elizabeth asked helplessly.

"According to the accountants, Michael's business ran at a dramatic loss for most of the last decade. And the upkeep of Ardfield apparently ate up much more resources than appeared on the balance sheets."

"So basically he was fiddling his tax," Myles observed.

"Not fiddling. Simply not paying any for most of the last decade," Cross said. "Revenue is demanding over two and a half million euro in back taxes and penalties."

"But, how?" Elizabeth asked.

"Your father liked a bet," Cross explained. "Not on the horses, but on shares and property. And from what I can gather he liked long shots: maximum payoff for minimum investment. In short, a mug punter. Long shots are long shots for a reason, because they rarely come in, and nothing of Michael's paid off. In fact when everything went economically south, he was left with lots of expensive paper worth nothing."

"Jesus fucking Christ!" George exploded, standing up and staring down at Dorothy. "Did you know this?"

She returned his stare. "No, I did not."

"Well, that's it then. The whole thing is fucked royally now. Did *you* know?" he asked Cross.

"I suspected Michael was under financial pressure but nothing like to this extent," the older man said.

"How much time have we got?" Dorothy asked.

"Officially they want the money now. But there are several delaying measures we can employ – if that is helpful," Cross said.

"You said there is money owed to others," I chipped in. "How much are we talking about, and to whom?"

"There's no outstanding figure, apart from the Revenue one. It's an accumulation of things, like an outstanding bill to the builder that put a new roof on the lunging ring for Dorothy's horses. And several art dealerships in Britain who have been patient for a number of years but are now anxious, given what happened to Michael. Their bills have arrived in the last few days. More will probably come. Up to now, there's about half a million in total in miscellaneous items."

"So three million in total," I said.

"Up to now."

"Well, that's it then," George said to Dorothy. "You're going to have to sell to O'Donoghue now. There's no other option. You just have to hope he's still interested in buying."

Alicia stood up and put her arm through her husband's in an obvious display of support.

"Mum, there's nothing else for it. He's wanted to buy for months now. It could be the answer to all our problems. There may even be a little bit left over. That could be useful to all of us."

Dorothy didn't move. She appeared to be looking not at Cross but at a spot above his head. There was nothing distracted or vague about her reply though.

"Ardfield has been in the Maxwell-Williams family since 1822. If you think such history can be erased just like that, then you have no appreciation of legacy, Alicia. Your father has left Ardfield to his family. Equal shares for you two girls, and me. I am executor. As long as that situation remains, nothing will be done rashly.

Harry, what are our options?"

"You have some leeway, as long as you are prepared to enter into high-interest arrangements with the debtors to pay back what is owed over time. But it is Revenue that is the problem. If I get a receptive official, I might be able to get a few months of breathing space for you, Dorothy, but that's all. That money has to be paid, and Ardfield is your major asset. Unless you can generate money from elsewhere." He looked at the others.

"Don't bother looking at me," George said. "I was depending on this to get us –"

"Shut up, George," Alicia, said, quickly disengaging her arm.

Myles and Elizabeth didn't say anything.

"Maybe you can borrow the money against Ardfield, but I don't think the banks are in a position to play ball like that," Cross continued. "Do I take it that someone is interested in purchasing?"

"Yes, you can take it!" George practically shouted. "Gerard O'Donoghue has been keen. He even put in an offer."

"Really?" Cross asked.

"Yes," Alicia snapped. "And considering the market it was very generous. Enough to pay off everything and with enough left over for everyone to get on with their lives."

"I do not like the man," Dorothy said calmly.

"You don't have to like him!" Myles snapped.

His exasperation caught everyone a little off guard. It didn't seem like him at all. Clearly the Dennings were feeling a similar financial pressure to everyone else.

"It's business," Myles continued. "No one likes anyone in business. It's irrelevant what you think of someone personally. You swallow it down through you and do the deal."

"I do not like the man," Dorothy repeated.

The atmosphere was poisonous. Alicia looked at her mother with undisguised frustration. Elizabeth appeared on the verge of tears. Both husbands practically vibrated with tension. Harry Cross clearly felt it as well.

"Why don't we finish for today, let everyone digest this information?" he said.

"I think we all know what it tastes like," George said.

"Nevertheless, it doesn't serve any purpose to make snap decisions. All of you should go away for a while and ponder this. I have copies of the documents for everyone." He began to hand them out. He looked at me. "I'm sorry," he said. "I didn't know you were coming. I can get my secretary to make another copy."

"Why not?" George interrupted. "One for everyone in the fucking audience."

"That's not necessary," I said, shaking my head.

"Disappointed?" Alicia sneered.

"Enough!" Dorothy snapped. "If we can't behave properly, then let's stop embarrassing ourselves so publicly. Harry, I'm sorry."

Cross smiled, gave his friend a hug and ushered everyone out, no doubt relieved to be free of so much drama. There was a brief moment downstairs at the door out into the street where everyone waited for the security door to engage. But nothing was said and once outside everyone went their own way.

"Take me somewhere quiet, will you, Luke?" Dorothy asked.

We walked to the car, me wondering if a trip out of the

city up into the mountains might be the best thing to do, or maybe just find a quiet café, or nip into St Stephen's Green. But instead we ended up in the Ormond Gallery. It was only a short walk.

Part of me wondered if Freud would make a meal out of a man taking his long-lost mother to his place of work but it didn't seem likely. Too much analysis usually led to paralysis I'd found when pondering what to throw onto canvas.

The Ormond was quiet. The guard at the door recognised me. There was no one else in the place. The couple of secretaries who kept everything running like clockwork were at lunch. I mentioned eating to Dorothy but she said she wasn't hungry.

The work was on the walls: thirty-five pieces, well over a year's work. I suddenly felt self-conscious. When working, the idea that people would eventually end up looking at them never occurred. Over the years watching audiences pore over them in galleries like this always provoked an initial unease and embarrassment, like they were peering in at something deeply personal about me. Which in a way they were. Obviously I wanted these paintings to be looked at. If I didn't the easiest thing in the world would be to paint and then park the results in the cellar, away from everyone. But the weirdness about people first seeing them never left. And certainly not with Dorothy.

She said nothing as we walked slowly. There was no one else around. And it all made me feel ridiculously self-conscious, like a schoolboy waiting for the headmaster's report.

"Michael would have loved this," she said finally.

"And he would have loved to have met you. He could have understood what you do. I don't. It just looks very lovely."

I took her through the gallery office to a kitchen where the staff made tea and coffee. Sure enough there were ample supplies of both, and milk in the fridge. I boiled the kettle. Such mundane domesticity was turning into a familiar routine.

"Were you expecting that today in Cross's office?" I asked.

"No. I knew Michael was always worried about money. Ardfield is expensive. Even a little thing like heating it costs a fortune. I even used to nag him about it, told him we should sell it to the state or something, take the financial burden off us, even flog tickets so the public could walk around it. But apparently it's not of sufficient historical interest for the state and it's not like a princess got stabbed there a hundred years ago or something like that so Joe Public would pay up to walk around."

I made a pot of coffee but failed to root out anything to eat.

"So Alicia and Elizabeth were depending on getting something out of the will," I said.

"I'm not supposed to know but George's property portfolio is worth only a fraction of what it was. Apparently having Revenue on your back is not something he is entirely unfamiliar with," she said.

"Ah."

"Elizabeth told me, a little while ago. She was telling me about her own financial predicament. Myles got quite a lot of land from his parents but he has three siblings who're all entitled to a slice and the deal was that he would buy out their shares. According to Elizabeth, the others did much better out of that than Myles. They're feeling their own pressure."

"And why don't you like Gerard O'Donoghue?"

"You know him?"

"Of him. Who doesn't? Anyone with even the faintest connection to racing knows him. One of the biggest racehorse owners around, billionaire, philanthropist, friend to worthy causes everywhere."

"Exactly," Dorothy said. "You won't hear a peep from anyone against him. Mostly because it's in their interests to keep in. But that doesn't stop him being a prick."

My eyebrows rose at that one.

"Any specific reason?" I asked.

"I trust my instincts when it comes to people. And I know that makes me a hypocrite. Plenty of horses over the years have changed hands between me and O'Donoghue. He practically robbed Mail Carrier I sold him so cheaply and he won at Cheltenham a few years ago. And there was a good mare called Dolly Bird who he's bred a couple of very good ones out of. And Myles is right. That was just business. But this is different. Am I making any sense?"

"Sure. It's obvious how important Ardfield was to Michael. Apart from you and the girls, it was probably the uppermost thing in his life. So in a way, much more than just bricks and cement, the estate is what's left of him."

Dorothy nodded.

"And maybe I'm speaking out of turn," I added, "but there's probably a bit of guilt at work here too."

She looked at me straight. There was a disconcerting strength to that glare.

"You never knew the scale of the money problem," I continued. "Cross mentioned the cost of a new roof for the lunging yard. You told me before, Michael never refused you anything, especially with the horses. It's hardly a cheap business, the horse game. You're an expert horsewoman but that isn't the same thing as being an expert businesswoman."

Nothing was said. Dorothy stared at me for a few more seconds. Then she took a sip of coffee and stood up.

I silently cursed myself. Such bluntness was not usually my style. It had been hurtful to a frail woman struggling to come to terms with the murder of her husband and the crumbling apart of her family. What was I trying to prove? She walked to the door and turned around.

"Okay, Mr Perceptive, what do you suggest I do?"

The enquiry appeared genuine, couched in more than a hint of the sardonic, but I was getting better at establishing when she was being serious. And she was now.

"What does your gut tell you?" I asked.

"To get shot of the whole thing!"

"No, seriously."

She didn't say anything for a moment.

"I don't like being organised," she said. "And I don't like being told what to do. And Michael deserves more than being just a cash-cow to his children and their spouses."

"That's enough for now then," I replied.

"Correct. And that's enough quiet too. Let's get some lunch. You're paying."

Chapter 12

The Ormond was keen on a preview night for press and a select group of dealers and general arty types. My presence was required.

There was a supposedly a 'buzz' about this exhibition, the first in Ireland by a Dubliner who had been making a splash in London. Even the girls in the office had started to sound like they talking in press-release speak. And it was fair enough. The more skulls through the door, the better the gallery did, which was pretty fundamental to me too. Everything revolved around getting the exhibition profile increased.

Dutifully I stood on the edge of the rooms, being steered from one to another every so often by a PR guru called Rod whose professional smile never wavered and who greeted every journalist with handshakes, kisses and loud expressions of conviviality.

There were a few quick interviews to be done. Nothing strenuous, most of them concentrating on me, not the paintings, teasing out a back-story that might grab a reader's interest. They latched on to the jockey line. It always appealed to reporters. And so I delivered the well-honed, shorthand version of failing to make it as a rider and how horses weren't usually a subject for me and no, there were no Delamere ambitions to go all Munnings: all of it on the web already but journos liked their quotes fresh.

It was hardly a torture. They were pleasant, made complimentary noises when talking about the stuff on the walls and all said they were sure audiences would lap it up. One or two asked if I would be staying in Dublin and I told them yes, for a while, just outside the city.

If that was news to them, it also felt like it to me. Almost a week had passed since Cross's bombshell. I remained in Ardfield, not saying anything about staying, and Dorothy not mentioning anything about my leaving. Most of the time it was humdrum, me travelling into Dublin a few times, helping Barry in the yard, lunging a few, even taking some out on to the fields for gentle canters, just to take the edge off them. Dorothy mostly said little, learning to cope with a very different world and the more mundane but still pressing reality of owing millions of euro.

Twice I had driven her to hospital for check-ups. On both occasions she insisted I accompany her to the waiting room – "Just in case everyone thinks I'm lying about the situation." The second time, her consultant emerged with her and smilingly indulged her with a bulletin for her chauffeur as she referred to me.

In the circumstances, Mrs Maxwell-Williams was doing remarkably well, he told me smoothly. There was no immediate rush to start treatment even. Whatever she was doing, she was to continue. The prognosis was entirely positive. If she'd emerged and told me that herself, I probably wouldn't have believed her. But there was an ease about the report and the consultant's manner that reassured completely. Typical of her, I figured, to exhibit such forethought: practical and helpful at the same time.

What remained unsaid was the idea that someone might come back to the house again. A police liaison officer called in a couple of times to see Dorothy but that was the extent of our contact with the investigation into Michael's murder. I rang looking for Mark Foley a few times. He rang back once, assured me everything that could be done was being done.

"Don't fob me off like that, please," I said.

"I'm not fobbing you off, Mr Delamere."

"Okay. But can you give me any indication? Off the record. Is there anything happening."

"Look," he said, sighing, "what I can say is that there is no definite line of enquiry at the moment. But we are doing everything we can."

That we both knew was another way of saying the police had no idea who to look for. As for the second break-in, Foley said the gun was unusual but essentially nothing had been taken and my description had been too vague for anything definite to be established. Maybe it was unfair but I got the impression things had moved on. Other people's awfulness dominated the front pages now. Other priorities had arisen. There weren't enough resources to cover them, let alone cater for vague suspicions and dead ends.

I didn't go anywhere unless Mrs Beasley or Barry were in the house. Both were happy to do it and put up a fight when I pushed a few quid their way. But they took it when I insisted. It felt very odd, something that Alicia and Elizabeth should be doing. But there had only been phone calls since that meeting in Dublin. I'd overheard some of them, Dorothy being polite and formal, and occasionally lowering her voice, sometimes even leaving the room, presumably when the subject turned to me and what the hell I was still doing in Ardfield. It was a question I asked myself, but still hadn't come up with a good answer. Until I did, I reckoned on remaining, out of some sense of something I guessed might be duty. It was all very odd.

"Hello again."

Her voice actually sent a shiver down my spine: dreadful cliché stuff but none the less real. It was Julia O'Neill. I'd been looking out for her, hoping she'd be one of the press-pack. I'd given up hope. Now that she stood next to me, it was all I could do to say something.

"Great to see you," I said eventually, feeling my feet start to dance. This was getting ridiculous. "And thanks for that piece you did. You were very kind."

It had been a genuinely impressive article, not because of anything she'd said about me, although there had been a generosity there that an awkward first impression can't have aided. More importantly there was a depth of knowledge behind the words that wasn't flash or attention-seeking but was unobtrusively used to help her make the points she wanted. There was a rare perception there. Or maybe I wanted there to be. She really was very beautiful.

"You're welcome," she said, her eyes glancing around the room. "Are you getting much feedback?"

"A bit. Everyone seems to be positive about it," I

replied. "Mind you, they would be, wouldn't they?"

"Why?"

"They're hardly going to come here and slag it off," I grinned. "Not when there's free drink!"

"That's one way of looking at it," she said coolly.

Very smooth, I said to myself. She had a way of looking at me that made my mouth shoot off without thinking: best to retreat with whatever shred of dignity I might have left.

"Sorry, there's a phone call I have to make," I said.

That was, strictly speaking, true. I had dropped Dorothy into town. The idea of returning to the gallery hadn't appealed to her. Too many people in one place, she'd said, asking too many questions. Instead a trip round the shopping malls was a better option – "Don't worry, no extravagant purchases. I have quite enough guilt already!"

"Checking up on me?" she said now on answering.

"Just making sure," I said, outside in the street near a couple of furtive smokers.

"Don't worry. Harry is with me. We're having a drink not too far from you. When you're finishing why don't you pop over to Magee's? For once in his life, he's not being miserable. He's even bringing a little cheeriness to the world."

"Okay," I laughed. "I shouldn't be long more here."

"Is it going okay?"

"Sure. I'll be spattered all over the place."

"At least that's what you want."

Back inside a new visitor had arrived, provoking my minder into a state of excitement.

I recognised Gerard O'Donoghue. The big stout figure

stared out of the racing pages every second day of the week, a round, open countryman's face usually smiling, and looking for all the world like a farmer instead of a billionaire businessman who'd originally made his fortune in building and now had his finger in every money-making pie worthy of the name.

Racing was his enthusiasm away from business. Prepared to spend millions every year on young horses, he was the economic backbone for half the training yards in Ireland, and quite a few in Britain as well. He was also a staple of the gossip-pages. If there was a charity in need of help, O'Donoghue was usually approached because his reputation for generosity was legendary.

There were plenty who regarded the man, whose name had inevitably been summed up as "GOD," as some kind of saint: the acceptable and philanthropic face of rampant wealth. He was genuinely popular, a folksy down-to-earthiness appealing to ordinary people who liked the idea of a postman's son from Waterford rising into Ireland's elite.

Not surprisingly for so public a figure, there were other less positive views. Murmurs of business ruthlessness behind the smile were persistent and hardly a shock. Nobody rose to O'Donoghue's level of wealth by being a nice guy all of the time, I reckoned. And so what: it actually made him more of a three-dimensional figure than the smiling, benevolent one in the pictures. Everyone, I thought again, even those not in the headlines, had a public face, the one chosen to face the world once out the front door. I had one myself. O'Donoghue's might be amplified by his wealth and power but it was none the less real for that.

It was interesting watching the impact his presence had on people. The couple of photographers hardly paused for breath as they snapped. More than a few of the arty brigade were trying to sneakily capture O'Donoghue on their phones. Rod scampered up to me, vibrating with excitement.

"I'd no idea he'd come!" he practically whimpered. "We sent an invitation of course. We always do to these things. But it's so rare he accepts."

The PR expert grabbed my arm and barged his way through a gaggle of people surrounding O'Donoghue.

"Mr O'Donoghue. Rod Boland," he said, grabbing the man's hand to shake it. "I sent you the invitation?"

"I got an invitation?" O'Donoghue said, smiling a little and then taking pity on Rod's discomfort. "You're very kind but I was in town and I wanted to see this exhibition anyway."

"Great," Rod rallied. "May I introduce you to Luke Delamere."

"Really?" O'Donoghue said. "Delighted to meet you."

"Pleasure to meet you," I replied, shaking his hand. He then introduced me to his wife, Marian, a short, thin woman with an open smile and a handshake as firm as her husband's.

"Gerry likes your work very much," she said. "We have that Newmarket morning-mist landscape you did a few years ago."

It was a picture of a single horse and jockey emerging from fog having worked on the gallops, the animal's head hanging low with tiredness, the rider trying to light an illicit cigarette while maintaining only a minor hold on the reins. I'd liked the ordinariness of it, centring the portrait on the jockey's cupped hands, sheltering his lighter from the elements. But I'd been pleasantly surprised when it made twenty thousand at auction to an anonymous buyer who wasn't so anonymous any more.

"Thank you," I said. "And a belated thank-you for buying it."

"Not at all," O'Donoghue said. "I have another one you did, of a jockey coming back from a race covered in muck."

That was one of the first things I'd ever done, a very quick sketch of a jump jockey I knew.

"You don't really do many horse pictures, do you?" he said.

It was amazing how he could chat so casually with cameras flashing only a couple of feet away. Familiarity, I guessed, made it seem almost natural.

"No. Just once in a while," I told him. "Although now I know you like them, things might change!"

"Quite right too," he laughed. "A guy like you who used to ride is too good not be producing quality stuff. Just remember: a picture of Sea The Stars eating grass is likely to make a lot more than a horse eating grass."

"Don't worry," I grinned. "Commercial realities are never far from my mind."

"Good man. Now if you don't mind, we'd like to look at your latest work."

The crowd parted as if by magic and the O'Donoghues walked on with tails of media and gallery pilot fish trailing behind them. Rod came from behind me and grabbed my arm again.

"Brilliant," he said. "He doesn't like to make a big deal of it but he's one of the most significant art buyers in the country. Actually fuck that – in Europe. You were great."

He took off to join the wake. I turned around and Julia O'Neill nodded in mocking acknowledgement. Then she left.

The star attraction spent barely quarter of an hour looking around. He could hardly take a step without someone wanting to speak to him, or shake hands, or have their photos taken. Each person was treated to a smile and was accommodated. It was noticeable the look of satisfaction each of them had when finished with him. I waited by the door, trying not to taste a cup of bad coffee. We shook hands again.

"I'm very impressed," he said, getting my mumbled thanks in return. "I think I might be coming back."

"I'd understand if you didn't," I replied, nodding at the people hovering just too close. "I don't know how you put with that."

He stood close and half-whispered. "What would you recommend I do? Tell them all to fuck off?"

"It occurred to me."

He laughed. "Me too."

"I think we might know somebody in common," I said.

"Really?"

"Dorothy Maxwell-Williams."

"Dorothy? Of course, I've bought some good horses off her over the years," he said. "How do you know her?"

"We're related. Kind of."

"What do you mean 'kind of'?"

"She's my mother," I said, the words feeling odd on my lips. "Birth mother, I mean. I was adopted."

He looked at me straight.

"We only just made contact again," I said. "I'm actually staying with her while things settle down again."

He put his hand on my arm and turned around to say goodbye to everyone else. Then he steered me out through the door. A massive dark Mercedes came out of nowhere and parked in front of us. We climbed in. Mrs O'Donoghue was already sitting inside.

"Oh," she said, surprised. "Is Gerry kidnapping you?"

"There's an unexpected side to this artist," O'Donoghue explained, sitting in beside me. He motioned to the driver. "Take us around the block, Larry," he ordered, then grinned at me. "I've always wanted to say that. Now, talk to me, how is Dorothy?"

"Who's Dorothy?" his wife asked.

"Maxwell-Williams. You know, the woman who sold us Danger King," he said. "It appears she has something of a past with our boy here."

I repeated what I'd said inside and filled them in on what had happened since Michael's death. She kept saying "How awful!" but O'Donoghue himself was silent.

"But one thing I've learned is she's a tough woman," I said.

"She is that," O'Donoghue replied. "You are aware of course that she isn't my biggest fan."

"I think she may have mentioned something."

"I bet she did," he said. "She's a desperate snob, you know. I'm nouveau riche apparently."

"She said that to you?"

"No. But she's not great at disguising her disapproval. She is, however, a woman to be reckoned with and no one deserves what has happened to her. Is she okay? I mean resources-wise?"

I hesitated.

"I don't know if you're aware of this but I've made several offers in recent months to buy Ardfield. It's a property I'd like to get my hands on if possible."

"It's come up."

He smiled. "I'm not used to being rebuffed but it isn't the end of the world if I don't get it. As a property it would be good for some of my horses. And the house would be a good investment when it's done up. But if it helps people out to sell then that would be a nice bonus too."

I hesitated again.

"All I'm saying is if it helps, my interest in buying remains," he said. "Nouveau Riche can have its uses!"

"I'll pass it on."

"She's actually a great old bird. It's hard not to admire her. At the very least, what you see is what you get. And she's brilliant with those horses of hers. They really get a good grounding. It's just a pity she hasn't had a good one in a while. Does she have anything at the moment?"

"I don't know really. She has a few horses there that mightn't be too far off a run," I said. "If one of them was any good, it might help out in a big way. I'll have to try them out one morning. Earn my keep."

"You're going to stay with her for a while?"

"I haven't really thought about it," I said. "But for the time being, I guess so. If she wants me to."

"Good man," O'Donoghue said. "And if I can help at all, just let me know."

He handed me a card with a mobile number on it.

"Of course, don't tell your mother you've got that!"

Chapter 13

I'd never really heard Dorothy laugh before. It was surprisingly high and girly and pleasant. It signalled her out in the busy bar immediately. She was at a table with Harry Cross.

"What's the occasion?" I asked, pulling up a stool.

"Nothing really. Just catching up," she replied. "Remembering Michael."

"I was telling her about the time me and Michael went fishing in Killarney," Cross said, smiling at the memory. "It was a long weekend and not once did we hold a fishing rod. We stayed up in the hotel one night, for the whole night, in the lobby, getting fed drink by the porter. There were Yanks coming down at five in the morning to go hiking and all that tourist stuff and they were met by a couple of sozzled old Paddies, barely able to stand up."

Dorothy laughed again and looked straight ahead towards the bar.

"I'm going to miss him terribly, aren't I, Harry?" she said. "It's going to be terrible."

"It's not going to be easy, dear. But you'll manage. You always do. And you have people around you who'll help."

"Really?" she said. "I've got you. And Luke here has been incredible. God knows what would have happened if he hadn't agreed to meet me that day."

She wasn't drunk or maudlin, just very sad. And I didn't know what to say. A lounge-girl stood over us and I ordered a round of drinks. Dorothy's tipple was brandy and port. I looked at her as if to ask should she really be drinking, and got a look back that put me in my place.

"Harry has come up with an escape route – of sorts," she informed me.

"I've spoken to a guy I know in Revenue and they could be willing to play ball in the circumstances. Nobody is going to smell of roses going after a widow in these circumstances. So off the record he says they'll be willing to accept instalment payments over a number of years."

I nodded. It made sense. Better little bits of something than a dramatic nothing.

"What Dorothy has going for her is land. There are one hundred and fifty acres. At current prices, that roughly translates into 1.3 to 1.4 million euro. But the likelihood is that prices will rise again. And it would be better not to have to sell everything. She does after all need land for her horses. But theoretically it does give her a little leeway."

"Theoretically?" I said.

"Yes. Dorothy is the executor of Michael's will but selling bits of the estate could result in a legal challenge by her family who quite clearly want Ardfield and everything with it sold off."

"They would do that?" I said.

"Quite a little coven I've managed to breed, isn't it?" she said, taking a pull of her brandy. "Anyway, Harry has a plan to prevent them getting their claws on Ardfield."

"I didn't say that, Dorothy. I said there was a small chance."

"Tell him," she ordered.

"Are you sure?"

"Of course I am. He's the only one that doesn't have his hand out."

"Fair enough," Harry said. "Revenue says they will take quarterly instalments over a period of time yet to be finalised. They obviously want it short. We want it long. I reckon we'll eventually meet somewhere around the ten-year mark. They also want a business plan."

"What kind of business?" I asked.

"Quality country-house hotel. A chap I know has already expressed an interest in starting up at Ardfield. Dorothy is thrilled at the idea."

She grinned crookedly. "Better to have some say on who tramps into one's house than none at all."

"It's no certainty it will work," he said. "Things are so uncertain economically now no one can know anything. But things will eventually change. And this gives you a chance. And with the figures we've got in front of us, a chance is all you can ask for."

"I'm very grateful, Harry," Dorothy said, squeezing his hand.

"Don't thank me yet," he said. "And I hope you develop a taste for relative frugality."

"Ardfield is what counts," she said simply.

"Maybe so. But don't forget the catch."

"How can I?" she said.

Harry turned to me. "Revenue wants evidence of goodwill: confirmation that we're serious about all of this."

"What do they want?"

"An initial lump sum payment of one hundred thousand euro," Cross said. "And I had to argue like hell to bring it down from one-fifty. It's ludicrous. If a person is in the shit financially, demanding more money off them achieves nothing."

"What will you do?" I asked Dorothy.

"Beg, borrow or steal, I suppose," she said.

"The problem is they want it by the end of this month," Cross added. "The mechanics of selling land make it very unlikely that Dorothy will be able to pay them in time, no matter what price she charges. I've tried arguing but they're digging their heels in on this – a cynic might suggest because they hope not to get it."

"And how does that benefit them?" I asked.

"It doesn't," he replied. "But bureaucracy is all about ass-covering. And no one wants to let their ass hang out over this type of money. It's the same with banks. No one is going to risk lending. Is there anyway, or anyone, who could supply you with a short-term loan?"

"No one springs to mind," Dorothy said. "I know plenty of people who might like to give the impression of that kind of liquid wealth. But not many who actually have it. In fact, no one."

"I might be able to help you there," I said, fishing in my pocket for Gerard O'Donoghue's card. "He was at the gallery. I even got a spin in the back of his car. And he said to ring him if you needed any kind of help. I think he actually likes you, even though . . ."

"Even though what?" she asked.

"Even though he knows you believe he's a nouveau riche piece of crap," I said. "But he seems like he genuinely wants to assist."

Harry, I noticed, had suddenly developed an interest in the contents of his glass. All the previous ease left Dorothy's face. It felt like a rocket was about to come in my direction. But her voice was low, soft and contained complete conviction.

"Don't get too close to that man, Luke. I've known him a long, long time. He may have a more socially acceptable face nowadays, and be richer than most anyone in the country, but a leopard doesn't change its spots. He is dangerous."

"He was just taking a look at my work," I replied.

"I know you must think I'm some half-witted old bitch but trust me on this. That man got to the top by pushing a lot of heads into the dirt. I would rather burn Ardfield to the ground than let him get his hands on it."

As definitives went, it was pretty hard to top. She looked at me steadily. I nodded.

Harry suddenly noticed his glass was empty and beckoned to the waitress.

"I'm driving, so nothing for me," I said.

"Brandy and port, and a gin and tonic," he told the girl, before turning to Dorothy. "I can rise to fifty grand."

Her expression was impossible to read. But I noticed she put her empty glass on the girl's tray a little unsteadily. Harry made it sound like he was giving her a loan of a tenner for a taxi. A friend indeed, I thought. She reached for his hand and squeezed.

"I'll rise the other fifty," I heard myself say. What the

hell: I could keep painting. "If that's okay."

Dorothy's expression never changed. Harry said "Good man" and no more. We sat there drinking, me with a cordial, and when they were finished we stood up and left the pub. Harry kissed her goodnight and walked a little unsteadily to a conveniently waiting taxi. My car was just around a corner. We got in and I started the engine. Reaching for the gear-stick, I felt her place her hand on mine. It felt cool, and strange and lovely. She kept looking out straight.

"It's quite a nice night really," she said eventually.

"Yes," I replied, starting the drive home.

Chapter 14

"Are you crazy?" Jerry blurted down the phone.

"Come on. What's fifty grand?" I replied.

"It's about fifty fucking grand more than you have right now!" he shouted.

Jerry was right. The breadline might not have been on the horizon but no way could I get my hands on that sort of money right away. I'd put a lot into getting the Foxes' Den up to par and sunk some of the profits from a few paintings into various investments and a pension fund. On paper, I was worth a bit: in reality, not much.

"Jerry, you know I'm good for it. What about that guy in Hong Kong who told you he wants first call on anything I do? And that woman with more money than sense in Cape Town is always keen on portraits. I can run a couple of them up and we'll be square."

"And what makes you think I can just pony up that sort of money?"

"Oh, don't be so modest! A business genius like you? That's only pocket money to you."

"Bloody deep pockets," he sulked.

"I'll pay ten-per-cent interest against it coming off future earnings, and/or royalties. Please?"

"Okay. Stop wheedling."

"And I need it by the end of the month."

"Jesus!"

"You're a good man, Jerry Barnett."

"I'm a moron. That's what I am," he sighed.

"Just think of all that lovely interest," I said.

"Yeah, I will – and you'll throw a sketch into the pot as well," he said. "Hopefully it might still be worth something by then."

I grinned. The sketch would be the interest. And the cash wouldn't be an issue for him. He was loaded. Old family money still floated through the Barnett accounts with gratifying liquidity. All of which didn't squash scepticism at what his client was up to.

"And you're not going to get anything for this money?"

"No," I said. "She wants me to formalise it: take a stake in return for the money."

"Do it!" he shouted down the phone.

"No. That's not what this is about."

"What is it about?"

"Buggered if I know," I muttered.

"Be careful," he warned. "I'd hate you to be diverted from the task of paying me back."

It was a beautiful morning in County Meath. I'd arrived down for breakfast to be met with Dorothy on the way out to the yard. She was dressed for work in boots, cap and battered oilskin.

"You deigned to rise then?" she said.

"I have to head in to Dublin again. The gallery people want to make the most of last night's events."

"Good luck with that," she said, sketching a slight wave as she strode out. The bounce was back in her step. Or at least it looked like it. Even if that was a front, it was still encouraging.

"Her spirits have come back a bit," Mrs Beasley said, handing me a steaming mug of coffee. "It's good to see."

I nodded, took a couple of sips, grabbed an apple and made for the front door.

There was a young man outside, holding a phone to his ear and looking up and around at the windows on the upper floors. In his other hand he held a long, narrow cylindrical tube, like a whisky case, but longer. I recognised it. They were handy for carrying canvasses.

"Can I help you?" I asked.

He looked at me, startled.

"Who are you?" he demanded. "You're not Michael."

He was in his mid-twenties, blonde, fit and tanned. His English was perfect but accented: continental Europe, maybe Dutch, or Scandinavian. Behind him was a transit van with an unusual number plate. Next to the blue and yellow EU insignia was "DK" – Denmark.

"No, I'm not Michael. My name's Luke. Michael is dead."

"*Dead!* But he can't be," he said, clearly rattled.

"I'm sorry. Did you know him?" I asked.

He started backing up towards the van, stumbling slightly on the stony surface.

"No. No," he said.

"Hang on. If I can help at all, I will," I said, following him. "Are they canvasses? I can help you with those if you like."

"You can?" he said. "You know Johann?"

"Yes, of course," I said, lying.

Afterwards, I still couldn't explain why. It was a hunch. There was something not right about the guy. He was too furtive, too jumpy. And it was too soon after Michael's murder to ignore that.

"So what do you want?" I quickly added.

"Here," he said, shoving the tube into my hands, and going back to the van. "And here are the other two. My job is done now, right?"

He was clearly looking for any excuse to get going. Stopping him didn't look likely. He was young, strong and his feet looked like they were on springs.

"Right," I said.

He skipped back to the van and took off in a flurry of dust and stones, with me suddenly realising it might be a good idea to try and find out a little more about what was going on. I ran after the van, shouting, and cursing my own stupidity. If he heard me, he didn't let on, making the most of his opportunity to scarper. This was turning into a bad habit.

The Ormond could wait. I quickly took the tubes upstairs to my bedroom and took out the contents. They were canvasses all right. The thread texture of the material was as familiar to me as running a hand through my hair. I winced as I rolled out the five paintings, each of them separated by a roll of polystyrene. It was never a good idea to roll up canvas, especially water colours. Unless the painting was completely dry, and not just touch-dry, the risk of cracks and peeling paint was high. But these looked okay.

The third one I recognised immediately. It was a

Bukovac self-portrait. There was another self-portrait by the Croatian artist in another tube. And there was a picture by the Spaniard, Avendano. And one I guessed was by the Indian painter, Raza. They really were very good. I suspected they were all fake: good fakes, but still not the real deal.

For one thing genuine canvasses by artists as good as these weren't used to being carted in transit vans. Prints maybe, but not something purporting to be what it wasn't. The real stuff was hanging in galleries or in private collections somewhere, or resting in vaults, accruing in value with each passing day.

Far from the clichéd image of tortured artistic purity, the business surrounding art was immense, generating hundreds of millions each year. Inevitably with that kind of money the temptation to cheat was irresistible. And was it even cheating? There were famous portraits out there that had been dismissed as fakes for hundreds of years and then with modern carbon detection declared real, only for many 'experts' to steadfastly believe otherwise: And the same the other way round.

The quality of fraudsters' work varied wildly. Some were as talentless as they were stupid, making schoolboy errors that only the blind could miss. One famously managed to get the spelling of an artist's signature wrong. But many more were genuinely gifted, producing reworks with real artistic merit. There were some that technically probably exceeded the standard of the original.

What they found out was O'Donoghue's dictum: Sea The Stars on the horizon resonates more than 'horse' on the horizon. All the talent and originality in the world sometimes isn't enough to make people want to buy you.

And when your mortgage payment depends on selling, the temptation to fake is only too real because the chances of getting away with it are so good.

The internet had opened up the purchasing of art work, and of cutting corners. And the business of investing in art had never been busier. For someone who knew what they were doing, the chances of making money had never been better.

It had never affected me, at least not that I knew of. If anything the idea of being copied would feel like a compliment, I guessed. But direct experience of being hit in the pocket might alter that.

There were no identifiable marks on the work itself. And the first two tubes had nothing on them, not even a barcode. But the third one had a faded postmark on it. Most of the red lettering had disappeared. And it was barely visible. But there was something there: a 'H' and an 'E', two 'L's' and an 'E'. Then there was nothing. Obviously part of a place name, I reckoned. Or all of it. There was a town in Germany called Halle. A tennis tournament took place there every year.

I unpacked my laptop and keyed in 'Helle' and 'Denmark' into a search engine. It gave me a district in Jutland. Geography classes from long ago jolted the memory into recognising Jutland as the sticky-out bit of Denmark, the peninsula near where the 1916 naval battle took place. Thank you, Mr Fitzgerald, for recognising that fighting could grab teenage boys' attention and focus it on even the most boring of geographical detail.

'Helle' was also the first name of a Danish politician. Hardly likely to be dealing in fake pictures. It was a popular Christian name all round. Adding 'Art' to the search gave more people, none of whom meant anything to me. Putting 'Gallery' into the equation threw up more place names in Aalborg and Roskilde. There was a music festival in Roskilde. That's all it meant to me. This was useless. I added in 'Bukovac' and 'Raza' and got more place names with plenty of Danish language text. One of the places was 'Hellerup'. I clicked on a couple of tag lines. One of the sites offered a Bukovac for sale, the same as the one I'd uncovered. And the Raza.

One of the watercolours had caught my eye when first going through the contents of the tubes. It was a dark piece, the inside of what looked a glorified hut, with peasants huddled around an open fire and vague shadows in the background providing a brooding threatening atmosphere. It was medieval stuff, more than a little gothic and not my cup of tea at all. But there was no denying its distinctiveness.

I flicked through some of the images on the screen. There looked to be about fifty available. Sure enough, No. 31 was the hut picture. It gave the artist's name – Qualic – which I didn't know and quickly looked up. He was Polish, late nineteenth century and currently staring up from my County Meath bedroom while being offered for sale by a gallery in Denmark.

After gathering up the canvasses and reluctantly putting them back in their tubes, I went down to Michael's office. Nothing had changed or moved but the atmosphere was different. What had he been involved in? Julia O'Neill was right. He had been involved in fakes, either storing them or selling them on. Dorothy had said Michael could barely draw a line so he was hardly producing this stuff. But he was in it up to his neck.

Enough to get killed? Was this stuff valuable enough to torture and then kill someone?

I looked around. I didn't know enough to distinguish genuine paintings from copies. They couldn't all be dubious. There were too many. The whole point of dealing in fakes was to be selective. Flooding the market was counter-productive.

And who was to say Michael was doing anything wrong? This could have been entirely legitimate, selling on good-quality copies to people who knew what they were getting. However unlikely that might seem, there was no way of proving otherwise. Contacting Foley and telling him about these paintings and a blonde guy and this gallery in Denmark might mean something but it proved nothing. What the impact of a suggestion of criminality about her late husband would do to Dorothy was unknowable too. The fight to keep Ardfield had rejuvenated her own fight, at least to some extent. Was that worth extinguishing on hearsay?

The words of a head lad who had basically thought me to ride in Newmarket came back. Fearful of what might happen if a horse ran away with me over the vast expanse of the heath, I'd been informed: "If in doubt, do nothing – he knows a lot more about this than you do." I'd taken it to heart. Maybe it was time to trust that instinct again.

They really were good though, I thought, flicking through the pictures. I couldn't tell what was real and what wasn't. There were impressionists and cubists known to those in the industry but hardly the sort of stuff to be found hanging in hotel lobbies. And there were classic prints like Van Gogh's self-portrait, Raphael's *Portrait of a Young Man* and a couple of Picassos. It was interesting just to look at them and ordinarily I'd have happily spent hours down in this eerily quiet room. But all this was anything but ordinary.

I'd barely climbed upstairs and closed the basement door behind me than the sound of raised voices carried across the halls. It took an effort of will not to sprint towards them. The voices were female, and angry. As it was I got back to the drawing room at more than a walk.

"Why do you have to be so horrible?"

Alicia was shouting at her mother, pacing around the room, her face twisted with temper.

"Don't speak to me like that," I heard Dorothy say. She was out of sight. "I am your mother."

"Don't I know that?" Alicia lashed back. "Only my mother could be so stupidly stubborn."

I stepped to the side. That gave me a view of the side of the drawing-room and Elizabeth was standing there, saying nothing. It looked like only the two girls were there – no way could George have stayed silent for this long.

"Why are you delaying the inevitable?" Alicia implored. "All you're doing is hurting yourself."

"Harry Cross says this can work," Dorothy said steadily. "And that's enough for me. It should be enough for you. This estate was your father's life."

"And look what it did to him: borrowing money left right and centre with no hope of paying it back. All to keep up this pretence, this family history," Alicia retorted. "We can't even afford to heat this place, never mind run it properly."

"That will now change," her mother said, her voice not changing a monotone. "Your father was a weak man in many ways. And he didn't face up to the financial realities. I will."

"Don't you dare insult Daddy when he's not here to defend himself," Alicia said, lowering her voice. "Why do you think he borrowed so much without telling anyone? So that you could keep living the way you want to! All the horses and the clothes and the way you look down on everyone. He was afraid of you. I'm not. Just do what's right."

"I will not sell."

"But it's not O'Donoghue," Elizabeth suddenly interjected. "Have you ever even met James Norton?"

"No, I haven't and I've no intention of doing so," Dorothy answered.

"But he's perfect, Mummy," Elizabeth continued. "He's willing to match O'Donoghue's offer. And we know he has the money."

Too right he does, I thought. James Norton was a household name, another businessman, a renowned player in the media world with stakes in newspapers and radio and TV stations around the world. He lived in New York, hung around with Presidents and the elite of the American business world. His hard-headedness when it came to business was legendary. How had he entered the Ardfield equation?

"So George has broken his back arranging this deal for nothing then," Alicia said helpfully. "He has called in every favour and contact he has. This is being given to you on a plate. It solves everything."

"It might solve your everything, Alicia, but not mine," Dorothy said. "And why doesn't your husband break his back working these contacts for a job?"

"Because we have no money!" she screamed.

"Everything's gone. We're borrowed up to our bloody necks. And Elizabeth's the same. We need this to work or we're ruined. Can't you see that? Or is your pride worth more than your children's wellbeing?"

"Don't be ridiculous, Alicia, control yourself," Dorothy said.

"You're a horrible old woman, and I hate you!" Alicia shouted.

She stormed out and saw me. It was impossible not to read the expression on her face. If she could have got away with it, Alicia would have happily hurt me.

"You," she said, and continued walking.

Chapter 15

It was very wet, rain pouring down in sheets. Barry handed me some waterproofs and an old pair of wellies.

"I don't suppose you could give a few of them a spin around the top field, is there?" he asked. "They've been doing loads of walking but they need to stretch their legs. And with all this rain, the ground will be gone soon."

I grabbed a bridle and a saddle-cloth and tacked up one of the four-year-olds. We cantered around the big, wide-open flat field. He was full of the joys at being able to stretch out. I was riding quite short, stirrups pulled up high, with hands low, giving signals to the half-tonne of power and muscle underneath with little pulls on the reins and a constant exchange of information through those same reins that almost felt like a second language. What it told me as we pounded over the grass was this youngster was going to be no superstar. I shook my head at Barry as I dismounted back in the yard.

"Not much, yeah?" he said. "I guessed as much. His mother never threw anything good. Mind, neither did this fella's."

He was holding the big white-nosed gelding for me and I swung up into the saddle. The horse skittered on the stone surface and put his ears back, clearly not in love with the rain. We plodded out, down a muddy lane and into the field. I clicked my tongue and off he went.

It was obvious even in the first few strides. With the really talented ones it only takes that initial feel to know. I'd ridden enough decent horses up the gallops at Newmarket. One of them had even gone on to be placed in the Derby. It was hard to explain but immediately obvious: the good ones just felt alive in your hands.

And this big, angular lump was good. He did nothing more than the other one, went no faster or further and yet it was there. The messages coming between my hands and the bar in his mouth were very different. There was a reservoir of power waiting to be tapped. And it felt like he was moving over carpet, almost floating over the squelchy ground. The effort involved in doing so was minimal. His ears were flicking back and forth, taking everything in.

At one stage a pheasant shot up from close to a ditch and the horse briefly skipped sideways, all the time keeping an eye on the bird climbing into the sky, and all the time cantering forward. I might have been more used to finding out about sprinters and milers on much more luxuriantly appointed gallops but the basics were the same. Unless my guess was way off-beam, this was a good one.

"I knew it!" Barry shouted as we trotted back into the yard. "He's good, right?"

"How do you know?"

"You didn't have a silly grin all over your face the last time!"

"Yes, Barry, I reckon he's decent," I said, sliding off and giving the horse a hearty slap on the neck. "And he feels pretty good. He might only be six or seven weeks off a run."

"He has been doing a lot of walking and trotting," Barry considered. "It's time to get in touch with Mr Barton. He trains them for us."

"Maybe," I said.

"What do you mean 'maybe'?" he asked.

"Potentially good jump horses go for quite a few quid. We know he's good. Why don't we sell him before risking him on a racetrack?"

Barry shook his head. "They have to prove it. One run would be enough, if he showed enough in it. Then you could have buyers from all over Britain and Ireland smelling after him. But you can't expect anyone to fork out without having some idea of what they're getting."

"Maybe," I replied. "Maybe not."

"Look, if he won a good bumper at a good track you'd have agents and trainers around him like bees around a honeypot. Who knows what he might make? Three, maybe four hundred grand, if you got on the right side of a bidding war."

It was impossible not to picture what the impact of such a sale might be on this place. The desperate immediate pressure would be lifted in an instant. Mind you, putting the thing into training would be a drain on resources that simply weren't there. And the world was full of morning glories, horses that promised plenty at first and whose careers subsequently were nothing but a long litany of disappointment.

Still, this white-nosed giant had managed to put a smile

on a couple of faces on a dirty morning.

"What are you two ladies grinning like schoolgirls at?" Dorothy demanded, arriving into the yard.

"Luke thinks the four-year-old out of Governess is good, ma'am," Barry told her.

"Yeah, there's definitely something there," I added.

"That's good to hear," she said. "Although you're so thin, I imagine he thought he was running loose."

"Barry seems to think one good bumper run could make him worth quite a lot of money," I said.

"Well, Barry knows these things," she replied casually, although I did notice a brief smile. She probably had a price worked out already, I guessed. "He throws that off-fore out a bit."

"You wouldn't know it on top," I said. "He's got a very easy, comfortable stride."

"Hmmn," was all she said, taking off towards a couple of two-year-olds who had a date with the lunging ring.

I'd noticed a slight lightening of her mood. The deep lines on her face, full of grief and worry, were still there but eased a little. Now that there was an objective to work towards, the feeling of helplessness had gone. There was a job to do and she intended to get on with it, regardless of illness or anything else. The previous night she had even arrived into the small television room off the kitchen with a bottle of champagne.

"What are we celebrating?" I asked.

"Harry just rang and said those horrible little Revenue people are willing to row along with this plan of turning Ardfield into a hotel. He also said the money that you and he provided as a lump sum convinced them of my seriousness," she said. "And besides, there are only a few bottles of this particular Bolly left: might as well polish it off before my daughters try and sell it."

"They sound like they're under dreadful pressure," I told her. "Stress can make anyone say nasty things."

"Don't worry. Alicia didn't rip my heart out or anything so dramatic," she said, sitting down on the chair opposite, ignoring the drone of the frantic chat show on the telly. "She's always tended towards the operatic. Even as a little girl, there was never any in-between: either hysterically happy or roaring. If she fell on the floor it was always like her leg had fallen off."

"And Elizabeth is the opposite?" I asked.

"She is much quieter. And she's a good girl really. But don't underestimate our little one. She misses nothing. They just made bad choices in the husband stakes. George and Myles are well bred, speak proper and are pretty much useless when it comes to surviving on their own."

"Meaning?"

"Meaning they both got good starts in life, inherited well and everything they've turned their hand to, be it either property, land or shares, has gone belly up," she said. "But then maybe I am being horrible. The same thing could be said for the girls. They looked to have everything handed to them too. And in effect they've got nothing only a mountain of debt and a stubborn bitch of a mother. So what about you?"

"What about me?"

"Ever come close to having kids of your own?"

I thought of the couple of girls that I'd once thought might be possibly ones to settle down with. One got tired of waiting for a commitment and moved on. The other didn't wait for that, hooked up with another guy, and left me feeling righteously wronged for a while before finally admitting relief. There had been others, plenty of them enjoyable and fulfilling on their own terms, leaving some nice memories, but nothing serious. Certainly nothing remotely like the commitment required for kids, even marriage.

"No, nothing like that," I said.

"I know your type, all right. The old 'hump them and dump them' boys." She laughed briefly, pouring herself another glass. "You artists are all the same, licentious buggers. And as for having been a jockey . . . ha!"

I grinned. It was nice, sitting here, having a drink, pretending to watch TV.

"I really am very grateful, Luke," she said. "And not just for the money – although the money was a fantastic gesture."

"Happy to do it," I said, meaning it. "I presume Harry is in for a lot of work with legal documents."

"Yes. And he's being a real old soldier about it too. Because everything is equal shares with the girls, he wants everything tied up watertight legally. In case the girls decide to go down the law route and argue their mother is out of her mind. What do you think?"

"Do I think you're out of your mind? Yeah, I guess so. I mean who wants to run a hotel?"

"Hah! That will be the day: me standing behind a counter. Maybe Alicia will be in the kitchen," she laughed. "And George will carry the bags!"

We watched the telly in silence for a while.

"I would have been lost without you, Luke. During all of this," she said out of the blue. "You're a very capable young man."

There wasn't anything I could think of to say at that moment, or do. So I just grinned sheepishly at her and tried not to appear as ridiculously gratified by what she'd said as I felt.

"Your exhibition officially opens soon, doesn't it?" she asked.

"Yeah, in a couple of days."

"Have you given any thought to what you're going to do?"

The truth was I had. There was work backing up at a major rate back home, new stuff I was excited about getting to grips with. And there was the rest of my life to get on with. The trainer I rode out for had been on twice wondering when I would be back. There were electricians waiting to get into the cottage to finish off a wiring job. Hardly earth-shattering stuff but the details of an existence I'd carved out for myself, an existence a lot more real than hanging around an old woman and an even older house and all the conflicting emotions that both were provoking.

"There are a few things to do over here still," I said after a while. "People I haven't seen in ages. Those horses of yours aren't going to exercise themselves either. And I suppose I can always paint wherever – if I'm okay to stay for a little while?"

"That shouldn't be a problem," she said. "You can be the first unofficial guest in the new regime."

"How much for the B&B?"

"Don't worry about that. You've given a deposit."

The following day and money was also on my mind. The white-nosed horse was good. Exactly how good was impossible to know. Barry's point was a good one about how much more he might be worth on the back of a win, but against that was the very real possibility of him never even making a run. Horses were like glass, always just a bad step away from injury, or even worse. All the talent in the world was no use if it couldn't be kept sound. Maybe it was time to try and cash in, without Dorothy having to know anything.

O'Donoghue's card was still in my wallet. She didn't have a problem with selling him horses, and he had said to ring if he could do anything.

It felt ridiculous ringing such a man out of the blue. He was dealing in millions every minute of the day. His time was valued by important people around the globe. But if I got on to a message box, he could ring back in his own time, if he wanted to. At best I reckoned I might get a secretary. On the second ring he picked up.

"Yes?"

"Mr O'Donoghue, it's Luke Delamere, the painter. I met you at –"

"Luke, how are you?" he boomed. "What's up? Have you got a masterpiece to show me?"

"I wouldn't go so far as to call him a masterpiece. At least not yet," I said. "Sorry about ringing you on spec like this but you did say to get in touch if there was anything you could do to help Dorothy."

"Of course, what is it?"

"She has a few three and four-year-olds, most of which she's trying to get ready for the sales," I explained. "But I rode one this morning that felt more than a bit good."

"Really, that's interesting."

"I realise I don't know much about the jumps side of things but I do twig when a horse gives me a good feel. And this one does."

128

"What are you proposing?"

"Would you be interested in buying this horse?"

"I'm always interested in buying potential talent," he said. "How much are we talking about?"

"Good bumper horses can go for six figures easily."

"Correct. But proven bumper horses – winners with the scope to go on and jump a fence. Are you asking me to pony up that sort of cash on an unraced animal?"

"What sort of figure would you be prepared to pay?" I asked, feeling more than a little weird, haggling with Gerard O'Donoghue.

"Hell, Luke, you're putting me in an awkward situation here," he said. "I want to help, but not at any cost."

He was right of course and the gaucherie of my approach was suddenly all too obvious. Even on the other end of a phone I felt myself blush.

"Please forgive me, Mr O'Donoghue. I can't believe how stupid I'm being."

"Hey, call me Gerry, and don't be embarrassed. You're trying to do the best for your mother. I respect that."

In the circumstances he was showing a level of class that no amount of money could account for.

"Tell you what, if things are really tight, I'll give seventy thousand for the horse," he said. "Actually, any more than that and your mother would throw it back in my face. She'd see it for what it is."

"I've made enough of an ass of myself this morning," I said. "I take it you won't be heartbroken if I try and forget this conversation ever happened."

He laughed. "The motivation was right," he said. "Technique might need a little work. But don't be a stranger."

Chapter 16

Rod was underwhelmed. The normally exuberant PR man surveyed the large throng milling around the Ormond and obviously didn't like what he saw.

"No one's buying," he seethed.

I wondered if he was on a percentage from the gallery owners. It didn't work like that. This wasn't some sales ring where each painting was bid over in a matter of minutes.

"Don't worry," I reassured him. "It usually goes like this. The first time a lot of buyers see their purchases is when they're delivered."

Rod didn't cheer up much.

"It's just when Gerard O'Donoghue came for the preview I was sure he'd buy something. And he hasn't," he said dolefully. "Selling to him would be easy to sell to the papers – bring us plenty good publicity."

I nodded. Each to his own speciality. Rod clearly knew what filled column inches. Selling to O'Donoghue would have been nice for me too. But I'd never been one to ponder too much on why someone didn't buy my work. It was still a thrill to find that anyone was willing to cough up for it at all.

O'Donoghue wasn't interested. That was his prerogative. Once the stuff left home, it wasn't mine any more. It existed on its own terms. Ownership really could be counted in pounds and pence. The idea that it might hang on anyone's wall was enough. If only other parts of the mind could be so easily cordoned off.

Julia O'Neill was back. Part of me resented how uncomfortable she made me feel. But there was straightforward admiration too. The woman looked spectacular. The fact I clearly figured on her radar purely as a professional duty irritated my ego a lot more than it should have. It would be nice, I reckoned, to figure in such a woman's life as someone worthy of more attention than that. She paced slowly around the room, chatting briefly to a few people, but examining the pictures closely.

"Honestly, the swill they serve at these things never wavers from awful. Here," Jerry said, handing me a takeaway coffee. "I had to go across the road to that café to get a decent cup. What are you looking at?"

He'd flown across that morning. The first thing he'd done when I picked him up at the airport was stuff a receipt into my hand. It was confirmation of the transfer of fifty-thousand euro into Dorothy's account. "You owe me large," he'd said.

Jerry followed where my gaze had been and identified his target.

"Ah, the lovely Miss O'Neill," he cooed. "And you getting all cow-eyed – *aww*!"

"I might owe you, Jerry, but that won't stop me

chastising you," I warned.

"Ooh, promises," he laughed and then called across to Julia. "Oh, Miss O'Neill!"

She turned around. Jerry's volume meant so did most of the rest of the gallery. I noticed the attention made her shift uncomfortably.

"What do you think of my boy's work?" he asked a little more quietly when she joined us. "Be honest."

"You didn't read the review then?" she asked him.

"I never read reviews," he said, affecting disdain. "Only regard what someone is prepared to say up to your eyeballs."

I looked at her and delivered a 'sorry, but I can't help him' look. Or at least I hoped it was.

"Okay," she played along. "I think it's excellent, the portraits especially. They give a hint of Le Brocquy and I can't think of a higher compliment."

"Indeed not," Jerry smiled. "And what do you think of my boy?"

"Jerry," I interrupted, "can you contain your mischief-making just for a little while? Or at least until I find a hole that will swallow me up."

She laughed at that. It sounded good: just a pity I couldn't enjoy it more. Damn Jerry. When he got playful he was capable of anything.

"He's not the worst looking in the world, is he? And he can be mildly interesting to talk to – when he wants to be," he said.

"Really?" she grinned, although I noticed a blush too. Damn, damn, damn Jerry.

"Come on," he continued. "My boy is obviously smitten. Why don't you throw him a bone here?"

"Are you normally his wingman?" she asked, staring at Jerry, maybe even hoping to unsettle him. If so, she clearly didn't know her man.

"Oh, this one doesn't need a wingman, darling. At least not normally. But you seem to have got him all tongue-tied and irritable," he smiled. "If I were you, I'd make the most of it."

This was getting ridiculous. If it weren't for the little matter of a fifty-grand docket resting in my pocket, I would have been sorely tempted to go through Jerry for a short-cut. As it was, my embarrassment was too much to let him carry on like this.

"I'm sorry about this," I said to her. "Jerry's a good guy but he doesn't know when enough's enough. And now is enough."

I looked at my pal meaningfully. It was sufficient to put a halt to his gallop, at least temporarily.

"Oh, don't be so sensitive, Luke, I was just . . ."

"I know what you were just. And while I might know that, Julia doesn't. So let's stop now, all right?"

He nodded, I apologised again to her, and turned to walk away.

"Hold on," Julia O'Neill said. "I'd hate to be the cause of a row between two friends. So I guess I'll just have to offer it up for my sins, and for friendship everywhere."

"Offer what?" I asked.

"I warn you, it's a long time since I've had a really good lobster, so dinner is going to cost you." She smiled slightly.

"Good on you, girl!" Jerry laughed. "I knew there was something about you."

I didn't know what to say. She looked at me, the smile

still in place, more than a little mocking, and challenging at the same time. Christ, she was beautiful.

"Well?" she asked.

"Friday night, at eight?" I said lamely.

"In the interests of friendship," she said and handing me a business card with her phone number on it, "I guess I'd better accept. Now if you'll both forgive me, I have other things to attend to."

I watched her leave, noticing a sway to her hips that provoked some very unartistic thoughts. This was getting ridiculous.

"You can thank me now," Jerry said.

"There will come a time when . . ." I began. "But, yeah, thank you."

The rest of the evening passed in a blur, shaking hands, making small-talk, a couple of interviews, the polite, meaningless words that oil the business of selling. One or two people remarked on how I was in such good form. Amazing, I reckoned, what being mortally embarrassed into a date can do for a person.

By the end, Rod had cheered up considerably. A couple of confirmed sales, and three other strong interests was a good score for one night in anyone's terms. The gallery owners seemed pleased too – a good night for everyone.

"When are you heading back to England?" Rod asked as I put my coat on to leave.

"Not for a little while yet. There are things for me to do here," I replied.

"So, you're available for some more press?" he asked.

Depends on who the press are, I thought.

"Sure, if it helps."

My step was lighter than I could have imagined

walking back to the car park. The following morning, Barry would load 'White Nose' up into a horsebox and we'd head for a neighbouring trainer's gallops where I'd find out if my first impressions were correct. My luck seemed to be still in, work-wise, and most of all there was Friday to look forward to. It was a heady cocktail, nearly enough to put everything else to the back of my mind. Nearly.

I still hadn't rung the police about the forged pictures, the jumpy Dane and my suspicions about the gallery. One reason was because suspicions were all they mostly were. Getting the paintings identified as fakes would be straightforward enough, but what would that prove? That there were more forgeries in a world awash with them? No doubt not passing on this information put me on shaky legal ground, and the idea of not helping out an investigation into Michael's murder was one that kept me from sleep almost as much as the flashbacks to finding his body, and the evidence of what was done to him. But still I didn't get in touch with Mark Foley.

Not being able to prove anything didn't prevent me from not knowing, or at least suspecting. Michael had been involved in something illegal enough to provoke someone into killing him, maybe. Foley's initial hunch could still be correct, just opportunists who went too far. But if opportunists killed it was due to panic. Burning someone suggested anything but panic.

The absence of any breakthrough in the police investigation was hardly encouraging either. Jerry had told me a police friend had once confided in him that unless they had a firm lead on a case within the first few days, usually their work fizzled out into nothing. Foley struck me as a capable man, but also a man under pressure from various angles. Was Michael's death just another example of inexplicable cruelty – sad, regrettable but unresolvable?

Most of all, though, I didn't want suspicions about Michael to ruin his memory. If they were correct, then so be it. But what amount of hurt could be caused by having them thrown out there? People presumed the worst: the old no-smoke-without-fire logic. What would that do to Dorothy? She was starting to rally again, fighting to make sense of a life torn apart, fighting to honour her husband's memory through the preservation of what much of his life revolved around. The fight was hard but it was sustaining her too.

She was still alive. Michael was still dead. Nothing could alter that. If I could find out why he'd died, without inflicting unnecessary pain, then that was worth doing. At least it would be the truth that would have to be faced up to, not innuendo and suspicion. Emotionally it made sense. Logically I wasn't so sure. Best then to leave the police out of it, for the moment at least.

I was so engrossed in the dilemma that I heard or saw nothing, just identified the object coming towards me as a baseball bat in the millisecond before it smashed into my face. The pain was excruciating. The world felt like it had dissolved. Everything was fluid. I was only mildly aware of lying on concrete, and of boots in front of my face. Mostly there was only pain. There was no feeling from the waist down. I tried to move my legs but nothing happened. Dear Jesus, I thought, don't let me be paralysed. And then the blows came.

Some were with the bat again, aimed at my head,

intent on really hurting me, or worse. A few boots dug into my ribs, and at my head and back. I curled into a ball, hands over my head and face, leaving the rest of me to fend for itself. I wanted to shout, scream 'Stop, you've got the wrong man!', but a split-second glance upwards convinced me they hadn't.

The figure with the bat had red hair, fair skin and freckles. It was the one from outside Ardfield, who'd treated me with contempt, the one that I'd chased until the cops stopped me, the one who'd pointed a gun. Dear Jesus, don't let him have a gun, I thought. It was the last one I had.

The blows were too much. There wasn't any feeling any more. It was just a blur of pain. One of them must have done the job because I passed out, tasting concrete, briefly recognising the squeal of car tyres turning and realising I was about to die.

Chapter 17

There was the sound of an engine and motion. I couldn't see anything, just black darkness. Even after managing to open my eyes everything was dark. I tentatively moved a hand to my face. Even in these circumstances, that provoked relief. I squeezed my eyes shut again, feeling the cake of what presumably was blood clinging to the lids. My toes wriggled when requested. I moved my hands over my body, checking everything was intact. But even that slight movement produced pain. Ribs protested at even the slightest touch or move. My back was sore beyond belief. I felt dreadful, even more so after a cough produced blood in my mouth and paroxysms of agony. But I was alive, able to move a little, and conscious.

Years before I'd taken a heavy fall in a race and been briefly knocked out. The sensation on waking up again was unpleasant: a queasy, sickly feeling, a massive headache and relief at actually feeling that way. This was a thousand times more intense. That horse hadn't meant to clips heels with another animal and come down. And I knew where I was: Yarmouth racecourse on a wet Tuesday evening. Familiar stuff, not like this.

It took every bit of mental strength not to panic. Dreaming might be nursed in darkness as another painter had told me once, but this was a nightmare. Concentrate on what's identifiable, I ordered myself. Moving my feet and arms around the confines, it felt like the boot of a car. There was a smell of oil in the corner. I moved to feel around and a metallic shape filled my hand. Probably a jack, I guessed.

Suddenly the car started to slow, then tilted slightly as if turning. It stopped, the engine still turning over. There were footsteps and the sound of metal screeching, like a gate opening. Then the footsteps came back and the car lurched forward. The surface became bumpy and rough for a while before the car stopped again. Briefly there was the sound of another engine nearby. That too stopped. Then more than one set of footsteps walked closer.

Any idea of springing up at anyone was ridiculous. Just the thought of moving my head was bad enough. I couldn't overpower a kitten. Long ago I'd learned fighting was only an option when there was a chance of success. There was none here. And somehow I was still alive. The trick was to stay that way. A voice sounded very loud outside, loud enough to make me want to breathe more quietly.

"What the hell is this place?" a high-pitched Dublin accent said.

"Only the perfect place to get rid of someone," another voice replied. It was the red-haired one. The confidence that had been there at Ardfield was still intact. Any idea that I might have survived the beating was clearly ludicrous. "It's a quarry. They tore a massive hole in the ground here, a hundred feet deep, when they were building houses all over the place. Now it's disused. And do you know what happens when you dig that deep?"

"What?"

"It fills with water, that's what," he replied. "See that pump over there. That's on all the time, pumping water out, or else it'd be flooding the country. No one will ever know, at least not until the whole thing is drained. And that won't be for a long time."

My last thought, before the boot opened and night air and moonlight flooded in, was not a new one: when in doubt, do nothing,

One of them grabbed me under the arms, the other by the belt on my trousers, then under my belly to get a better grip.

"Jesus, he's heavy," the first one said.

"Dead weight," Red Hair said, grunting with effort.

The movement was too much. I groaned with pain.

"He ain't that fucking dead," the first one said, his voice rising. "Put a bullet in him."

I felt so weak. It was enough to barely move, never mind run or even walk. But my mind was different. Put a bullet in him, he'd said. Jesus Christ, this was it, I thought. Bitterness and fear welled up in my throat. This had to be a mistake. This wasn't supposed to happen to an ordinary guy, an ordinary painter, not some gangster getting dumped like so much refuse in the middle of nowhere, a gun placed at the back of the head and nothing but oblivion ahead. And mixed up in all of it was shame, at not doing more to fight.

"Go," the first one repeated.

There was a metallic sound. I braced myself, closed my eyes, tried not to cry out in terror.

There was a click. And then nothing. Another click and then a curse.

"Fucking thing's jammed," Red Hair said viciously.

I felt piss running down my leg.

"Fuck this. We haven't time for pricking around. He's fucked anyway. And we're getting paid to leave no trace. Best not leave a bullet in him."

My car was just in front of us, with the back door open. They unceremoniously shoved me in. If Red Hair decided to reach for his gun again, there was nothing I could do. They slammed the door on my coiled-up body, clearly keen to get away quickly. Red Hair leaned in the driver door, released the handbrake and shoved the car forward.

"Right!" he shouted and jumped clear.

The car jumped forward and downwards. I didn't move, terrified they might be looking down. The first thing that hit me was the thud of the car shuddering to a halt. And then water started to flood in.

It didn't seem possible anything could be so cold.

Red Hair had left the driver-door window open and the car quickly slid under the surface, tilting to its side as it did. To hell with who might be looking, I told myself: time to move. There was a moment when the thought of moving seemed worse than simply lying there and waiting for the end. But fear, and the cold, proved a hell of a motivator.

Parts of me I didn't know existed protested loudly at twisting and turning in an attempt to get to the nearest back door. It wouldn't be long before water filled the car.

Pulling at the latch and trying to push the door out didn't work. The force of the water was too much. Panic rose into my throat again. I didn't have the force to break glass. There was no handle to turn, just some buttons, a technological advance that was about to kill me. I despairingly slashed at the buttons and miraculously the back window came down. Water engulfed me. There were only seconds to get out. I took a deep breath. The cold was making me numb. It was now or never. One last effort got my head and shoulders out. And somehow the rest of me followed.

The memory of an old war film where a sinking ship dragged desperately swimming survivors down with it provoked a few feeble kicks. Even panic couldn't produce more. A final almost obscene gulping sound saw the car disappear further into blackness. So much of me was prepared to follow it, just to stop the pain. But survival was a more primal instinct. I kicked desperately again for the surface.

An almost full moon provided enough light to gaze around. The sides of the vast crater towered above, grey and forbidding. There was no sound from above. The nearest side was about twenty yards away. It might as well have been twenty miles. I all but floated to the side, touched rock and tried to put my feet on something solid. The drop under the water was all but sheer. My hands scrambled to get a hold but there was nothing except scree. It all came away. There was nothing to cling to. Panic returned, and it was so cold. It didn't seem possible for cold to hurt so much. This was no theoretical concept; this was hard physical reality. The realisation that even in the whole of my health I wouldn't last long at such a temperature only increased the panic. I kicked my way along the face, searching desperately for anything that might hold me. Small, sharp grey bits of shard rock kept tumbling down on my face. It felt like being mocked; so close to dry land but with no chance of getting on to it. And then my hand touched something different.

It was a hose. I glanced up. Its three-inch-diameter length stretched upwards out of sight into the darkness. That made sense. All the underground streams and channels forced to concentrate into this crater by all the quarrying didn't stop running just because it might be close to filling up. I didn't look down into the water's dark depths. But it could easily be hundreds of feet deep. It would have to be for Red Hair to be so confident of the car remaining undetected. However, a pump would have to regularly come on to keep this level constant. I grabbed the hose and tried to heave myself up and out. My body felt terrible but fright trumped the agony.

"Come on," I pleaded out loud to myself. "Come on, come on!"

Eyes clenched tight with the effort and, almost without knowing it, my arms somehow worked enough for me to feel a different kind of cold. Clear stars indicated a bright, clear and chilly night for everyone with the good sense not to be swimming around in lethal quarry water. Soaked to the skin, a breeze that might otherwise be bracing now cut through me, containing its own danger. But the immediate danger of drowning had gone away.

My feet scrambled, trying to find some purchase, and miraculously found some. It was a few feet above the water, a tiny ledge, just inches wide. But it was enough. With the last reserves of fear-inspired energy, I hauled myself up the hose one last time and fell on to perhaps the one piece of level surface around the crater. Gulping down air, shivering uncontrollably and sobbing with relief, I peered up and despaired at ever being able to get out. And that was the last I remembered.

Chapter 18

Julia O'Neill sat at the side of the hospital bed. A tube stuck out of my bare arm and a drip was hanging near the headboard. The unmistakable odour of disinfectant filled my senses. Weak winter sunshine came in through the window nearby. I moved my toes and fingers again, just slightly but enough to know. And then I kept looking at Julia O'Neill. After a few seconds she glanced up and caught me staring. I smiled.

"Busted," I said, not recognising my own voice.

"I think that's an understatement," she said, placing a magazine on a table and standing up.

"What are you doing here?" I asked, swallowing sorely.

"Funny question," she replied, sitting on the side of the bed.

She was wearing a light perfume that overwhelmed any chemical smell. I reckoned this might be what love felt like: or at least lust. Feeling that, after everything that happened, filled me with joy. I was alive.

"I get a phone call from the police at five in the morning, asking if I know someone about five-foot-ten, dark hair, skinny. I wonder if they could narrow it down and they say: 'Can you identify a person?' And I think: 'Oh Christ, someone's dead.' But they say no, he looks like he might be, but he's actually okay. We just need somebody to confirm who he is. Apparently the only name, or form of ID on you was the business card I gave you at the exhibition."

"I'm sorry," I said.

"So you should be. I show up here and find you looking like a butcher's window, tubes sticking out of you, dead to the world. It was all I could do not to puke."

"I can have that impact on women," I croaked again. "How long have I been here?"

"Let's see, that was yesterday morning bright and early, so thirty-six hours since then. How are you feeling?"

"Okay," and surprisingly it wasn't a lie, or at least not much of a lie. I'd caught a glimpse of myself in a mirror built into a cupboard at the foot of the bed. My face was hard to look at. There were a few stitches and bandages and lots of black bruising which I knew was going to be at its worst a couple of days after taking the blows. A sneaky look down under the hospital gown revealed much more bruising. But it all looked superficial, until I moved.

"You've fractured a couple of ribs, and they're worried about concussion but apart from that, they seem to think you're okay," Julia said. "So what were you doing jumping into a quarry? You're incredibly lucky. Normally there's never anyone there. But a farmer looking for some stray sheep went in purely by chance to see if they might have fallen in. And there you were."

"I didn't jump. I was thrown in. All this," I said, pointing to the bruising, "was done before it."

She looked at me like concussion was making me talk crazy.

"Why would anyone want to try and kill you?" she said, asking the only question that mattered.

It obviously wasn't some random thing. Bumping into Red Hair once was misfortune enough: twice simply wasn't on. And he was being paid. That's what he'd said. That fitted too. He was way too assured to be some gouger chancing his arm. Someone wanted me dead.

The idea was horrifying. That clicking sound of the gun failing to fire would haunt me. Just the thought of it made my stomach heave. God, I'd been so scared. Still young enough for mortality to be really just a concept rather than anything tangible, thinking about someone wanting me killed was hard to comprehend. Even more so when trying to tease out who it might be.

If he'd wanted to, Red Hair could have shot me the first time at Ardfield. There would have been time to clear any jam, no one around, ideal. But he hadn't. And I'd chased him, I remembered, shivering involuntarily at my stupidity and naivety. I wasn't a target then. Something else was.

It had to be something to do with the fake paintings. It was too coincidental. Michael murdered in the most horrible way on the back of clearly being mixed up in something way out of his league, after which people with guns start breaking into the house and nervous continentals with fake paintings show up. There had to be a connection, I figured, trying but failing to ignore another possibility.

Jerry Barnett had once advised the first question to ask whenever trying to reason out why shit happens is: "*Qui bono*, old boy?" And asking who would benefit from me being off the scene inexorably led to Dorothy's family. George and Alicia, Myles and Elizabeth: all of them under financial pressure, all eager for Ardfield to be sold, all desperate to bend Dorothy to their will.

Did removing me help their cause? They knew the old woman much better than me, enough surely to know that Dorothy's steely resolve meant she was unlikely to be swayed by anyone, least of all someone she'd known for a wet week. But how did it look? I show up and suddenly there are plans to reinvent the old house as a hotel, maintaining the family legacy. Maybe Alicia and Elizabeth didn't believe in coincidence either. Or maybe they wanted to remove any chance of having to divide up the inheritance more than fifty-fifty.

But could that provoke them into killing? Alicia was passionate and quick to anger but hiring someone to actually murder? It didn't seem possible. Elizabeth had a quiet intensity that made such pre-planning seem more likely but, even so, she had been civil to me, pleasant almost. It was hard to credit she could be that good an actor. Or was it their husbands. I'd humiliated George the first time we met. He wasn't a type to forget that. Could he nurse a grudge this far?

There was a knock at the door. A man in a pin-striped suit came in.

"Ah, Mr Delamere, you're awake, I'm glad to see," he said. "I'm John Sexton. I'm the consultant surgeon here. Do you mind if I take a quick look at you?"

He briefly shone a light in my eyes, told me to follow

his finger in front of me, asked a few questions and then looked at Julia.

"I can see you're a lucky man, Mr Delamere." He smiled at her.

I noticed she blushed, hardly the expected response of a woman appearing so self-possessed.

"And your luck has extended to this as well," he went on. "We've done a lot of tests, taken X-rays – and apart from a couple of fractured ribs, you're remarkably intact. Can I ask you what happened?"

"Fell into a hole," I said.

Julia looked at me but said nothing.

"Really," he said. "So these cuts and abrasions are because of a fall, not the result of a beating?"

"Yes."

"You do realise I have to report any suspicions I have to the police?" Sexton continued. "And I have."

"I hate to put you in an awkward situation," I said. "How long before I can get out of here?"

"Are you in some rush?"

"Kind of."

"You're going to be under supervision here for at least the rest of the week. Falling down and hitting your head is a complicated injury. We have to monitor you constantly."

"But you said there's nothing fundamentally wrong with me."

"We have to monitor you," he insisted. "Now, if you'll excuse me."

He glanced back at me with a quizzical look as he closed the door behind him. I didn't blame him. It must have seemed ridiculous to maintain a simple fall had caused these injuries. And it was obvious he had to call the police. Sexton knew what he had to do. I didn't. But my inclination was to follow the old advice: when in doubt, do nothing.

"Would you mind telling me what that was about?" Julia asked. "Why didn't you tell him?"

"It wouldn't change anything, so why bother?" I replied. "I shouldn't have said anything to you either."

"You're welcome," she said. "Anything else I can do?"

"Yeah, you can help me get dressed."

There were objections from Julia and commonsense reasons galore for staying in bed. But I got up anyway. If Red Hair and his pal believed me to be dead, it wouldn't do any harm to maintain that illusion for a while. I had no idea what I proposed to do with such an advantage but the idea of taking some sort of initiative back felt important.

"Right," she eventually said. "Let's get the martyr into his pants."

Any romantic illusions the gorgeous woman might have had about the artist and his sensitivities rapidly disappeared. Mystery could hardly be maintained in a hospital gown, or in groaning efforts to climb into a pair of sweatpants bought in a hurry. A hoodie and a pair of sneakers also purchased by Julia in a nearby supermarket were also fun to put on. At the end it was all I could do not to crawl exhausted back into bed.

"A thought has occurred to me," Julia asked, tying my laces. "Where are you going?"

"I don't know. A hotel. Just somewhere to rest up for a day or two."

"Christ, normally it's 'Can I come in for coffee?'," she said.

"What?"

"Someone's got to keep an eye on you. You'd better stay with me."

"That's not what I meant," I protested.

"I know," she said, smiling slightly. "That's why I'm going to play nursey."

Normally that would have been an image to put a pep in my step. But not now. Every step was a challenge. And of course the elevator had to be out of order. Three flights of stairs were great fun, but not as bad as getting past an admissions officer reluctant to let me sign out. Phone calls were made. I heard Sexton's name being mentioned. And eventually I was allowed scrawl on various bits of paper.

"You're a silly man," the admissions woman said in an Eastern European accent that somehow made the words sound more ominous.

I couldn't argue with her, but left anyway.

The motion of the taxi had me asleep in minutes. Only when it jolted to a stop did I snap awake, briefly disorientated and looking around. We were at an apartment complex, three storeys.

"Sorry, I'm at the top," Julia said, reading my mind.

The taxi driver earned a tip by giving me a shoulder to lean on as we traversed the outdoor steps. It wasn't as bad as before, except for ribs that protested with every twist and turn. The body was getting used to its circumstances, adapting, making the best of it: remarkable in its own way, reassuring too.

Not having a phone or my wallet was disconcerting. They must have emptied my pockets before getting to that quarry. Part of me wanted to ring or text Dorothy, let her know I was okay, come up with an excuse for not being around: the same with Jerry. They deserved not to worry. But I put it off. Instead I rang the airlines on Julia's landline.

It was a small apartment. An archway from the sitting room led into a tiny kitchen where a kettle started to boil.

"The bathroom is down the hall on the left," she said, leaning backwards in the kitchen to catch my eye. "Your bedroom is across from it."

"I can't thank you enough," I said. "And sorry for dumping on you like this."

"If you think you'll be waited on hand and foot, you're sadly mistaken," she said briskly. "I have work to do. And you have to heal. So sit there, watch the telly and make yourself as inconspicuous as possible."

"Yes, Sister."

The spare room was tiny, had just a single bed, and that night felt like a little oasis. Julia had sent out for Chinese food and I devoured mine and half of hers: all in all a good sign. Then we talked.

She was from Galway originally, comfortable upbringing, two younger brothers, and although she loved home it was never going to be home forever, not when there was so much art to see out in the world. At sixteen her school went on a trip to Italy that included a day in Florence.

"It changed everything for me," she smiled. "That so much beauty could come out of the human imagination just seemed incredible."

Her eyes sparkled at the memory. She was actually much more of an art-lover than I was. Yet I was the artist, supposedly.

"Can I look at some of your work?" I said.

"Not a chance," she laughed. "It's not here anyway. I don't have the space. Most of it is at home in my parents' place."

"A pity. I'd like to see it."

"Not going to happen," she announced. "I paint for fun, for myself. Having it examined by someone like you would be weird."

"What do you mean someone like me?" I asked.

I got a look that felt like an X-ray. There was an uncomfortable few seconds of quiet which was strange. Normally I appreciated silence. Julia O'Neill, it appeared, was the same. But eventually she seemed to make a decision.

"I think you're a major talent," she said bluntly.

I felt myself blush.

"Even before we met, I knew your work, loved a lot of it," she continued, "and some of what you're showing in the Ormond is beautiful. So the idea of a virtuoso examining cack-handed amateurishness isn't too appealing for the ego."

There wasn't a lot to say to that. She was way too generous.

"But I guess you're used to being fawned over," she grinned. "All those London art groupies flinging themselves at the brilliant Delamere."

It was true there were women who liked artists, for the association with art they provided, the whole artistic-muse cliché. A pal of mine referred to them dismissively as 'the fishing fleet', an assortment of trendies eager to trade affection for, who knew – credibility, excitement, abuse? And they could be great fun. I wasn't any more immune to flattery than anyone else. Like most men, when an attractive woman insisted I was wonderful, I found it hard to disagree. And the appeal of easy sex could be intoxicating. The idea of Julia O'Neill thinking I might view her in such terms was unsettling.

"They're hardly flinging themselves," I grinned. "Maybe the odd gentle lob."

"God, men!" she said with a sigh that resonated with the history of thousands of years' worth of female indulgence for male vanity and stupidity.

"Oh, come on, I'm kidding. Anyway, I bet a hell of a lot of blokes have flung their hearts at you – and meant it."

"You can forget flattery."

"I'd mean it," I said, immediately embarrassed at the obvious vehemence in my voice. "If I could move."

It was a weak effort at a save and neither of us was fooled. There was another silence, and then Julia switched off the telly.

"I'm bushed," she said. "You must be too. Any plans for tomorrow, besides watching TV?"

"Just a trip to the airport," I said.

"Why?"

"There's a flight to Copenhagen at noon. There are new credit cards coming here in the morning. I hope you don't mind."

"What's in Copenhagen?"

I didn't want to lie to her. And I'd already blabbed about somebody trying to kill me. So I told her. It sounded almost melodramatic when spelled out in black and white. She didn't interrupt once, except to gasp at the point where Dorothy and I found Michael. There was an intensity about her focus on me that might have been part journalistic but not all. At the end she said nothing for a long time. I was getting used to her silences.

"So you're going to Copenhagen to try and find this guy who dropped the frauds off?" she said. "That's a bit of a long shot."

"I have the name of a gallery. The Frederick. In a part of the city called Hellerup."

"What's your plan? Pile in like Rambo? Especially when you're barely able to walk."

"Rambo isn't my style," I said. "But I do want to find out what I might be dealing with."

"You're in no shape to go anywhere."

"I'll be all right."

"Got enough in your account to cough up for two tickets?"

Chapter 19

I woke at half two in the morning, sweating, sitting up, scared and briefly unaware of where I was. Then it came: Julia, her apartment, the spare bedroom, Dublin. Thank Christ, I swore to myself and flopped back onto the bed.

That had been unexpected. Dreams were a rare nighttime visitor to me. Usually I slept like a drunk sailor, passed out and dead to the world, the subconscious happily dormant and not screaming for attention.

It was the damn click of Red Hair's gun. The sound was so vivid and in my dream it still happened as it had, no bullet ending it all. Except Red Hair followed up in my mind, clubbing me with the heavy piece of iron that smelt of grease and oil and smashed into my face, blood coagulating with the spit and sweat of exertion from the body looming over me, viciously sending me into oblivion, purely for a few quid. All I kept saying was 'I'll pay you more to leave me alone!' screaming it, pleading. And still he kept hurting me.

There was no sound outside in the hall. I hoped I

hadn't screamed out in my sleep and woken Julia. That would have been mortifying.

Age was catching up. There had been a couple of times when I was riding which had got hairy. That was the thing with falls on the flat. They were unexpected, and worse than over the jumps because of that and the fast speed. I'd walked away knowing it was important to ride in the next race. Even as a kid, it was obvious that pondering on the possible was the road to giving up. I won the next and was fine.

But that was then when I was fit and young and able to bounce. Still reasonably fit I might be, and hardly a fossil yet, but there was no guarantee about bouncing back from this. Any sleep I got later that night was fitful.

There wasn't much chance to catch up in the plane either. I'd never been to Denmark. It seemed quite a long way away. But the flight took just a couple of hours. And we didn't even land there. Instead we landed in Malmö in Sweden. The sales rep at Dublin airport assured us it was just a short bus drive from there to Copenhagen. He wasn't wrong. The Oresund Bridge, joining the two countries was almost five miles long and even in winter gloom felt breathtaking in its scope. Julia, sitting next to me, showed me a brochure with pictures of it.

"They know how to build a bridge," I grinned.

"It's a good job you can paint," she replied.

"I'll leave the words to you, Mrs Shakespeare."

All told, and nightmares aside, I was feeling a lot better. The ribs ached, but not intolerably so and the rest of me looked worse than it felt. There were a few stares in the plane from other passengers. There certainly wasn't much regret apparent when I didn't sit next to anyone.

And there was no regret from me when Julia slid in beside me.

"Why are you coming again?" I asked, suspecting it was a question much better left unasked.

"Why? Don't you want me to?" she asked, more than a little coquettishly.

The sight of that wide-eyed glance gently mocking me banished thoughts of aching, in favour of some rather more primal emotions.

"Relax," she ordered. "I'm not working on the side for the opposition."

"So, what is it then?"

"Well, first of all, I said I'd keep an eye on you and I usually try and do what I say I'm going to do. And secondly . . ."

"Yeah?"

"Jesus!" she exclaimed. "Because I like you – even if you are a dense klutz."

All aches disappeared at that. I felt myself grinning.

"And because you're paying," she pounced. "So you can wipe that smug smile off your face."

The bus depot looked like any similar building anywhere. The cold, however, was unique. A wind whipped in from the sea and cut through clothes more suitable for soft Irish rain than rasping Scandinavian ice. Braced against the conditions we found an information desk.

"Sorry, do you speak English?" I asked the woman behind the glass.

"Yes, sir. The majority of Danes can speak English rather well," she replied. "Can I help you?"

"We're trying to find a hotel," I said. "A good one. Ideally somewhere near or in Hellerup. Is that far away?"

"No, sir. I'll just check here for you," she said, fingers moving quickly at a computer. Within a minute we were booked into a four-star.

"That's great," I said. "Can you tell us where the nearest taxis are?"

"Sure, about five hundred metres to the left. But you would be quicker going by train."

She wasn't wrong. Computer screens on the platform said the next train would leave at 8.26 and it left exactly on time. A short time later and we got out at Hellerup station where an attendant told us in perfect English the directions to our hotel.

"They know how to run trains too," I said.

"Fascist," was the response.

The staff at Reception were tall, blonde and remarkably pleasant considering one of their new guests looked like he'd fallen off the bridge on the way into town. And they knew the Frederick gallery.

"It's just off the main street, not far from the main post office: on the left as you walk from here. It is no more than a kilometre," said a tall young woman. "One double room, yes?"

Maybe it was the bangs to my head but the subject of sleeping arrangements hadn't crossed my mind once. The idea of sharing a bed with Julia had seemed as unlikely as it did exciting. But then that was before she let it be known she liked me.

"Yes, just the one room, but do you have twin singles?" Julia said smoothly.

"Yes, of course," the receptionist said and swiped my card for any additional charges.

"We don't want that card to melt with expense," Julia

said, glancing at me with an expression I couldn't read.

It was taking a bit of getting used to, trying to figure out what was going on in Julia O'Neill's head. And it didn't seem I was getting any better with practice.

The room was spacious and functional and as devoid of individuality as anything else owned by an international chain. And there were a pair of lonely-looking single beds in the middle – a pity.

"I don't know about you but I'm famished," I said. "How about room service? Or would you prefer we go out?"

"No, I'm tired. Room service sounds good. And then a long bath."

She scanned the menu and settled for a club sandwich with no fries. I ordered considerably more.

"Where do you put it?" she asked when I hung up. "You used to be a jockey for God's sake and you're still built like a whip."

"I don't know – maybe just lucky," I said, remembering again the torture of surviving on little but fresh air. "The weight was rough when I was riding, but it's settled down now. Doesn't really matter what I eat."

"Oh, just shut up!" She headed for the bathroom, then halted. "We'll take a look at those bandages later – but do you want to go first in here?"

I shook my head. Feeling a lot better was one thing, but now that the journey was over, an overwhelming tiredness started to take over. All I wanted was a little telly, some grub and a lot of sleep.

The waiter arrived with our meal just as Julia was finishing her bath, and waved away my offer of a tip. We sat on the bed, eating, and watching the international news. It was the usual assortment of global horror and despair, packaged into digestible sound-bite size and with a cute kicker-story at the end just in case the tone might be too low and stop people watching the ads. Bleak thoughts, I said to myself, all mixed up with death, and fright, and pain: best not to dwell too much. Life could have its up-sides too, like having Julia O'Neill, in a bathrobe, hair wet, generally looking spectacular, sitting next to you on a hotel bed.

I ate and pondered, not on man's ability to hurt and kill for the sake of it, but on what might happen the following day. What was I hoping to see in the Frederick gallery? Some basement factory churning out high-quality fakes, talented artists being whipped into fraud by gangster types carrying guns? It was ridiculous in its gung-ho simplicity, a result of watching too much pap on telly. But at the same time it was something that couldn't be ignored. It was worth checking out, just by someone who had a clue about what they were doing. I was still pondering when Julia stood up.

"Right, let's have a look at these cuts," she ordered.

I took off my shirt and stood up too. The bruising looked terrible but the worst was over, I reckoned.

"You'd swear I knew what I was looking at," she said, touching one of the bandages lightly. Her fingers were like charges of electricity through me. "There's no sign of infection that I can see. But I'm not really an expert."

"It feels itchy as hell," I said. "But that's good, shows things are starting to heal up."

"How do you feel in yourself?"

"Not bad," I said.

"Good," she said, and walked around to the far side of her bed. "Think we'll be able to push these together?"

164

Chapter 20

I woke first. Julia was sleeping, on her side, her back to me. There was a large beauty spot halfway down her back, prominent on that otherwise tawny, unblemished skin which had temporarily banished the world outside our room. Only a thin sheet covered her; the temperature in the room was warm. It was impossible not to slide closer and kiss that spot. Despite her being asleep, the response was immediate, a tiny grunt that carried an impossible erotic charge and a push backwards into me.

She had teasingly promised to be gentle with me the previous night. And there had been moments of almost unbearable tenderness mixed in with some rather more primal demands that must have given whoever was in the room next door an earful.

I didn't care, couldn't care. She seemed the same, urging me with words and hands and lips to sensations only barely guessed at before. It was all-enveloping. There was me and her and nothing else.

"Oh, you bastard," she'd gasped at me during a short

lull. "What's happening here?"

I hadn't trusted myself to speak and simply showed again how beautiful and sexy and plain fascinating I found her.

At some stage exhaustion must have set in and we slept. And it wasn't a nightmare about any clicking pistol-hammer that had woken me, rather the insistent sound of my phone alarm. Any irritation had been banished at the sight of that beauty spot.

"Hello, you," she said, turning over.

"Hi there, yourself," I replied. "Are you going to give me a chance to recover?"

"Only if you need one," she said, reaching under the sheet. "And apparently you don't."

It would have been lovely to stay in this ordinary room with this extraordinary woman forever. There was a straightforward appreciation of what we were doing physically that dovetailed seamlessly with a depth of intelligence I found almost intimidating. What would be so wrong with simply putting 'Do Not Disturb' on the door, sending down for essentials like food and liquids and just getting lost in each other? It was an attractive idea all right. But hardly a runner, at least not for a while.

"How are those scars bearing up, stud?" Julia asked later, through a mouthful of pastry.

"The old ones are fine," I said. "These new ones you've given me sting like hell."

That got me a kick.

"What do you call a Danish in Denmark?" she asked, kneeling on the bed wearing just a shirt, seemingly unaware of the effect she was having.

"A bun?"

"A bun," she snorted. "You are such a Dub! How long have you been living in England? Twenty years? A bun – Ma!"

"Oh, you're not getting away with that," I said, pouncing.

It was close to midday when we left for the gallery. The cold wind was still around but there was bright sunshine too. An air of quiet purpose was all around, from the people walking quickly past us, to trams snaking their way into the city centre.

Hellerup was a well-to-do suburb, a sign of social success. Several embassies were based there. A boat moored on the water nearby was something to be proud of. Everything was scrupulously clean, evidently well-organised, and eminently sensible.

We stopped at a sports shop and invested in a couple of eminently sensible padded jackets.

"Any plan?" Julia asked.

"I'm afraid not," I said.

The gallery was small, or at least the front of it was – just an adapted cottage in a long terrace. They were all painted differently, brightly coloured reds and blues. The Frederick was comparatively muted, a simple pale cream, and spotlessly clean. A couple of watercolours were framed in the tiny front window, and a smattering of Danish, including the word *Frederick*, was painted above the door. There was nothing remarkable about it at first glance.

A bell rang quaintly above us as we entered. It was a lengthy space, going back almost thirty metres. The walls were covered with pictures, packed closely together, lots of impressionist stuff on one side, portraits and Dutch interiors it seemed on another. There was nothing remarkable about them. Nothing looked especially valuable, or fake. It was common gallery stuff – run-of-the-mill, intended to shift quickly.

"Hi," said a man at the end. He was checking an inventory against a list, his focus on a clipboard. "Okay?"

There seemed to be some signal we gave off of being non-Danish, hence the English. I wasn't complaining.

He was in his late sixties, I reckoned, a large man getting slower through weight and time. There was an obvious world-weariness to his gaze as we approached but the sight of Julia managed to put a glint in it. His smile was unforced.

"Always happy to see new customers," he said. "Especially pretty ones."

"Oh, I don't think he's that pretty," Julia said, glancing at me.

"You are a lucky man," he laughed. "How can I help you today?"

"I see on your website that you have a Bukovac for sale," I said. "Can we see it?"

"I'm sorry," he replied, putting down his clipboard. "It wasn't in great condition so it's being rejuvenated. It will be in store very soon, maybe even next week. Are you interested in purchasing?"

"I might be. But I would need to see it first. Is there a Raza in store?"

"You are a connoisseur, young man, but unfortunately an unlucky connoisseur. That is also out of the store at the moment," he said. "But now that I know your tastes, maybe I can interest you in something else here?"

He guided us towards the right, pointing out various

pictures and enquiring about our possible budget.

"Up to a thousand euro," I said, then paused. "Excuse me – have you a toilet I could use?"

"Of course – just through that door at the back and immediately on your left," he said, returning his attention to Julia.

It was typical backroom stuff. Buckets, a mop and an overpowering smell of disinfectant. There was a toilet to the left and another door straight ahead. I glanced around, opened and shut the toilet door, and carefully opened the other one.

It was a large storeroom, filled with filing cabinets and the other assorted staples of running a business. In a corner was a sink and next to that a coffee machine. But in front of them was a small pile hidden under a tarpaulin. I was lifting the heavy cover to look under when another door opened and a figure appeared.

I scampered backwards, hunched down, and huddled behind a packing crate, praying to remain invisible. Only when the gurgle of the coffee machine started increasing did I chance a look.

It was the young guy who had driven into Ardfield and couldn't get away fast enough. There was no doubt: blonde, strong but with no nervousness now. This was his patch. Every move confirmed how at home he was here, even the automatic reach into a drawer for a fresh bag of coffee.

He brewed up for what seemed an eternity. Julia would be wondering what had happened to me. So would the old man. I hoped fervently Julia could keep him busy for another bit. There was no reason for the young man to guess anyone was there but it felt dreadfully vulnerable just hunched there waiting for the chance to get out. Even breathing felt unnaturally loud, no doubt a reaction to the beating. I didn't want another. Even in full health, it would be a close match. But right then, I knew it would be a losing battle.

He leaned on the sink, seemingly looking straight at me, occasionally taking sips. He groaned loudly and farted. Then he moved. I hunched down further and waited. A door opened and closed. It was the back one. I was on my feet and down at the other end of the room in a second. After flushing the toilet, I re-emerged.

"Sorry about that. I'll spare you the details," I grinned sheepishly at the old man. "I might take a canary in a cage in there, if I were you."

"Excuse me?" he said.

"Nothing, a bad joke," I said. "See anything you like?"

"It's wonderful," Julia enthused. "And Mr Andersen has been a great host."

"Please – Johann," he beamed. "She is a very knowledgeable young woman. And she has also warmed an old man's heart on a cold day."

"That's great," I said. "But we're going to have to head along. Have you a catalogue? So we can make our minds up?"

"Of course," he said, heading off to root behind the counter.

Julia's eyes bore into mine, pleading mutely for information. I shook my head.

"Here you go. And this is my private phone number. Please ring at any time. I love to talk to people who know what they are talking about."

170

"I don't know about that," I said. "But we'll be in touch."

As we left I noticed times written on a small piece of cardboard stuck to the door: '9-5' it read.

I walked away quickly in case Blondey was around, not stopping until we reached the end of the long street and ducked into a café.

"Well?" Julia asked as we waited to be served.

"The guy who came to Ardfield was out the back. I almost ran into him. There's definitely something going on."

"I think some of the stuff hanging up are knock-offs. If they are, they're good ones, but I can't be sure," she said, lowering her voice as a waiter served us coffee. "But that would make sense, right?"

"Yeah. What did you make of Johann Andersen?"

She smiled immediately.

"He comes on a bit lechery but he's actually lovely, harmless, a real old gent. And he knows his stuff, local and international. He was fascinating. I actually find it hard to believe he could be doing anything dodgy."

I'd always been suspicious of conspicuous charm, believing it to be little more than a self-regarding performance. But Julia was not someone to be taken in lightly. And she clearly liked the old guy. Presumably charm could disguise plenty.

"It sounds a bit dramatic but I'd like to know a bit more about Andersen. His shop closes at five. I'm going to follow him. It would be better if you didn't come with me."

"I'm sure it would, but I'm going to anyway."

"Put it like this: you made quite an impression on him.

And it's not like you're built for invisibility," I grinned.

"How charming. Okay. Just promise me one thing."

"What's that?"

"I don't want to have to get you out of a hospital again."

"Believe me, I never want to be in one again either."

Chapter 21

I hoped Andersen wouldn't drive anywhere and he didn't. At 5.15 he locked up the gallery and walked towards the tram station. It was easy to keep my distance. The old man had a distinctive Homburg hat and moved so slowly the danger was in loitering too conspicuously.

There was no problem in keeping an eye on him from another carriage as we sped into the centre of Copenhagen. Once there, the only moment of drama was when a young drunk, standing to the side of the street, arbitrarily singled me out for abuse.

"Fuck you!" he shouted. "Fuck you!"

Even that was in English, I noted, and walked quickly sideways, avoiding any attention. Plenty locals looked askance at the drunk, embarrassed and unsettled at his performance. It was to Copenhagen's credit, I reckoned. He would have fitted in a lot more easily in Dublin, or London, or most places I knew. In Newmarket no one would have given him a second glance.

Andersen didn't seem to notice anything. Instead he

continued walking until he turned down a side street and entered a four-storey terrace building. I waited a few minutes and then went to the front door. They were apartments. And among the names was Andersen. 'Apt 5,' it said. I pondered on whether or not to ring the button and idly pushed against the big front door. It opened. So did the smaller inside door.

The wide hallway was dominated by a big ornate wooden table covered in magazines. There was a lift beside it and a stairs discreetly tucked into a corner. I climbed quickly and found Apartment 5 easily.

There was so long between the knock on the door and him opening it that I wondered if it was the right place.

"Yes?" he said, squinting slightly at his unexpected visitor.

"I met you earlier today, in your gallery," I said. "With the pretty girl."

"Oh, yes. Hello," he said. "What are you doing here?"

"I'm not quite sure," I said, truthfully. "But it's best we talk. Can I come in?"

"I don't know," he began, and I pushed my way past. "Hey!"

"Don't be alarmed. I'm not trying to rob anything, or harm you," I said.

"I'm calling the police!" he shouted.

"Do that, and they can listen to your explanation for the fake paintings you're selling," I said.

Through an opening in the door to the next room, I caught a glimpse of something very familiar.

"Where are you going?" he shouted again, but this time, I noticed, with a lot less vehemence.

It was a huge room, even by the scale of this generously

sized apartment. At least one wall must have been knocked down to make it. There were canvasses lined up against one wall, four others on easels, and one other that was clearly being worked on placed in the middle. It was an abstract, of a landscape, big proportions. On the ground next to it was another canvas of the same picture.

"Who are you copying here?" I asked, as he shuffled in after me. "Derain?"

He looked at me weakly, his shoulders slumped.

"Tanguy."

A French painter of the early to mid-twentieth century, I remembered. It fit. A well-regarded painter, but not high-profile: valuable but not stratospherically so.

"You're very good," I said.

Even in the circumstances, he seemed to straighten slightly, pleased with the compliment. A slight smile even played on his lips.

"How did you find me?"

"Your pal dropped the paintings in Ardfield, even though I told him Michael was dead. He presumed I had something to do with all this."

"And you don't?"

"No."

"So how do you know so much about paintings?"

"I'm a painter myself."

"Really?" he said, with a trace of scepticism.

"Yes," I replied, and decided to forsake any modesty. "My name is Luke Delamere. You may have heard of me."

"Ah," he said, turning around for a chair, and sitting down slowly. "I knew your face was familiar. I've seen catalogues, and your picture in magazines."

"Michael was married to my mother," I told him.

"I didn't know. I'm sorry. It was very sad news about Michael."

"Then why did you kill him?"

I felt no fear of this man. He was too old and too frail to hurt me. But he stood up quickly at the accusation.

"What are you saying? How dare you!"

I let him rail for a little while. He was clearly distressed, maybe a little too much, I suspected. Or maybe it was just his way.

"What do you mean *kill*?" he shouted.

"Michael was murdered."

"But that's impossible," he spluttered. "Why would anyone want to kill Michael?"

"And he was tortured beforehand."

He slumped into his chair again, and rooted in a pocket for a packet of cigarettes. He lit one automatically, looking away at the window.

"Tell me," I said. "How did you know him?"

Andersen took his time replying, clearly struggling to comprehend what was happening. When he spoke, it sounded like someone reading automatically, without comprehension.

"It's nearly five years ago now; in London, at an exhibition. We got to talking. He is such a nice man – was. And it sort of just happened.

"What happened?"

"This is not a business to make you fabulously wealthy," he said.

"You don't look to be doing too badly," I replied, looking around.

"My grandmother's: inherited long ago," he said. "I'm

very lucky that way. And I've no family. So I don't cost myself too much – except for these disgusting things."

He took a long drag on his cigarette.

"Why should I tell you anything?" he said, regrouping.

"Because if you don't, I go straight to the police."

"Aren't you going to anyway?"

"I'm here, aren't I?"

It almost seemed possible to hear his mind whirring, running through various permutations, calculating the risk, and possible benefits, maybe even trying to reckon my motivations. But since I hardly knew those myself, finding an answer was unlikely. Eventually, though, he came to a decision.

"You know what it is to paint. And you know what it is to paint well. I can paint well. But not well enough. Not like you. There isn't that spark, or originality, or what you choose to call it. But I love to paint."

I let him talk. He was clearly expressing something he had thought long and hard about, possibly justifying it to himself. There was relief in the way he spoke, like easing a guilty conscience.

"Do you know what it is to be completely passionate about something and yet know you will never rise above being just a hack? Of course you don't. But I do. My whole life has been an exercise in trying to be more than that. I have cried with the frustration of being competent but no more. And then this came along."

"What is 'this'?"

"There are people I know who put a proposition to me. They said it was harmless, nothing would happen to anyone, except some rich people would lose a little of their money. And it gave me a chance to paint, to find out what it is like to create beauty, at least someone else's beauty."

"'People'? You mean criminals?"

"Yes. If I had the choice again I would do it differently," he argued, not even convincing himself, it seemed, never mind me. "It seemed like a bit of fun at first."

"Who are they?"

"Are you going to the police?"

"It depends."

"Then I will not tell you," he said. "They are not from this country."

"How did Michael get into this?"

"Someone reputable to sell on the paintings was required. My shop is a little too close to home. And when I first spoke to him in London, I got the impression he could be useful. So I put it to him. And he jumped at the chance. Be under no illusion, Mr Delamere. He wanted to be involved. I got the impression he was under a great deal of stress, money stress perhaps."

"So you produced the paintings, delivered them to Michael, who sold them on," I said.

"Yes."

"And what was the role of your non-Danish pals?"

"They supply me with everything I need."

"And?"

"And they take the originals."

"What do you mean?"

"They steal the original and bring it here for me to copy."

"And then sell back the copy?" I said. "Leaving you with an original to flog to someone else?"

"Something like that."

It was illegal, immoral and so simple. There were plenty wealthy buyers whose finances were greater than their knowledge. And Andersen's stuff was good enough to pass muster with a lot of them. Even Julia couldn't be entirely sure and she knew more than most. Anyone buying directly from an unscrupulous agent or dealer was at their mercy. How could they know? And would they even want to know? It was hardly in their interest to have their investments suspected. Better to sell on the pup if in doubt. And, for the crooks, all the while there was an original that could be traded at any time, or maybe even copied again and again.

"We make money," Andersen continued. "But that's not why I do it, not really."

"Why then?"

"I am not a vain man, Mr Delamere. But I am not without imagination. The idea that something I have done might be looked at many years from now, long after I have gone, is appealing. They might not know my name, but even if they don't realise it, they will be looking at my work. A copy, yes, but still my work."

"And Michael?"

"He didn't like it. He said once he felt dirty about it. But he took the money. He knew, made his choice. I don't blame him, but he was no innocent. That's for certain."

"How are you so sure?"

"Because it was not just me he dealt with."

"What do you mean?"

"I mean with me it was just fakes. But he dealt with others too, people who were just stealing work and going through the various processes of selling it on."

"Like money-laundering?"

"Exactly. For an artist, you know very little about the business of art. Maybe that is the creative way."

My experience was the most creative people were also realistic enough to care about the cash very much indeed. So what did that say about me? He looked almost amused.

"It is like any luxury item: if there is a demand, people don't care how they get their hands on it, as long as they do. The illegal trading of art is worth billions every year. What I do is tiny. There are traders out there, the epitome of respectability, who are getting their hands dirty to a far greater degree than I, and for much greater sums of money too."

"So you figured you'd get in on it," I replied.

"No – well, I guess, yes. But it's not really for the money, more the excitement," he said vaguely. "You don't understand."

Except I did. Perfectly proper people who ordinarily disapproved of anything shady could forget their disapproval if they were in the know. I'd seen it in racing often enough. Punters shouting about betting scams usually shut up if they were in the loop. Most of us rather relished a bit of roguery, I reckoned. But only if it remained that: not if it extended to torture and murder. Michael had got in badly over his head.

"Are you certain Michael was a middleman for stolen work?"

"If you're asking me for evidence, then no, I cannot provide you with any. If you're asking me if I know he was doing that, then yes, I am certain."

And that would mean the list of candidates who might

have a motive for killing him would be long, and difficult in the extreme to narrow down.

"I can only presume Michael got greedy," Andersen continued. "With the amount of money to be made, the people involved are not sentimental."

"So why aren't you afraid?"

"I am. But I talk to you because I think you understand why I do it," he said, before smiling slightly. "And I also think you will not make trouble for me."

He was right. For one thing it would achieve nothing. And what could I tell anyone? That an old man was copying obscure paintings? All he had to do was say they were for his own pleasure and what happened to them after he gave them away as presents had nothing to do with him. And there was nothing concrete to tell anyone anyway, except maybe that Michael was crooked, and what would that achieve?

"Young man, I genuinely regret Michael's death, especially his violent death. But you pretending to be some John Wayne figure out for revenge is not going to bring him back."

He didn't mean it unkindly, and it didn't come out that way. There was a deep regret there, plus an old man's willingness to accept that so many things are out of our control. And maybe he was right.

"I suspect that Michael's death, unfortunate as it is, will remain a mystery," he went on. "For you, I think all this is over."

But he wasn't right about that.

Chapter 22

"Where have you been? And what's happened to you?"

Dorothy's voice was strained, frantic almost. Her face reflected that. She reached out and grabbed my hand, squeezing it tight.

"I've been ringing your phone, and ringing and ringing, and asking people," she continued. "There's been no trace of you, or your car. We thought something was wrong. We got in touch with the police. Is everything okay?"

I glanced to the other side of the kitchen and saw Barry sitting at the table, looking relieved. He smiled at me.

"Good to see you back, Luke."

With everything else going on, the idea of ringing Ardfield hadn't really occurred to me. Maybe it was the faintly ridiculous idea of keeping anonymous and unknown for a while, or simply the wonder of getting to know Julia. Either way, it wasn't exactly considerate.

"I'm sorry. I had an accident, and had to lay low for a while. Is everything all right here?"

"No, not exactly," Barry said, standing up. "But I'll let you tell him, ma'am. I'm going to go home, if that's all right."

"Of course, Barry. And thank you so much. I'm sorry for being such a pest," Dorothy said. "Age is making me anxious."

"It's no trouble," he said, and quite obviously meant it. Only after he left did she let my hand go.

"What's wrong?" I asked.

"I didn't know where you were," she said accusingly.

The bitter irony of such a statement could hardly be any more obvious to either of us. I said nothing and waited.

"There was somebody outside a couple of nights ago," she said.

Jesus, I thought.

"Are you okay? Did anything happen?"

"I wasn't sure at first. There were just shadows. And it was nothing more than a feeling at first. So I locked everything. Then I saw someone running across the rose garden at the side, crushing some of the young plants I'd put in. It was a man, young, moving very fast. That's when I called the guards. Except they didn't come, not for ages. And when I peeped through the curtains again, I thought I saw another man. At the back, looking through a window."

Jesus Christ.

"And I couldn't get through to you, Luke. You didn't answer."

I grabbed her hand again, told her I was sorry, and promised to sort things out.

"But you won't even tell me what happened to you," she said, pulling her hand away slightly. "You're wincing just standing here."

The circumstances could have been better but I told her everything: about getting attacked and left for dead, going to Copenhagen, finding out her husband had been mixed up in criminality and with people he shouldn't have. Dorothy didn't flinch. But she took it in all right, even the obvious implication that whoever had tried to kill me could now be stalking her.

"I think we should get you away from Ardfield for a bit," I proposed. "We'll tell Foley what's happened, and then lie low for a bit. Let the police do what they're supposed to."

"I am not going to be scared out of my home," she objected. "I have spent most of my life here, and no bullying will get me out."

"No one's talking about being scared out," I insisted. "It's just prudent – for a while. Until we find out what's going on. Everything is way too dangerous and up-in-the-air right now to be so intransigent."

She shook her head.

"Why not visit somewhere, or someone?" I asked.

That provoked a slight grin, but no budge. And neither of us broached the obvious matter of why her family couldn't help.

"I'm so sorry, Luke, dragging you into something so awful. And I don't know what I would have done if you had been killed too," she said, her voice catching. "But I will not run away."

Such resolution was maddening and illogical and hard not to admire. I looked at this woman who had turned my world upside-down in a matter of weeks and tried to cope with a torrent of conflicting emotions, but mostly right then downright frustration and indulgence.

"I'm very tired, Luke. And now that you're back, I think I'll be able to sleep," she said. "Why don't we see how things look in the morning?"

I nodded. She put her hand on my face.

"You really are a remarkable young man."

How remarkable could anyone be if overmatched in a battle of wills with a frightened old lady, I thought.

Upstairs, I peered out of her bedroom window while she was in the bathroom. It was dark but not so dark you couldn't see movement. There was none right then but even the idea that Dorothy's eyes might have been playing tricks was ridiculous. She was hardly a fanciful woman, prone to histrionics. Was whoever she'd spotted a local chancer hoping to prey on the vulnerability of a woman on her own? Or was it deeper than that? Deeper questions than I could answer. Maybe things would be clearer in the morning.

"No need to stand guard over me, Luke," she observed on re-emerging. Over the fright, I reckoned.

"Luke?"

"Yeah?"

"Do you think Michael suffered very much?"

The evidence of what men are capable of doing to each other was still tattooed all over my body. The bruising would fade and the ribs would heal. But the memory of that horrible vulnerability would remain, the shock at other human beings so casually snuffing the life out of another. And I'd been lucky: passing out spared me. Michael wasn't so fortunate. And what happened with his arms and face was calculation beyond comprehension.

"I think so, yes," I said.

Her face betrayed so little. I could only guess at the pain generated by the thought of a loved one suffering.

186

My mum had suffered greatly, but I'd been young, wrapped up in myself. Everything revolved around the impact on me. What Dorothy was experiencing was very different.

"He was a good man, Luke. Not a perfect man. He could be weak-willed when it came to lots of stuff – like me, maybe, I don't know. He indulged the children terribly. There were times when he would drive me mad with his indecisiveness, and over silly stuff that didn't matter. He liked to gamble, obviously more than I ever realised. But he was a good man, kind, and generous, and loyal. What he did, he did for us, to maintain the family tradition. That might have been illegal but I struggle to believe it was wrong."

She was much too smart a woman not to know how easily such a line could blur when inclination wanted it to. But as an expression of loyalty, it took some beating.

"Get some sleep," I said. "I'll stay up for a while."

Ten minutes later she was asleep. I made some tea in the kitchen and rang Julia.

"I'm staying here tonight. And maybe for a little while," I told her.

"Dumping me already, huh?"

"Someone has been prowling around the place, scaring her."

"Shit, I'm sorry."

"She won't leave either, which kind of complicates things."

"Just be careful. You've taken enough punishment," she said. "I'd hate to have to nurse you again."

"I don't know about that."

"Go on, mind your mother."

After that I rang Jerry.

"Oh, you've decided to check in, have you? Very good of you, I'm sure."

We parried mock-insults for a minute, him bemoaning how he'd given an advance on future earnings that looked decidedly shaky on the back of sales at the Ormond.

"Doesn't anyone over there have any money?" he asked.

"If they do, they ain't spending it on me. At least not right now," I said. "Jerry, who do you know in the world of forgeries?"

"Whoa, kid, we're not doing that badly," he objected.

"No, it's not that. But there are things I need to know. Apparently, Michael Maxwell-Williams was dealing in fakes. And it came back to bite him. I tracked down one of the people he was dealing with. I don't think there's a suggestion of someone capable of killing there, but he said there were others."

"Christ, Luke. I'm sorry to hear that," Jerry said, and I could almost hear his brain working. "It's not really my field. But I'm no innocent. It goes on all the time. I've been caught by these bastards, everybody in the business has. How important is this?"

"Very."

"Okay, just let me have a think. And I'll try and dig somebody out that might be able to help."

"You're a star."

"Just protecting my investment."

Finally I rang the police, asking for Detective Inspector Mark Foley. He was in a meeting so I left a message to ring me back at Ardfield. Then I walked down to Michael's office.

In the Picture

It was just as I remembered it, pictures stacked against the walls, an atmosphere packed with Michael's absence. What here was real, I wondered, pondering how much disposable cash might be raised on the back of it. Maybe it didn't need to be real.

There was nothing obvious, no stupid signature sticking out like a sore thumb. There hardly would be. Michael knew his stuff. I began taking out random pictures and examining them with an eye I quickly realised as being desperately inexpert. There were no obvious brushstrokes that jarred with the little I knew, no technical glitches, no obvious evidence of new paint bleeding into age-cracks. Some black light would have been handy but I doubted there would be anything as crude as a smoking brush anywhere.

Some of the paintings I didn't know, but the quality looked good. Other stuff was of the value I suspected Michael liked dealing in: lucrative but not too obvious, mostly canvas, but watercolours and acrylics too. I peered closely at the backs of them. Sometimes they told stories as much as the front. The features on them looked genuine enough, the names of suppliers, manifest numbers, supplier-tags. There was no guarantee they were all legitimate, but no sign they weren't either. The stretcher-bars weren't obviously tampered with. They didn't look purposefully aged. The nail marks looked consistent. This was useless, I figured. I didn't know enough.

There were prints too, all framed run-of-the-mill stuff. A few Van Gogh, Munch, Gauguin, classics as familiar to any art enthusiast as a footballer's signature move to a sports fan. I stood staring around for a good half an hour, not knowing why, almost silently pleading with Michael's

189

memory for a steer. There might not be anything here, I reckoned, but why had that intruder I'd chased been heading this way? Had he been simply been wandering around for something else? But that hardly made sense. And what Andersen told me meant Michael's death must have had something to do with paintings, maybe even those here. It was too coincidental otherwise. But I couldn't figure it out: too tired, and sore, and anxious.

I climbed up and continued climbing, checked on Dorothy – out cold – and started checking the windows in the rooms to make sure they were tightly closed. It started raining outside, miserable weather, and I suddenly felt like getting away, to go to Julia, curl up next to her, and forget about pain, and death, and families and the illogical obligations they entailed.

Dorothy was a good woman, just as she felt her husband was a good man. But the ties that bound us were emotional, sentimental even: certainly nothing that I felt for my adoptive mother or how she must feel for her daughters. Who was I kidding? To Dorothy I must have been a loose end to tie up. The business of rearing her girls was done, now time to tidy.

The windows were secure. I walked down a hall and heard a rattle. It was above my head, an entrance to the attic. A draught of wind whistled and made the timber fitting rattle again. There was a handle on it beyond reach. I looked around. A wooden pole with a hook on it lay on the ground nearby. It latched on to the handle and I pulled. The wooden panel opened and plastic stairs unfolded down to the floor.

A string hanging in front of me as I stuck my head into the cold air turned on a light. No wonder the house got so cold. There was little or no insulation, no distinctive fibreglass tang. A narrow wooden passage went down the middle of the rafters, allowing access to a lifetime of discarded items and memories placed on pallets to the sides. Packed clothes-bags piled into a couple of wooden baby cots. Other bags contained toys, the neglected residue of years before, irrelevant now except for the nostalgia that refused to discard them.

A couple of dust-caked old timber trunks sat at the end, one closed, the other with paper peeping out under the lid. There was a picture of a horse race on a newspaper, just visible. I pushed up the top of the trunk and looked in. There were bags with old files, bills, receipts and documents kept in order by being punched through straightened old iron coat hangers. There were bulky folders too. I left them alone: not my business. But some of the newspapers were loose.

They were racing papers, from some years before, the material yellowing with time. It was remarkable how dated the layout looked even though it came from just over a decade before. The paper was folded in half on a page containing reports from various race meetings. I glanced casually and recognised my name.

It was a paragraph on winning a race at Leicester on a horse called Ultimatum. I remembered him, and I remembered the race; lashing rain, a mile handicap, nothing very special, another ordinary middle-of-the-week fixture. Ultimatum was a big angular chestnut that didn't like trying very hard but had no problem galloping on soft ground. The trainer said on no account to hit him or he'd curl up underneath with resentment. We'd got to the front with a couple of hundred yards to go as instructed only to be tackled by another horse. I'd given Ultimatum one slight backhander, just a little reminder and the shock of it spurred him on to one final effort. Clearly the instructions not to hit him were not new: the surprise of getting a tap was the winning of the race. The report had a sentence from the trainer praising the ride. If we'd lost he would have been steaming. But that was the way of the world: winning fixed everything.

There was another paper open underneath. I recognised it immediately. It was a profile of me done when I'd first started to ride a few winners. The journalist had come to the hostel in Newmarket to do the interview. It was like another world, that someone would come from London like that. All the other lads ripped the mickey but it was jealousy, I knew. The man, and he must have been at least forty, arrived, shook hands and we went into town, found a hotel lobby and he started asking questions.

It was embarrassing, for both of us. He must have wondered what he was doing pretending to be fascinated by the banal statements of a shy kid. The idea of confiding in someone I'd never met just seemed ridiculous to me. But we got through it, shook hands and he was kind in the piece he'd written. There was a small picture of me over it, small smile, big helmet, colourful silks and hamster cheeks that hadn't yet started to feel the impact of serious wasting. It was like looking at a television personality – familiar but unknown.

Underneath that was another open page, with another race report. A couple of paragraphs from Warwick circled in faded biro. And they went on. Not always open on the page, but always an edition that contained some mention of a winner I'd ridden. There was no other common denominator, no orderly dates, one copy from a fallow month was followed by six or seven from a productive few weeks. A segment, outlining a contender for 'ride-of-the-week' on an old stayer called Herculean Heights at Chepstow was circled in biro too. They went all the way back, to that first ever unforgettable winner, Pay The Piper at Goodwood.

I sat there a long time, unaware of the cold and the dust. More digging around in the trunk exposed a couple of magazines and a few more newspapers where I'd featured with my art work. I smiled at that. Dorothy definitely paid more attention to the horses. Maybe Michael had pointed them out to her. Did he resent me? Were they thrown at her in resentment? But they were kept. That was important. I started putting them back and saw a piece of newsprint sticking out from underneath some books at the bottom.

It was just a sheet torn out, the edges crooked, I recognised it, but couldn't remember from where, until I recognised some familiar place-names from my youth: the local paper from where I grew up. There were no bits circled, and I was about to put it back when the photo hit me. There were three little boys, showing off medals for football. I didn't need the captions underneath. Jimmy Talbot and Mikey Flannery stood tall and grinning and cheeky, just as they did in school. They towered over their pal in the middle, staying close, just as they did against the bullies in school. My gap-toothed grin was wide, and happy, and secure, safe between my two pals. Luke Delamere, aged eight.

Tears rolled down my face.

Chapter 23

Dorothy twisted and turned the jeep through the racecourse stable-yard, blissfully unconcerned at the tiny margins by which the horsebox hitched behind us was missing everyone else. It was a dull, misty morning, heavy with the threat of rain but none of the hundred or so people at Fairyhouse racetrack seemed to care or notice. Everyone was too busy.

It wasn't a race day. Instead, for a nominal sum, horses could run around the track in what was known as a schooling gallop. There was no prize money and no competition. But there was a valuable opportunity to get some exercise and experience. We had brought White Nose. Barry said he needed to get away from home. He was getting bored and more than a little boisterous. What was required was a gallop and something new to occupy his mind. And for a hundred quid he was getting both.

All the stables were full so I tacked up the horse in the box. He couldn't see much, but he could hear. When I backed him out down the ramp, he skittered around briefly, ears pricking at all these strange new sights, sounds and smells. And then he extended his neck and roared out a challenge, like a stallion claiming territory. New it might be, but this wasn't a horse withdrawing into his shell due to nerves.

My own gear consisted of an ancient helmet, riding boots that were twenty years old if they were a day – and a size too small – plus jeans and a cheap anorak bought in a supermarket on the way.

I didn't care about how I looked, but controlling half a tonne of thoroughbred would be a good test of my physical condition, especially on a horse that could be shying and spooking at everything and nothing.

"The unraced horses are going a mile and a half," Dorothy said. "So you'll start up the side from the stands. Just follow Maguire there in the yellow cap." She pointed at a tall rider, impeccably togged out, and sporting a bright yellow cover on his helmet. "He's Mark Maguire, rides all the top bumper horses here, champion amateur. This is his patch."

The morning was open to all horses so experienced runners were going first over two miles. About forty of them clattered out of the yard, past the parade ring and out on to the course. I noticed quite a few onlookers, not connected with any of the horses it seemed, but simply observing, no doubt trying to pinpoint future winners.

Dorothy went to organise the paperwork and I led the horse around. It was all new to him and his flanks heaved with excitement, but not nerves. Chilled at home, this was very different and he was definitely tuned in.

"Ten minutes and we'll be able to head out," Dorothy said on returning. "There are about twenty-five others going in our gallop. A couple of them belong to O'Donoghue, bought off the point-to-point fields. One of them is supposed to be the next big thing. Maguire's going to be riding him."

I noticed quite a few people approaching Dorothy, shaking hands and offering both condolences and concern. It felt formal, almost like a dance with set moves and expectations, but no less touching for that. One man in a cap and a battered anorak spoke to her for about a minute and then approached me.

"Are you working for Mrs Maxwell-Williams?" he demanded.

I nodded.

"Do a good job, now," he ordered. "No blackguarding. She doesn't deserve that. Anything you need, just ask."

And he pressed something into my hand and walked off. It was a fifty-euro note. I opened my mouth to call him back but thought better of it. The gesture clearly meant something to him. And it showed a respect and affection for Dorothy that I liked.

"Who's that guy?" I asked her, nodding towards my benefactor as he legged up a rider.

"Colm McDonald," she replied. "He's one of the top trainers in the North – bought a lot of horses off me over the years. A bit pompous, but a decent man. Why?"

"Nothing. He seems to think a lot of you."

"And why wouldn't he?" she demanded with a smile.

"Why not indeed?" I said, and jumped on to White Nose's back.

The ground was very soft. We squelched to the start, the horse looking around and clearly enjoying the novel experience, me wondering how the ground would be restored after all this traffic taking lumps out of it. But that wasn't my problem.

What definitely was my problem was making sure I remained in charge of this partnership. The horse was taking in too much to think about running away with me but that could change when the gallop began. The key was getting him relaxed and settled.

There were riders of various sizes, weights, and I guessed competence around us, mostly concentrating in case their mounts whipped round suddenly, but otherwise the scene was the same as at the start of any race. There was always a joker, always someone cribbing about money, a Lothario boasting, quiet ones eager to be off or just shy.

"All right, lads," said an official in a pristine wax jacket. "And lassies."

We set off. I buried the horse at the rear of the pack, surrounded by others, trying to get him to relax. It was the greatest gift with horses, the ability to make them not fight you. The phrase that summed it all up was hands: some people had hands that could make horses respond, others couldn't. It had nothing to do with size, or strength or willpower. If the biggest and strongest had hands of concrete, they had no chance of winning a tug of war with half a tonne of thoroughbred. Subtlety trumped force every time. It was a language through the reins, between man and beast, containing a full dictionary of expression that was almost as mysterious to the initiated as those who would dismiss it as fanciful nonsense.

I hardly moved, keeping my hands still. Changing them would be a signal to go quicker and that wouldn't be good for either of us. I pointed him at the backside of the horse in front, careful not to get too close and clips heels, pleading silently to him to take it easy, just lob along and enjoy the view.

A glimpse at the front saw others more anxious to make an impression, dashing off, galloping way too hard for there to be any hope of lasting all the way to the finish. Exuberance and inexperience on the part of both horse and rider winning out, understandable in its way but useless: after all there was no prize money for first here.

Despite the gruelling ground White Nose moved with a fluency and ease that I remembered from Ardfield. Horses that couldn't act on the soft were obvious straight away. Every stride felt like an effort, pulling their feet out of the slop. This one seemed to glide through it. And he had twigged maybe responding to the insignificant human on his back mightn't be a bad thing.

I didn't feel too bad either. Each exaggerated tug on the bit sent a jolt to the ribs but nothing to shout about. Like anyone who'd ever worked with these animals, I knew when pain was serious and when it wasn't. And this was okay.

After the first uphill climb, we turned right downhill. The ones at the front went even faster. But Maguire in his yellow cap was only about ten lengths in front of us. That was good. He was the one who knew what he was doing here, familiar with the pace of these things, and what these horses could do. He was riding a big chestnut that looked to be going very easily, lobbing through the mud, ears pricked and enjoying himself. If we kept him in our sights, I reckoned, we wouldn't be doing badly.

The horse we were tracking suddenly dropped out,

forcing me to yank the reins sideways to skip around him. White Nose was only fifty-per-cent fit, I figured, but there were others here who must have barely broken out of a trot. What was good though was that suddenly faced with open ground he didn't take off. He had a good look around at the wide open spaces but felt no need to quickly explore them. And there was plenty in the tank. Half-fit he might be but he wasn't half going well.

A white pole with "6" on it, signifying six furlongs to go, was a hundred yards away on the inside of the course and meant we were at halfway. It was time to check what there might be under the bonnet. Lobbing along was all very well but the real talent was in quickening up. I gave White Nose a squeeze in the belly and he bounded forward. I noticed the yellow cap quickening up at the same time.

The ones that couldn't wait were coming back to us now, some being urged along with kicking heels and whip-taps down the shoulder. Their riders were doing more harm than good. Pressurising tired young horses to keep going on bad ground would make a bad first impression of this racecourse lark. Maddening, impulsive, instinctive creatures they might be but they weren't stupid and were certainly capable of associating a bad experience with a place. My guess was they were being ridden by stable lads using their chance to live out their racing fantasies.

Mr Maguire, though, was much more hard-headed. He never varied his pace, kept a tight hold of the horse's head, kept him resolutely balanced and sure enough sliced through the front-rankers as we approached the turn into the straight.

White Nose it seemed had twigged we were tailing the big chestnut and followed him through the other horses without missing a beat. He was doing better than we could ever have expected. There was a naturalness to him that only the real good ones possessed. It didn't matter what age they were. I was more used to two-year-olds, maybe immature three-year-olds, but it was obvious from the first quick canter if there was talent there. It might be gangling and unfurnished and raw but the feeling of power always radiated through the reins. This was a big National Hunt stayer bred to last three miles over fences but the talent was fizzing in my hands.

We passed the two-furlong pole. Only the big chestnut was in front of us. This was a brilliant piece of work for a horse that had barely been out of the yard. But our competitive juices were running. I gave another squeeze. White Nose responded immediately. At the furlong pole we ranged upsides. Maguire looked across.

There was an etiquette to riding work. The horse around which the gallop revolved was expected to have his nose in front at the line. It meant nothing, probably a relic of some habit that became ingrained. But the real jockey clearly expected it to be followed. He changed his hands and the chestnut changed legs and extended. My fella went with him.

It was no race that anyone in the stands would recognise. Neither rider moved his hands again. The whips weren't raised. But there was a hundred yards of real competition nonetheless, until good sense won out. I eased up and let the other horse get half a length up. We both crossed the line standing up in the saddle. But the point was made. The chestnut was good. However, he was also fitter, had run in a point-to-point and was a year older. Anyone with any kind of an eye would plump for White Nose as the horse with more potential.

I let him slow down in his own time. He was tired but far from exhausted. His ears were pricked at the trot, long after Maguire's horse had stopped to a walk. I could see the champion amateur looking at us. He knew better than anyone, I reckoned. The only question he was asking was: 'Who the hell is that horse?'

It would be hard to tell him since White Nose didn't even have an official name yet. But what he was a horse with a future. And I told him that as I patted him on the neck, telling him he was a great fella, and meaning it. He reluctantly turned around to canter back to the yard.

Dorothy was waiting for us amidst the mass of people removing jockeys and saddles from snorting, stamping horses, steam rising from their sweating backs into the cold mist. Her cheeks were glowing and it was nothing to do with the bracing winter conditions. She knew what she was looking at. It had gone better than we'd dare dream. For her it was a moment of rare satisfaction. And the prospect of having a valuable commodity on her hands wouldn't even figure. Or at least not much.

It was having bred this horse; planned the mating of mare and stallion, figuring out what nick and cross would suit best, paying the stud fee, delivering the helpless foal in the middle of the night, watching it take its first steps, worrying about it out in the paddocks, whether it was suckling properly, moving right, getting stuck in a rogue piece of wire. And then four years later watching him do what he was bred to do, and doing it well.

"Well?" she asked, knowing the answer.

"He's good," I replied, slipping down, and noticing the buzz of riding had made me completely forget about ribs and everything else. "I don't know anything about these jumpers, of course, but there's definitely something there. He's a natural."

She grabbed the reins, and patted White Nose's neck repeatedly and with a force that testified to the depth of feeling he'd generated. Idly, I wondered if the two girls had looked at similar enthusiasm in the past and felt envy. Irrational it might be but jealousy didn't have to obey any logic except its own. She led him in off the course, back onto tarmac and towards the parade ring where debriefs of varying enthusiasm were taking place. More than a few hopes and dreams had been punctured out there, maybe even Gerard O'Donoghue's.

He was standing in the middle of the ring, a luxurious overcoat protecting a business suit, and listening to Maguire. The jockey suddenly turned around and pointed towards White Nose plodding back to the yard to be hosed down. His finger jabbed animatedly, hopefully I reckoned with strict instructions for O'Donoghue to get over right then with his chequebook open. My hand was hanging on to White Nose's mud-and-rain-sodden tail. What the hell, I figured. The horse had done the talking that mattered out there. But it wouldn't harm to talk him up.

"I'd say his price just went up a good bit," I said, walking towards the businessman.

He looked at me, his face a blank. He didn't recognise me. I pulled off the helmet.

"Luke Delamere," I told him, feeling myself blush despite the cold. How often must people approach

O'Donoghue, feeling like they knew him? "Sorry, I rode that horse with the white nose out there."

"Ah, Luke," he said. "Sorry, you caught me on the hop there. Just a moment."

He leaned into Maguire, who for some reason shot me a dirty look, and listened to him whisper into his ear. O'Donoghue nodded and turned back.

"You weren't joking, Luke. That's a nice horse you've got," he said. "We think quite a bit of our lad."

"Sorry for putting you on the spot there."

"Don't be silly. What are your plans for that animal?"

"He's still for sale," I smiled.

"I'm sure he is," O'Donoghue said. "But it's one thing doing it in a gallop – another altogether in a race."

I nodded, and he slapped me on the shoulder.

"I've got half an hour to get to the airport and on to the plane, so I'll have to dash. Give my best to your mother."

I didn't bother. Nobody else figured on Dorothy's radar just then other than the horse. She looked truly happy, standing in the yard in wellies, hosing mud and sweat off her pride and joy, affectionately telling him to move, or lift a leg and all the while delivering more hearty pats to his neck and backside.

White Nose wasn't as skittish any more, hardly surprising considering he'd just put in a mile and a half of hard work. But he was a long way from out on his feet. Dorothy reached into a pocket and produced an apple which he sniffed and devoured, hardly an act of distress.

"Sorry about that," I said, grabbing the head-collar. "I got a little carried away, chasing Maguire."

"Oh, Luke, it was fabulous," she gasped. "I couldn't

believe how good he was. Right from the start, he settled and travelled and when he came alongside that good one, oh . . . And you weren't too shabby yourself: quite the flat stylist among all the jump farmers."

"I don't know about that. But it sure perked me up. He really is very good. You're going to have to name him now."

"God, I hadn't thought of that. What do you think?"

"Nope, that's your task," I said. "Mine is just to get this guy back into the box."

I scraped the water off him, slung a rug over his back, tied it up, and gave him one more pat on his face. He tossed his head, annoyed at the attention: back to his no-nonsense self again.

Chapter 24

Both the Huxleys and the Dennings were waiting for us at Ardfield. Their cars were parked outside. Dorothy steered the horsebox into the stable yard and it seemed to me dallied over unloading the horse, taking extra care of its bedding and grub. She took a deep breath entering the kitchen.

There were no hellos, or greetings, simply George and Alicia looking stern and Elizabeth and Myles, their faces sheepish. But they were allied, no doubt about that.

"This is a nice surprise," Dorothy said, delivering a kiss to each of her daughters. "What's the occasion?"

"It's very simple," George boomed. "This is Gavin Devlin."

He nodded to a man standing by the fridge. If George hadn't pointed him out, he could have stayed there for quite some time unnoticed. Short, thin, bland suit, bland face; lawyer, I reckoned.

"Gavin is our solicitor. And he has something for you, Dorothy," George added.

"Mrs Maxwell-Williams, we have been given an injunction from the High Court to halt any development of this property while a judicial review into the instructions left by your late husband takes place," he said smoothly.

"What?" Dorothy almost whispered.

"It's all here," Devlin said, handing her an envelope.

"I'm sure you can break it down to one sentence," I said to him.

But it was George that answered.

"We don't believe the will reflects Michael's true wishes at the time of his death," he said.

"How do you know what his true wishes were?" Dorothy exploded. "What do you know about anything?"

"We believe Michael didn't get the chance to update his will," Devlin said. "It was drawn up five years before. Legally it is suspect to have the powers of executor left solely to one member of a family. And it is reasonable to argue that as his children have grown older, their father would have invested more trust in their executor powers. It is also our argument that Mrs Maxwell-Williams has been under a lot of stress since the tragic death of her husband. There is also the issue of her illness and that combined with everything else this has led to a certain inability to take in the long-term picture of what is best for all concerned."

"Oh my God, you're questioning my sanity!" Dorothy gasped. "You're saying I'm incapable, aren't you?"

She spoke to Elizabeth, but it was Alicia who responded.

"Mother, it has been a trying time for everyone. We're

only trying to do what's best for everyone."

"Best for yourself, you mean!" her mother spat. "Let me guess: O'Donoghue still wants to gobble this place up, right?"

"As it happens, he would like to buy Ardfield, and at more than generous terms," Alicia said.

"You're tilting at windmills," Myles piped up. "This is pie-in-the-sky stuff, about leisure breaks and a hotel. Who's going to come here?"

"You'd never know," I chipped in.

"You stay out of it," Alicia shouted. "If it weren't for you, we wouldn't be in this position. You're sticking your oar in and encouraging her in this. And for what? So you can play the hero for your lost mummy?"

George laughed. It wasn't a happy sound.

"Who's paying Mr Devlin?" I asked the big man.

"What?" he said.

"I presume Mr Devlin doesn't come cheap," I replied. "How is he being paid?"

"There's no need to answer that," the lawyer interjected. "My financial arrangements with my clients are completely irrelevant."

"It's just that these guys are supposedly broke. And you look expensive," I said to Devlin.

He didn't even blink. Money clearly wasn't an issue here. Maybe he was on a future percentage? Maybe he wasn't.

"All work on the hotel project, and any other re-development, apart from fundamental maintenance on this site, is to be ceased immediately," he continued. "Naturally, we are anxious for this matter to be resolved as quickly as possible. If it is necessary to go to court, every effort will be made to secure an early date. But my clients recognise it would be in everyone's best interests if the matter could be resolved privately and to the satisfaction of everyone concerned."

Everyone's attention turned to Dorothy. Her face was inscrutable. Elizabeth's in contrast looked tortured. If eyes could speak hers were pleading with her mother to give in. Alicia's expression was stony, all hint of the previous torrents of anger and frustration carefully wrapped up in front of the lawyer. The two men were practically sitting on the edges of their chairs. They hadn't learned much about their mother-in-law over the years, I reckoned.

"You are always welcome here," Dorothy said eventually. "This is your home. And it would be great if you all stayed for dinner. But I am not going to be strong-armed into doing something I fundamentally disagree with. And I don't care what kind of legal representation you bring here. If it goes to court, it goes to court."

There was silence. Elizabeth looked like she was about to burst into tears. The two men didn't look far behind her. Only Alicia's expression didn't change.

"We're having beef for dinner, and there's plenty for everyone," Dorothy said. "Are you staying?"

"Mum, please," Elizabeth pleaded.

Dorothy smiled sadly at her, then looked at me.

"Looks like it's just you and me, Luke," she said. "Do you like beef?"

Alicia stood up first, looked briefly at her mother, and strode out. She was followed by her husband. As the Dennings trailed them, I asked Myles a question.

"Do you know anything about quarries?"

"What?" he said, clearly annoyed.

"Quarries: are you familiar with them?"

There was no flicker of recognition, no link betrayed on his face, no guilt. Myles wasn't that good an actor.

"I haven't time to play games with you," he said, and left.

"You don't really think they had anything to do with trying to kill you?" Dorothy asked.

"I don't know. Maybe not," I said. "Are you all right?"

"Of course. I'll get in touch with Harry and see where this puts us."

"It's not good: you don't have the resources for anything drawn out. And I reckon they do, wherever it's coming from."

She was about to speak when the front door bell clanged.

"God, what now?" she gasped.

Mark Foley stood outside, looking apologetic.

"I wish I could have come sooner but I only got the message this morning," he said. "What's the problem?"

Dorothy explained, without emotion but clearly unenthused, and tried to give as good a description of the shadows she'd seen outside as she could, but it was obvious there was nothing to go on. Foley knew it too. But he took everything down and promised to do his utmost.

"Does that include a police presence here?" I asked.

"I'd like to be able say 'yes' but there's no way we can spare the manpower right now, especially in something like this. You haven't actually reported anything concrete."

"There were men out there," Dorothy protested.

"I don't doubt it. But there's no way I can justify

twenty-four-hour protection," he said.

"So after somebody gets in here and does something horrible, you'll have a reason to devote some manpower," she replied, scornfully.

"I wish it were different," he said.

"Can you at least tell us if there has been any progress in the investigation into Michael's death?" Dorothy asked, not bothering to keep the exasperation out of her voice.

"I realise I'm not the most popular person around here," Foley shrugged with a slight grin. "The answer, I'm afraid to say, is no."

"I'm sorry," Dorothy told him. "It's not fair taking it out on you. I realise you're doing your best."

"And when we get a lead, our best is pretty damn good. It's just there hasn't been a lead yet. But one will turn up. It's rare that criminals don't slip up, either through greed, or arrogance, or stupidity. It's often a case of waiting."

He was okay. Reassurance probably wasn't a priority in the job-description: it was decent of him to try and provide some. I walked with him to the door.

"She isn't making it up. She's not the type," I said.

"I realise that. I really do wish I could sew this place up tight. But if we were to do that for what could be just some bastards messing, we'd be doing nothing else," he said. "Unfortunately, if messers were a renewable resource, the world would have an inexhaustible fuel supply."

I was tempted to fill him in on what was really happening. It would be the civic thing to do. But I held back, going with my instinct again. One day it really would get me killed.

Chapter 25

Saplings had grown into trees, the houses looked smaller but shinier, and the quality of cars lining the road were flashier. But fundamentally little had changed. It was familiar. If I closed my eyes, it would have been no chore to find my way. A few hundred paces down Laurel Walk, turn right at what used to be Cooper the publican's house. Then fifty yards, cross the road, and the griselinia hedge would rustle in the wind: the sound of coming home.

I leaned against the glass of the bus shelter a hundred yards past. It was new, a sign of the increased human traffic in the area. There was an estate at the end of the road where before there had been a field full of rusting scrap, a natural playground for youngsters eager to play, explore, take a furtive swig out of a cider bottle, sneak a first kiss with Aoife Donegan. No doubt the kids now had found somewhere else.

As usual the house was pristine in appearance, a new coat of paint put on during the summer glistened in the frosty morning air. The garden would be perfect too, carefully manicured and trimmed despite most everyone else having gratefully stored up the mowing chore for the winter. I bet myself there would half a dozen small shrubs carefully spaced out in the short brown verge leading to the front door: everything in its place.

A bus pulled up and two boys, happily late for school, clambered noisily aboard. The driver glanced up and I shook my head. It drove off, leaving me alone, except for whatever eyes were peering from behind curtains at the stranger who preferred loafing around to getting the bus. There was nothing for it; time to move.

We'd met occasionally over the years: at funerals and weddings. Conversations were brief, pleasant on the surface, churning underneath with stuff left unsaid. At first I'd been angry about what I regarded as slights and everyone else chose, maybe correctly, to regard as coincidences: like being placed at a corner table at one of the twins' wedding, finding out about the arrival of a nephew on Facebook, everyone forgetting to inform me about Mum's anniversary Mass. Now all I felt was regret, and fatigue at such an impenetrable cloud of emotion and resentment.

Needs must though: I wanted help now. Dorothy finally gave up and admitted it wouldn't do any harm if she took a short break from Ardfield. A vacation, she called it, which put the idea in my head. We needed an out-of-the-way place which would have no impact on anyone else. The cold reality was that someone had tried to kill me, and someone else was prowling around Dorothy's home, soon after her husband had been murdered. There was also a dollop of fraud and organised crime in a cocktail that felt overpowering but which still needed to be faced up to. If I had any chance of doing that, getting Dorothy somewhere safe was vital.

The gate opened without even a squeak. Sure enough there were the six plants, flowers not shrubs, but spaced an exact distance apart. One tiny rogue weed had survived in a corner by the wall. Maybe he was slowing up with age, not able to reach down as far. The doorbell tune hadn't finished before the door opened.

"Oh, Luke," my father said. "What are you doing here? I wasn't expecting you. Is everything all right?"

"Yeah. Sorry for coming unannounced."

"No problem. Come on in," he said, standing aside.

"Thanks."

Nothing much had changed since the last time I'd been here, about five years previously, when everyone had congregated before heading to Uncle Val's funeral. The carpet was new, a loud, brashly colourful covering that didn't seem like something my father would choose. I wondered idly if there was someone new in his life. It felt odd to think of him that way. After Mum's death, he'd retreated into himself so deeply that the idea of another woman didn't even occur to me. It still hadn't, until now.

I looked at the photo display that hung over the table with the phone on it. There were a few new shots of his grandson, more old ones of the twins. Nothing of Mum, or me.

"Would like a cup of tea?" he asked, striding into the kitchen. I remembered how he made it, strong, builders' tea, bag squeezed tightly against the cup.

"No, thanks."

He looked well. That weed was living on borrowed time. Still tall, well over six foot, ramrod straight, a little

Brian O'Connor

heavier than I remembered, but that was hardly surprising. The sands of time didn't run north. His hair was almost white now, which contrasted even more with the redness of a face that off and on had been affected by high blood pressure. He was fit though, and still as intimidating a physical presence as he'd always been.

"I read in the papers you were in town with that exhibition," he said.

"Yeah, sorry I haven't been in touch," I replied. "Everything's been a bit hectic."

"Of course, of course."

We spent a few minutes name-checking various people, ticking off the diplomatic obligations one by one and studiously avoiding anything non-neutral. Eventually there was nothing else for it.

"I need a favour," I said bluntly. "Do you still have the summer house in Brittas?"

"Yes. Needs to be done up a bit, but it's still there."

"Can I use it for a little while?"

"Now? In the winter?"

"Yeah, a friend of mine needs a place that's out-of-the-way and private – and so do I."

It didn't feel right to tell him about Dorothy just yet. Or maybe it was, and I just didn't want to. Either way, there was nothing to be gained from filling him in, not yet anyway.

"Sure, if that's what you want. There's never anyone in it during the winter. I'll get in touch with the woman who cleans it up occasionally and she can make it habitable."

"No, that's fine. I'm sure it will be great. We can fix up whatever needs fixing."

"Right," he said, taking his time over brewing a cup of

tea. "Did you drive? What kind of car have you got?"

"No, I came in a taxi."

"I can give you a lift back into town, if you like, or to the train. You know, later."

I should have agreed to tea. My hands felt desperately conspicuous, eager for something to do. When the letter box slapped shut, he was on his feet in a second, striding purposefully out, and coming back with a couple of letters.

"Nothing but damn bills," he shrugged.

He opened them immediately, scanning through the documents carefully. That had always been his way. "Never put off to tomorrow what you can do today," he used to intone. Enough of it had rubbed off on me, I knew that: just the idea of an unopened letter made me uneasy. There was probably something obsessive and compulsive about that. But had that come first or was it years of listening to and watching this man? Punctuality too: he hated being late, even more than being kept waiting. Tardiness was ignorance, a statement that your time was more important than the other person's. He was right too.

"My birth mother has made contact," I said.

"Really?"

Why had I blurted it out like that, I wondered? It wasn't like I hadn't thought about it. After a lot of consideration, the logical thing to do was leave it alone. What good could it do?

"Yes. I've met her."

"And?"

"She seems a nice woman," I said. "Did you ever have any dealings with her?"

"No."

"Did Mum?"

"No. At least . . ." he faltered. "She didn't tell me everything."

I knew. She hadn't told him about being ill until it became obvious something was wrong. He'd erupted, accused her of betrayal, said secrets had no place between a husband and wife. She'd tried to explain. I heard her, from the stairs, in the dark, telling him she'd tried to spare everyone, that him knowing too wouldn't change anything, that it didn't look good even to medical people who were paid to know these things. And I'd heard him continue to shout, knowing the volume was in proportion to the fright, but hating him anyway.

"I don't think she did. There was certainly no indication to me," he said. "What sort of woman is she?"

"Posh," I said, knowing the idea would swerve his prejudices. "Anglo, I suppose."

"A West Brit?"

"I don't know about that: just, different."

"And you get on okay?"

"Yeah. We get on okay."

"Well, that's good at least," he said, nodding his head. "How's life in England. Are you still riding the horses?"

"A few mornings a week."

"I don't know how you do that," he smiled crookedly. "A mad, dangerous way to spend your time."

He wasn't being hurtful, just straight. To him, the idea of being perched on top of a living, breathing creature that could collapse underneath you at 40mph was mad and dangerous. Trying to explain the thrill of not being completely in control would be futile. Control was what he aimed for.

"Would you like to come to the gallery some day? Have a look around?"

"Oh, I don't know. I don't know what I'm looking at with pictures. It would be a waste of time in many ways: pearls before swine, and all that stuff."

"There aren't any rules to it. Nobody has to look at anything a certain way. It's just whether you like it or not."

"It's not really me though, is it?"

"Do you want to come into town anyway, go for a pint?"

"Yeah, that'd be nice," he smiled. "We can catch up more – have a drink. Yes."

I knew he wasn't going to have a drink with me, and he must have known. The idea of staying any longer seemed silly. People got more set in their ways with age, not less. Expecting some sort of tearful reconciliation was wishful thinking. And it wasn't like that was something I wanted. I didn't hate this man any more. Neither did I like him. But it was ridiculous to ignore the influence he continued to have: maybe almost as ridiculous as imagining we could peep underneath the veneer of civility we had. And at least there was that veneer. He was after all giving me the keys to his holiday home.

"The big one opens the front door. The other is for the coal shed out the back. But you probably remember."

I did. It was our summer routine growing up. Every August we decamped thirty miles south, usually sitting inside, bored out of our minds with no TV, staring out at Irish summer rain, desperately trying not to upset him or get in his way. The upside was driving home, knowing it would be another year before having to endure another concentrated period of holiday happiness.

"I appreciate this. What sort of rent would you like?"

I knew as soon as it was out of my mouth. His face darkened, automatically on guard. The veneer had been breached. I hadn't been having a dig but, to a man like him waiting for a slight, it was enough. He would rather burn the place down than accept money from me.

"I mean, will I paint a few walls, or chop some timber for you?" I stammered.

"What? In winter? Don't be silly."

And that was it. I mumbled my thanks again and we sat into his car. He drove to the train station in silence. It started to drizzle as we parked.

"I didn't mean anything by the rent thing. I don't even know why I said it."

"What? Don't worry about that. It's a thing of nothing," he said, climbing out and walking with me to the ticket machine.

"It's getting a bit wet," I said. "You should head."

"Yes, I suppose so. Hopefully the place will be warm enough for you."

We shook hands. I watched him walk back to the car. My train was approaching in the distance. It arrived just as he drove past. Neither of us waved.

Chapter 26

"He's got a name," Dorothy announced in the car.

"Yeah?"

"Spirit of Michael."

We were driving south, past Dublin, heading towards Brittas. Rain was turning to sleet. The car heater was up high.

"It's dreadfully sentimental and mawkish, I know. And Michael would have done himself an injury laughing at even the thought. But it's all I could come up with it."

"Sounds all right to me."

"And he's gone to Colm McDonald's," she continued. "I rang him up and asked could he put the finishing touches to him in the next month. And we would settle up later. He was very good about it."

"Sounds like you've got things ticking along nicely on that score," I said.

"All we have to do now is get your licence sorted out so you can ride him in a race."

"What?"

"They're not going to let you ride without a licence, Luke."

"You are kidding. Riding work is one thing. I haven't ridden in a race in nearly fifteen years."

"Thirteen. But you'll be great, an ex-professional flat jockey riding against amateurs: it will be easy for you, and it will help Spirit of Michael. You know what he's like, and what he can do. He's used to you now. You have to ride him."

I didn't even know if the rules allowed an ex-pro to ride in a bumper. And I'd seen enough of Mark Maguire to realise what real race-fitness looked like. At the same time, the idea of riding competitively again stirred up dormant instincts. It wasn't like the horse had to be pushed and shoved the whole time. He travelled generously at Fairyhouse. And I'd never been a whip jockey, preferring to view my role as doing the steering and remaining as inconspicuous as possible.

"We'll see about that," I said, trying, in the midst of everything else happening, to contain the flickering excitement generated by just the idea of another race. "Can I ask you something?"

"Depends what it is," she replied.

"Why do you hate O'Donoghue so much?"

She didn't say anything for a while.

"He is a vindictive man, and such men are very dangerous," she responded eventually. "He holds so much power over people, and isn't slow to use it. And because everyone wants to be in his good books, no one is prepared to say boo to him. His jokes are always the funniest, his parties are always the best, his generosity is always the most. And maybe they are: but you hear the flip side too."

"Such as?"

"Such as a man I knew in Cork, a trainer who was once one of O'Donoghue's favoured few, built up his stables on the back of that patronage, and then fell out of favour when he recommended an O'Donoghue horse be sold on because he felt it was no good. The horse won at Cheltenham a year later for someone else. It happens, to everyone. No one's infallible when it comes to horses. Mistakes happen. But next thing the numbers in his yard start to shrink, other owners too, not just O'Donoghue's. And then all of the great benefactor's strings are taken away, leaving a good trainer with nothing except debt and depression."

I wasn't convinced. Everybody did make mistakes in the horse game, and everybody usually looked for someone else to blame. O'Donoghue's supposed vindictiveness could have been an easy excuse to explain away a cock-up. I didn't doubt Dorothy in terms of the facts, but who knew the motivations?

Dorothy spoke again. "He was found hanging from baler-twine just a few months after by his daughter."

"It's tough to pin that on O'Donoghue though?" I ventured a minute later.

"You think? The man was effectively ostracised. It was like something from the Mafia in Sicily. And yes, it's impossible to pin. But don't think I don't know the power of vindictiveness. You're still young. You'll learn too."

If anything the rain got worse as we approached what we'd called 'the holiday gaff' growing up. There was no other traffic on the coast road that snaked its way to the two-mile-long beach, the seaside-destination of choice for generations of Dubliners keen to get out of the city . . . but not too far. A series of holiday houses lined the road at the foot of a small hill, the other side of which descended to the beach. Some were palatial, others looked like the howling wind could knock them. The Delameres' was a small but well-maintained bungalow, largely hidden up a short lane by small trees my father had planted when he first bought the place.

Not a lot had changed here either. The thin concrete walls were bright red now rather than the usual white I remembered but promised no more warmth for that. The chill of disuse met us inside. I dropped the bags, flicked the heating switch to 'on' and went out the back to the small boiler house. The back panel of the boiler came off easily. The reset button was covered in dust and cobwebs. I pressed for a number of seconds, heard the rush of fuel and prayed it caught. It did. After a minute I checked the oil tank, ignoring the rain hopping off me as I put a dry brush handle into it to check the level. There was half a tank, more than enough.

Back inside, Dorothy was building a fire out of old newspapers and a small bunch of kindling kept in a basket in the corner of the sitting-room.

"Tell me there's a match here," she said.

On the kitchen windowsill was where he used to keep the matches: said it was a sure way of finding out if the place was getting damp. Behind the curtain was a big matchbox, full to the brim, and dry. Predictability had its upside, I smiled to myself.

"One thing before we light it," I said, kneeling down, and sticking my hand up the chimney. Sure enough some crumpled-up newspaper came away with a little pull. A gust of wind blew soot down, proof no nest was blocking it. "My father is a man of routine," I explained.

That worked out for us a few more times before we sat down to eat a hastily constructed stew filled out with rice. We ate silently, listening to the unfamiliar sounds of our temporary home. The roof creaked alarmingly in the wind, just as it had years before when only exhaustion would allow sleep for the first few nights of our holidays. Some things never change, I reckoned.

"Do you really think that about the girls?" Dorothy asked suddenly.

"What do I think?"

"That they tried to kill you."

"I don't know," I said. "I don't think so, but I don't know. They seem to be desperate. And desperation can make people do things they wouldn't normally think of."

"They are many things, Luke. And their husbands are probably more again. But they are not criminals. They're not . . ."

"The type?"

"Yes, the type. That might sound snobbish but snobbery is something I understand. Not financial snobbery, or intellectual snobbery; but standards, the sort of standards that are ingrained in a person, from childhood. And I put those standards in my children."

"Children grow into adults."

"The character is formed by the age of five. A teacher told me that once. And he was right."

I tried to think of myself at five, and couldn't. Apart from a few snapshot memories, blurry recollections of a first day at school, and breaking a finger in the park, I couldn't.

"I presume that teacher believed in standards too," I

said. "School can seem very straightforward sometimes."

"My children would not do that," she asserted defiantly, in a tone that suggested the conversation was finished. But after a minute she piped up again. "I'm staying here for only a few days, Luke. You can call this whatever you like but it is hiding. And I'm not going to hide."

"I realise that. But I can't think properly if I'm worried about you."

"And what are you thinking?"

"I'm going to Liverpool tomorrow and meeting a guy who can tell me more about the trade in forgeries and who's doing what."

Jerry Barnett had e-mailed a name – Alex Whinstone – a number, a time and a place to be at. Its sparseness alone was evidence of his disapproval, not just of what I was doing, but of the whole business. Earlier he'd urged me to reconsider. I would be in well over my head. These were ruthless people, gangsters. Forget about what they dealt in, he argued. Art was just another part of their criminal portfolio. This Whinstone guy apparently wasn't a total animal, but still more than a bit shady.

"You're going to meet a criminal?" she asked.

"I don't know that either," I replied. "But I do know I have to get some idea of what Michael got himself involved in. And if I go over there, I need to know you'll be okay back here."

"It's not worth risking your life, Luke," she whispered. "Nothing is worth that."

I reached over the kitchen island at which we were sitting and put my hand on hers. There was a slight flinch, and then she took it and squeezed.

"Michael felt Ardfield was worth getting involved with God knows what and look where it got him," she said. "And he did it for money, and pride, maybe even me. That's something I'm going to have to live with. But I can't live with the idea of someone else putting himself at risk because of some misguided loyalty to me."

"There's nothing like that involved," I said quietly.

"You should feel no loyalty, Luke. I didn't show you any."

"Please, you did what you felt was right."

"I did what I felt was opportune. And I don't even have the excuse of complete selfishness. It was opportune for others too, my family especially. And I was selfish, worried about the future, my prospects. It was diffcrent back then. Now being unmarried and pregnant means little or nothing. Systems kick in to help, so do families. But when I gave you up, it was still something to be ashamed of. And I worried about people thought, God help me, as if they don't think the worst anyway, whatever you do."

The tiny figure seemed desperately frail, sitting in a tiny cold house, frightened out of her home, facing an unknown future, conflict with her kids and little peace of mind. I needed to say something, find a way to make everything seem less bleak. But I couldn't. Nothing came. I cursed myself. What kind of man couldn't at least try to make an elderly woman feel a little better? All I did was hold on to her hand, look away at the front window rattling in the wind, and try to imagine any way a rotten situation could be fixed.

Chapter 27

I wasn't sure what I had been expecting but it wasn't the Alex Whinstone that appeared in front of me.

"Mr Delamere?" asked a slim figure in an expensive suit.

I tore my gaze away from the Merseyside panorama, all expensively priced high-rise buildings that had transformed the waterfront from its traditional industrial heritage. One of them was the hotel in whose lobby I was sitting.

He was tall, dark-haired with a strong face and a pleasant smile. His accent didn't have that distinctive phlegmy Scouse drawl; it was more Scottish, but not harsh.

"Very happy to meet you," he said. "I'm an admirer of your work."

"Thanks. And thanks for seeing me like this."

"That's okay. I really do like what you do by the way. It doesn't try too hard. That's what's wrong with this all too-cool-for-school material that's all the rage now, don't you think?" he declared, sitting down and accepting coffee from the large pot in front of us. "Nothing dates quicker than trendy."

I agreed and instinctively smiled back at him. He looked more like a business executive than some crook in a tracksuit. But as I'd told Dorothy, appearances could be deceptive.

"If you don't mind me asking, what do you do?" I blurted.

"Oh, you know, bit of this, bit of that," he said stone-faced. Then he laughed. "I am something of an agent. Rather like Michael Maxwell-Williams who I gather is connected to you in some way."

"He was my mother's husband."

"Oh. I'm sorry."

"Did you know him?"

"No, barely heard of the guy, until recently."

"What did you hear?"

"That he was shifting on some very decent material."

"Which means?"

"Look, you're a creative person. I don't know how much of the business side you're aware of. After all that's why you have Barnett looking after that side of things. But art is big business, both legitimate sales and the side of things that prefers to remain anonymous."

"You mean illegal."

"Not necessarily. A lot of people appreciate flying under the radar of auctions and headlines. It might currently be fashionable to flaunt everything in public but not everyone's like that."

"Especially when trading in stolen or forged items."

"Again, not necessarily. A lot people simply like

privacy. Take you for example. I've seen interviews with you. But you're not like some of your contemporaries, flogging their arses all over the media. You prefer to keep a lower profile. If I may so, I admire that: shows a bit of style."

"Thanks – I think."

We stopped when a waiter approached asking if we wanted more coffee, or anything else. I shook my head, although not with impatience. Suddenly it wouldn't have been bad if he'd hung around for a bit. What was I going to ask this man? How much stolen gear have you fenced? Can you give me the secrets of your success as an art-con? Ever done a stretch?

"If you're asking me do I know who killed the guy, then the answer is no. If you're asking me who might have, the list of possibles is massive. As I said, art is big business, and lots of people around Europe and the world have invested a lot of money and time in making it pay for them. There's no knowing who might have done it."

That was pretty definitive. I poured more coffee.

"Forgeries are as old as art," he continued. "You know that. What about Van Meegeren?"

The story of the Dutch painter was well-known to everyone who'd ever seriously picked up a brush. He focussed on Vermeer, produced *Christ at Emmaus* that was acclaimed as genuine by the top experts in Europe in the 1930's and sold for millions. His misfortune was to see the painting sold to Hermann Goring. And he was hardly alone. Elmyr de Hory forged hundreds of Matisses and Modiglianis. There was even a movie made about him.

"And it's in everyone's interests not to rock the boat," Whinstone continued. "You never hear the auction houses complaining, right? Why should they: they're getting their cut whether stuff is genuine or not. I'd estimate about half of the art on the market right now is fake."

My face must have looked as stunned as I felt.

"The police here have a full-time unit dealing with forgeries and stolen work. It's an industry, from guys working at home knocking out stuff so they can make a few quid, or send the kids to a good school, up to big organisations in Antwerp or wherever, practically factories, churning out stuff to meet the demand from all these wealthy Chinese and Russian who're throwing money around. You can even buy books showing you how to do it. And it's in far too many people's interests to turn a blind eye."

"People like you?"

"Sure. But I'm only an individual. This is much bigger than just me, or anyone else, no matter how rich they are."

"Meaning?"

"Want to know what's trendy now, in my game? Terrorists. With all this mayhem in the Middle East, there's stuff floating around you wouldn't believe. And a lot of it is organised by these Arab fanatics who need funds. It's the same in South and Central America, except there it's the drug cartels. What you have to understand is that art is a commodity, like sugar, or oil. And you can trade it, say for weapons. That cuts out any money trail you might leave after you. And if you take art as payment, the last thing you want is any suspicion it mightn't be the real thing. So, if you're worried, you sell on the pup to someone else who doesn't want to know."

"It's hard to get the head around that," I said.

"Okay. What about something more basic: you're the insurance company that's faced with a massive payout when an expensive piece is nicked. What do you do when the people who took it get in touch and offer to give it back in return for a ransom that's half the amount it's insured for?"

"You pay the ransom."

"Of course. And the guys who took it know that too. They will always make it worth the company's time to play ball. Am I disillusioning you?" he smiled.

"A little," I laughed, shakily. "So really the artist, the one who does the actual painting is at the bottom of the food-chain."

"Now you're getting it!" he laughed. "For what it's worth, your pal Barnett is legit, one of the good guys. A bit of a boy scout in fact."

Again, thank God for Jerry, I thought.

"There is one thing I heard about Williams," Whinstone continued. "Apparently he had something of a speciality in dealing with old guys."

"What do you mean by that?"

"Relax, nothing weird. It's just that a lot of the generation that were even little more than kids around the time of World War Two are dying off now. And towards the end of the war was when an awful lot of art moved around, or changed hands, or just plain disappeared. The scale of it is incredible. I've heard figures of one third of the art in Europe in 1939 disappeared. No one can know for certain.

"But think about it: some GI comes across something in Bavaria, decides he'll have a keepsake and somewhere in Redneckville Iowa right now, a Van Dyck is hanging on

233

a wall. Or a Russian soldier finds something in the ruins of Berlin and decides I'll have that. There's no knowing what ended up where. And that's just one-off stuff.

"The Nazis ransacked every significant piece of art they could get their hands on. They even photographed some of it, stuck it in albums for Hitler to pick out his favourites. There are Botticellis out there somewhere, either in an attic or being traded around by people who don't want to go through dealers for whatever reason, and either know, or don't know, what they've got."

"Which is where you come in," I interrupted.

"To an extent, I suppose, yes," he said. "It's not like I'm breaking into museums, so you can put your prejudices back in their box. I facilitate sales and purchases. And I know what I'm talking about. I know art. You'd be amazed how many supposed experts don't, particularly on all the work that disappeared after the war."

The waiter came back again, and I practically shooed him away. Despite myself, it was intriguing to listen to Whinstone.

"For every *Road to Tarascon* that got burned, there's a *Place de la Concorde* that shows up years later and is described as the real thing," he continued.

Place De La Concorde was by Degas, one of his signature portraits, one of the great impressionist works.

"It was generally presumed lost after the war, and then fifty years later it shows up in Russia. It was just one of any number of paintings looted by every side. Look at that Raphael the Poles are so hot on, the *Portrait of a Young Man*. That vanished in the last days of the war. There were any number of rumours and supposed sightings but it remained unknown for decades. And then it turns up. Cue delirium."

"I notice you say 'is described as the real thing'. You don't believe them?" I asked.

"No. It's just that I'm a student of art and even a cursory look at the history shows how definitively the 'experts' say such and such a work is real or fake. And then years later, the opposite is decided."

"But what about all these dating techniques?" I argued.

"That might prove how long something has been around but no one can be really sure it's the real thing. Maybe there was a really good painter around the same time as Caravaggio who got his kicks from copying the old lunatic? No one can know for certain. And as I say there are plenty people out there in whose interests it is not to rock the boat."

"Would you be interested in looking at some paintings?" I asked tentatively.

"What paintings?"

"There's quite a lot of material in Michael's office still. And I'm not sure what to do with it. It could be all worthless, or it might not be. Would you be able to value it?"

"I might. What's in it for me?"

"I'll pay you a fee obviously. Basically to tell me what's fake and what isn't."

"It can be very hard to tell for sure, almost impossible with a real good one."

"Your guess will be better than mine," I said.

"If there's anything valuable there, it'll probably be fake," he said. "Real good fakes can generate a lot of money. What's to say I'll be straight with you?"

"Nothing, I guess."

"And aren't the Irish police interested in the origins of this stuff?"

"They don't know. And it's not important they know. Michael's dead. There's no point tarnishing his reputation now."

He looked at me quizzically, clearly weighing up his options, calculating risk and reward.

"What do you hope to achieve here?" he eventually asked.

"I'm not sure. I'm trying to find out why someone would want to kill him." I said out loud, keeping the need to find out who wanted to kill me to myself. "Basically I need an expert view on what might be there that's worth killing for."

Whinstone said nothing for a little while.

"What the hell," he decided, handing me a card. "Ring me when you want me to come over. You never know: there might be something interesting there."

Chapter 28

The prone brown shape filled the stable-door entrance, one leg bent against the frame, neck and head facing inwards. His eye was half-open, milky white and lifeless. I steeped over the bulging belly and knelt in front of him. No amateur had shot him. There was one wound, in the middle of his forehead, right at the juncture of the 'X' between right eye and left ear and vice-versa. A slight cordite smell still lingered in the tiny straw-covered box. A small trickle of blood from the wound had caked. A flash from the police photographer's camera seemed even more accentuated in the stable's gloom.

"Never thought I'd end up taking shots of fucking horses," he muttered, wielding the heavy old-fashioned apparatus. He shot me a glance. "Sorry."

Outside, flashing blue lights on top of the police cars cut through the morning rain. There were two of them in the stable yard, along with a couple of ordinary vehicles too. They presumably belonged to the detectives. It all felt desperately incongruous. Such an elemental environment was supposed to be a refuge from such apparatus, or at least it used to be.

They were all dead, all the horses that just a few days ago I had been lunging around the shed or trotting around the fields, feeling all that power and life through the reins. All had been despatched the same way, shot, through the head. The only consolation was that it had been quick. There had been no messing, no need for second shots to terrified, agonised creatures who'd never done any harm to anyone.

A stepladder had probably been used with some of them. Even a tall man couldn't have reliably got into position to fire without one. The trick was in angling the bullet parallel with the skull so it went into the brain and didn't ricochet. And there had to be at least one other person to hold the animal. They rarely shied from a gun or a bolt. Even the oily smell didn't normally spook them. Years of conditioning to man's attention and care meant most of them didn't baulk at even the most unusual requests. In my experience the sound of gunshots would have provoked curiosity and little more.

"No sign of any ladder of any sort anywhere," Foley said. I'd told him my theory. "Not surprising, I suppose. They don't seem to be amateurs. Just lucky there was no one about." He glanced in Barry's direction and lowered his voice. "Although it can't have been a pleasant way for him to start the day."

Barry was sitting on a bale of straw outside the tackroom, still numb from the shock. He'd worked with these horses every day, looking after them, getting to know them, their every foible and quirk, likes and dislikes. To most of the rest of us, this was a desperate waste. To him it was much more: to him and Dorothy.

She'd been the first person he rang. It had been before six in the morning, still black dark. I'd been in a deep sleep that no amount of rattling from the roof in Brittas could disturb. Dorothy's voice got me up in a hurry though. Panic was only just being controlled.

We'd driven fast around Dublin and were met with the paraphernalia of crime that neither of us ever expected to see again. Dorothy went straight to the stable, brushed past Barry's attempts to keep her back and went to each stable individually. She stood in front of each carcass for a few seconds and moved on. Then she went into the house to see the damage there.

"The forensics guy has just had a few minutes but he thinks it was a pistol. A .45 calibre, maybe," Foley continued. "Can you come with me inside and see what's missing?"

There was no sign of a break-in. The front door hadn't been tampered with. None of the windows were broken. The drawing room was messed around a bit but nothing was smashed, just thrown about a bit. Foley strode down the hall towards Michael's office. The door had been destroyed. There was no other word for it.

"We think they used picks, crowbars, other heavy tools," Foley continued. "They obviously knew the house was empty."

The office was torn to shreds. Everything had been thrown around and lay all over the floor – the computer, desks, filing cabinets – even some of the light-fittings had been torn out. The pictures had been systematically taken apart. Glass from the various framed prints lay strewn around the place, crunching under the feet of various officers doing their technical examination. The sight of canvas torn away from frames made me wince. A lot of the canvasses were torn and ripped and looked to me beyond repair. Fake or not, they didn't deserve that.

"Clearly they were looking for something," Foley said, standing next to me. "Any guesses what it might be?"

Everything was destroyed as far as I could see. There was no way my memory extended to a detailed knowledge of what remained and what didn't.

"Whatever it is, I don't know about it," I said, truthfully.

"You do know it is punishable to obstruct the course of an investigation," Foley continued, his voice not changing tone but his body straightening ever so slightly.

I didn't know what to say to that. So I said nothing. It hardly mattered anyway. Whatever they'd wanted was gone with them. Maybe now everything could get back to some semblance of normality. Maybe Dorothy could grieve her husband with only an estate on its uppers, and an angry family fighting for her attention, to impinge on her thoughts, not the prospect of even more awfulness.

"Has there been any progress in your murder investigation?" I asked.

He stared straight ahead, but couldn't have missed the officiousness of the question. I didn't like slapping him down like that. He seemed a decent guy in a very difficult job. But I did it anyway.

"Enquires are ongoing," he said. "We should be finished here by the afternoon. Please be available should we need to contact you."

Dorothy was in her bedroom, brusquely going through clothes on various hangers, I guessed purely to avoid doing nothing.

"I'm sorry," I said.

She spun around.

"The bastards," she said simply.

"If there's any consolation, it's that there was no suffering. Whoever did it knew what they were doing."

She said nothing, just spread a couple of outfits out on the bed, brushing imaginary creases out of them.

"They say it was a pistol," I continued.

"Of course it was. Did they tell you what kind of pistol?"

I shook my head.

"Then I'll tell you. It was a Glock .45," she said, the harsh phraseology sounding wrong on her lips.

"They did mention a .45 calibre."

"I'm not surprised."

It shouldn't have been a shock to hear her talk about guns. Spending a lifetime with animals, breeding them, and looking after them, meant she was as intimately familiar with death as life.

Anything as delicate as a thoroughbred, with a vast bulk supported by thin fragile legs capable of bending under intense pressure but snapping at a single bad step, was always vulnerable. Often there was nothing else for it but to prevent them from further suffering. That was a reality too blunt for many people but remained a reality. Dorothy might have pursued the task with an unsentimental competence but never thoughtlessly.

"Can you drive me down the country a bit?" she asked.

"Of course. Where to?"

"Elizabeth's."

There was a little more tidying up done, a walk back

to the yard where Barry got a hug and an instruction to go home, accompanied I noticed with some money pressed into his hand. Not once did she look at the carcasses which would soon be removed by the knackers I'd called earlier. Then we sat back into the car.

Nothing much was said. Dorothy made a couple of calls, one of them to Harry, asking what the state of play was with the injunction and requesting a meeting as soon as possible. Then we continued our way towards Carlow.

"Thank God White Nose had left for McDonald's," I said eventually.

"Just because he can run fast, right?" she snapped. "Sorry. That was unfair. But I knew those horses better than most people – liked them better too."

"Were they insured?"

She didn't answer. Jesus, I thought.

"There are financial investments, Luke, and there are other kinds of investment," she said.

Yes, and the other kind is usually a luxury you have to be able to afford, I thought, but didn't say.

"One of the policemen told me Michael's office was wrecked."

"Yeah," I replied. "You didn't look?"

"No."

"They were definitely looking for something specific. Foley was fishing but I didn't say anything."

"It doesn't matter. They just want to get me out. They didn't have to destroy Michael's place. That was just malevolence. They knew how to get to me."

"Who's 'they', Dorothy?"

She said nothing. We drove for another half hour, through increasingly smaller country roads, until she motioned to turn left. Massive stone walls that managed to dwarf even Ardfield's led to a black wrought-iron gate that gleamed with fresh paint. It opened automatically. We drove in.

"This is where Elizabeth lives," she said.

The house was more modern than Ardfield, and the drive up to it wasn't as long but the effect they presented was the same: affluence, which showed how deceptive appearances could be, in both cases.

We got out in front of the house but Dorothy made straight to the left towards a farmyard, climbing over a gate and striding towards a massive stone building that looked like an old mill. I had to trot to keep up. She went in, veered right into what was obviously some kind of storeroom, and began pulling out drawers, rummaging intently.

"Mother? What's wrong?"

Elizabeth was at the door, anxiously looking at us. She must have heard the car.

"Where is it?" Dorothy demanded. "Tell me."

"What?"

"Has he got rid of it?"

"Mother, you're scaring me. What's wrong?"

"Where is it?"

Myles suddenly appeared behind his wife, warily trying to take in this strange interruption to the everyday routine. He wasn't wearing the usual smart sports jacket, but jeans and a fleece that looked like it had seen better days. The landowner looked to be working his own land.

"What have you done with that gun?" Dorothy said with ominous calm.

"The gun?" Myles responded. "I haven't had that in a long time. It's dumped."

"Isn't that convenient?" she sneered.

"Mum, what is going on?"

"The horses, all shot, in the head, with a pistol. All of them, you heartless creature!" she practically spat at Myles. "I hate you."

"Mum! Please."

"And you," Dorothy said, turning her venom on Elizabeth. "You were in on this as well, along with that sister of yours and her good-for-nothing brute of a husband: trying to intimidate me, to get your hands on some easy money so you can compensate for the messes you've made."

"Dorothy, please don't say such things," Myles pleaded.

She stopped, took a deep breath. I noticed her hands shaking. Only then did I see how her whole body vibrated with temper.

"You're right. There's no point talking to those who don't wish to listen. So I'll simply say one thing," she said, turning to Elizabeth. "Whatever I have to do to keep Ardfield out of your hands, I will do it. Believe me, if I have to knock it down, or burn it, or blow it up, that will be done before you or your sister get your hands on it. I promise you that."

Elizabeth burst into tears. Her husband looked stunned. Dorothy strode away.

Chapter 29

"If you think us sleeping in the Big House is going to make me forgive you, then you're wrong," Julia said, running her fingers along my belly and nestling her head into my chest.

I ran my fingers through her hair and tried to get my heart-rate back to some kind of normality.

"Have you been feeling ignored?" I gasped.

"As a matter of fact, yes. Flying off with someone to exotic continental capitals, shagging like stoats, and then not communicating when you get back might be the norm for you, but it isn't for this chick."

"It's not like that. Everything has been in a heap and I –"

"Don't be so sensitive," she grinned. "For a tough ex-jockey, you're remarkably easy to wind up."

"I'm a tough ex-jockey who believes in retribution," I grinned and kissed her deeply. "I'd watch out, if I were you."

Afterwards, she got up and looked out the window,

down at the stables where just the day before the dead horses lay sprawled on the ground.

"You'd hardly know," she said sadly.

Too much had gone on to ponder such things too deeply but she was right. The carcasses had been removed, the police were gone, the house cleaned up. If only everything else could be patched up so efficiently.

We'd driven back from Carlow and Dorothy had been so morosely distracted and angry she'd only put up token resistance to the idea of continuing her vacation in Brittas.

"It would mean a bit of breathing space," I'd argued. "Away from everyone."

"Sure, why not?" she'd said.

I'd seen many sides to this woman in the few weeks since she'd entered my life. But resignation was new, and not welcome.

Julia had phoned when I was driving back to Ardfield to stand guard after dropping Dorothy off. The sound of her voice alone was a rare upbeat moment.

"Are you trying to tell me something?" she'd asked, and even the idea of her being unhappy with me provoked panic. I explained what had happened and she demanded to see me. It felt good. It still did.

"How is your mother?" Julia asked, still peering outside.

"Okay, I guess, considering her world has been turned upside down."

"Do you really think her family tried to kill you?"

The same question had been coursing through my head. Logically the possibility existed. But, still, I doubted it. That was just a hunch. There was nothing concrete to back it up.

"I don't know," I said. "But I do know I'm tired of thinking about it. Let's talk about something else."

"Okay," she said, returning to the bed. "Let's talk about something close to my heart."

"Oh, yeah?" I grinned.

"Let's talk art."

I groaned.

She persisted. And I reckoned Julia O'Neill could persuade me to do most anything she wanted. Anyway she did most of the talking.

It was exciting to listen to someone so obviously in love with the subject. Her hands flew about praising the Impressionists and damning with disdainful venom anything Cubist. Best of all was her adoration of Modigliani, the neurotic, drug-addled Italian that painted damn near the sexiest pictures ever hung up on a wall. My clumsy attempts to make comparisons between Julia and the famous *Nude Sitting on a Divan* image were playfully slapped away.

"Concentrate," she giggled. "I'm making a point here."

"Which is?" I murmured while kissing her shoulder-blade.

"That you are so fortunate. Being able to paint the way you do must be wonderful."

"It's nothing to do with me," I murmured again.

"What do you mean by that?" she gasped.

I looked at her.

"It's a gift: from God, or whoever. But that's nothing to do with me," I said. "All I can do is try and make the most of it. That's my input. It's just a pity it isn't a gift for something more useful."

"What? Art isn't useful?"

"Hold on. I just mean relatively: like someone with a gift for curing cancer might be more generally important than someone who can throw paint on canvas."

She looked at me with open incredulity.

"You don't agree," I said.

"I don't believe you can say that. If making something beautiful isn't important, then what is?"

"Oh, I don't know: life, love, the pursuit of this ass," I smiled, reaching for her again.

"I can't believe you," she said, and she wasn't smiling.

"Is that the mood broken then?"

Julia didn't say anything for some time.

"I don't understand how you can be so flippant," she said then. "Art, and I don't care if it is music, words, sculpture, paint, or whatever, is the best of us. It means communication, beauty and truth. At its best it produces a greater truth than anything else. I would give anything to be able to create like you. And you don't even care."

"I care all right. And I'm sorry for sounding flippant. It's just I would rather not talk painting right now. Or if we have to, I would rather ponder the inspiration that got old Amedeo so hot."

She tried not to smile at that.

"Let's pretend we've got a chaise longue here," I added.

And we did.

It was evening when I left her sleeping and went downstairs to Michael's office. It still had the acrid stench of cigarette smoke and police chemicals. Plus the invisible smell of invasion. Everything had been tidied up, the smashed computer removed, with Foley's assurance he would examine the hard-drive personally, materials stashed into corners awaiting a possible insurance inspection. The floor had been hoovered free of glass and debris. But it felt very different.

The stacks of paintings and prints were gone, replaced by a tiny few that had survived intact and bits and pieces of frames the police judged might be retrievable. Even a cursory glance indicated they were erring on the side of hope. The remnants of torn canvas and ripped paper had been piled into a corner in the office.

I stood in the middle of it all, looked around and tried to think. What had they got out of here? Had they in fact got what they wanted? What, if anything, was missing? Why all the destruction? Why everything?

I picked up a surviving print that was leaning on the wall. There was no identification on it. I didn't recognise it. It looked a run-of-the-mill landscape, but who really knew: except perhaps Michael. I let it drop back against the wall and picked up another. This was a canvas. Again I didn't know it. There was a confidence and a swagger about the brushstrokes I appreciated but Pollock-like slap-dash wasn't to my taste. There was a small tear at the bottom right-hand corner. It looked to have been made by a knife. Somebody had checked underneath: for what?

I let the frame drop against the wall and stopped. The thud as it hit the wall was different. And it wasn't just the difference between canvas and timber. I put my hands on the wall, moved them around, trying to feel. There was nothing obtrusive. But there was something different. Slapping the wall produced nothing but the hard reverberation of concrete. I kept slapping and then heard it again, the hollow echo of a plaster partition. More slapping indicated it was small, no more than three feet by three, at ground level. It had been previously covered in any number of pictures. My heart was racing: time to take a deep breath, I decided.

Feeling tentatively around a little more didn't reveal much bar proof that everything had been plastered over to a perfect sheen. No one could know from looking. A quick examination of the other wall suggested there was only one such partition. I gently pressed against the plasterboard but nothing popped open. There didn't seem to be anything else for it. Picking up a small bronze figure of an elephant I tapped with increasing force around what felt like the border. It took a couple of laps before a chink came, encouraging harder taps. Even kneeling down, and with the air cool, sweat ran down my face. A blast of new colder air hit me as another hard tap brought a result.

The partition simply popped out, surrendering immediately when pressure was inadvertently put on the right place. Its material looked no more than an inch thick. Peering in revealed only darkness, and dust: lots of dust. I waited momentarily for it to settle, then stuck my head in.

To the left there was nothing but thick wall. Straight ahead, but a couple of feet away was the same. To the right was a vent: just big enough for a person to squeeze through. Cool air was streaming in, throwing up the plasterboard dust and milling it around. It was dark down that small space. The thought of venturing down it made me sweat more. All kinds of irrational claustrophobic fears swirled around. The idea of getting stuck, or not being able to turn around or something collapsing was scary. Given the choice, I'd have retreated, shouted my discovery and let someone else venture through it. But that was no choice at all. Time to suck it up, Delamere, I ordered myself.

I located a torch in a desk drawer and wriggled into the vent.

It was a good job I was skinny. Even with that, there was little or nothing to spare in terms of space. Face first, and tummy down, I forced myself to go into the darkness. After what seemed like an eternity, but probably was less than ten metres, the shaft veered sharply left. That somehow made things even scarier. And then the battery in the torch chose to give up which made it a lot more scary again. It took an effort of will not to retreat in funk. Whatever progress I made was tortuously slow. And then my head collided with something. It was all I could do not to whimper with fear.

This wasn't the tin surface of the vent. It was fabric, wool or cotton, with something solid behind it. Trying to feel around, hands outstretched, was difficult lying down. But I gave it a shove and it moved. It wasn't heavy, whatever it was. And then my nerve failed me. My hand got a hold of the object and I pulled. It was much heavier than a fabric cover but it slid easily on the surface, although its bulk was considerable. Squirming my way backwards, I returned to the light much more quickly than I'd gone in.

Relief made me flop onto the office floor and remain there for a few seconds, breathing in deeply. Fluorescent light never looked so good. And then I sat up. It was an old rug, tattered and frayed but exceptionally thick and warm. Underneath it was what looked like a bag carried by pizza delivery people to keep their products hot. It felt like polyester on the outside. I unzipped it.

A number of unframed prints fell out, laminated stuff of famous paintings by Rembrandt, Gauguin and a few other hardy standards. They surrounded a canvas, mounted on a thick frame. It measured little more than a foot and a half by slightly shorter. I didn't recognise the muted dark reds representing some kind of wasteland with vague skeletal shapes mixed into the darkest shades. There was nothing exceptional about it, just good professional work. Nothing special about the framing either it seemed. And then I saw the margins.

There were two margins of stretched canvas at the back, the edge of one peeping out from underneath the other. Something else was there. I stood up, found a small thin knife in the office and began trying to remove the nails. It was delicate work. Avoiding tears was paramount. Trying to minimise the holes left behind was important too. But it was as automatic a process to any professional artist as cleaning brushes. I carefully removed the red canvas and looked at the painting underneath.

It was so familiar and yet so incongruous the implications took a few moments to register, like looking at a parent's face on a 'Wanted' poster. The bright oils, vivid colours, the famous shadow, all that wonderful ambiguity that so inspired Francis Bacon. All of it was there, as recognisable to even the most casual art fan as the *Mona Lisa*. Except it shouldn't have been in my hands; it shouldn't have been in anyone's hands. This was supposed to be burned, just one of so many desperate art losses in WWII: lost to fire when the Allies bombed

Magdeburg. Van Gogh's *Painter on the Road to Tarascon*, there in my hands.

"Jesus Christ!"

I swung around. Julia looked the way I felt, dumbfounded. Her eyes were on stalks. She almost seemed afraid to approach.

"Is it real?" she breathed.

Who could know for certain? Maybe Michael knew. Why else would he have stashed it like that: why else would someone kill him? The torture made sense now. It wasn't pain for its own sake, rather to make him talk. God, Michael, why didn't you just tell?

"Can I touch it?" Julia asked.

I understood. It was like witnessing a mythical figure appearing from thin air, too much to comprehend all at once. Some tangible sensation of it felt necessary. She knelt next to me, barely touching the canvas with her fingers.

"It's real," she suddenly laughed. "Feel it."

Wanting it to be real didn't make it so, I reckoned. If desire alone was enough everyone would be lottery winners. But this was definitely a prize of some sort.

"Where did you get it?" she asked.

"In there," I nodded towards the hole in the wall.

She looked at the hole, startled, but her eyes were immediately drawn back to the painting.

"It wasn't burned," she beamed, keeping a hand on this tantalising object. "It survived. Isn't this wonderful? It survived!"

I grinned. It was impossible not to. And it was impossible not to keep staring. The thought of money went through my head and it almost felt unworthy. If this was genuine there was no knowing how much it was worth. I couldn't put a price on this. It was doubtful if anyone could. No wonder criminality was involved. What I held in my hands was truly priceless.

"I have to call the police," I said, standing up.

"Wait," Julia interrupted. "Don't do anything hasty."

"What do you propose I do?"

There was a light in her eyes that made her if possible even more appealing. For a woman so passionately in love with art, the idea of parting with such a picture must have felt like parting with a bit of herself. If I condemned her to a life in this basement office devoted to nothing else but looking at it, she would meet her fate with a contented smile.

"I know you're right," she shrugged. "It's just . . ."

"I know. But this makes sense of everything. We have to."

I handed her the picture and she took it as if she were handling her baby for the first time. We walked slowly upstairs to the kitchen where I retrieved my phone and scrolled down to Mark Foley's number.

"Mr Delamere, what can I do for you?"

"You asked me if I had anything more to tell you," I said. "I do now."

"Really, what about?"

"About a picture that I've found."

"Okay, where are you?"

"Ardfield."

"I'll be there as soon as I can."

Minutes later *The Road to Tarascon* sat in the middle of the kitchen table, leaning against a tall pepper grinder that Dorothy playfully referred to as Ardfield's very own

Rubirosa. Julia had made coffee. She didn't look up when I came back but kept staring at the picture, still hardly daring to believe it was there.

"It's so beautiful," she gasped, and I noticed tears on her cheeks.

"We don't know for certain it's genuine," I warned.

"For once, try not to be so damn sensible," she said, her voice catching.

I poured a coffee and joined her. Joining her in adoration would have been lovely. Julia was wrong about my supposed flippancy about art. It really was the best of us. I didn't know about truth since everyone vehemently believed their own was real. But beauty for beauty's sake was something I understood. Not that anything was ever free of context. But there were things I looked at and knew instinctively they were beautiful, and maybe even true too. If this thing was fake, it was a beautiful fake. If it was real, then it was the most remarkable thing I'd ever laid eyes on: context again.

The mundane interrupted us. My phone started beeping, complaining of a low battery and demanding to be charged.

"The charger's upstairs," I said. I nodded at the painting. "Try not to break it."

That got me a withering glance but she was too busy to deliver a quip.

The bedroom that had been home for longer than I could ever have imagined was in the sort of mess that made me smile. It had been some day. Not every day did one maybe find a priceless art treasure, and all the rest. The pencil sketch I'd done of Julia while she slept was on the floor by the side of the bed. Just the sight made me smile again. It fit easily into the small shoulder-bag I'd taken to carrying around. Already inside was the charger. I took it out, plugged in the phone and glanced out the window towards the yard.

Three shadows flashed past in the moonlight. They were men, moving fast towards the back door. Suddenly one of them looked up. I had the same sensation as I'd had with the painting. His face was pale, and his hair was red. It was the man who'd tried to kill me.

Chapter 30

It was cold, well below freezing, and we weren't dressed for it. Julia had a pair of jeans on. I had a light pair of sweatpants. Both of us were wearing thin T-shirts. She had black high-heeled boots on her feet. I had nothing. It didn't matter. All that was important was getting out. I'd grabbed the painting, screamed at Julia to move and took a chance going out the front door. The shock of running on cold stones in bare feet was nothing compared to the relief of not running into someone.

A hard frost meant the grass was already crunchy cold. Our cold steamy breath as we frantically ran made it seem even colder. Running produced sweat which dried. But the only thing that mattered was getting away. My car keys were in my jeans, back in the bedroom. There hadn't been time; the same with the phone. Behind us I could hear faint sounds from the house. We jumped a fence into a paddock and ducked behind bushes.

"Are you sure it's him?" Julia gasped.

"I'm sure," I breathed, grabbing her hand and

continuing to run.

About five hundred yards from the house was a dense clump of bushes and briars. We squatted behind it to get our bearings. Two shapes emerged through the front door. Neither was redheaded. One of them suddenly shone a strong flashlight to the side of the house. Instinctively I ducked. It shone in our direction, wavered for a moment, and moved on. Neither man budged.

"What do we do now?" Julia was shivering.

"I'm not sure," I said. "But we can't stay out here for too long. It must be at least minus five. Come on."

We continued through the paddocks, going out of our way to try and make the most of whatever cover was available.

"Jesus, you must be freezing," she gasped.

"I'm okay."

It wasn't the cold so much as the terrain. My feet were being torn by rogue stones and foliage of all kinds. Ordinarily it would have been enough to have me sitting down howling with pain. This was anything but ordinary. The frame in my hand was proof enough.

"Foley said he'd be here as soon as he could. Keep your eyes peeled for any lights coming down the drive," I said.

We got to the main gates first. If anything the night had got even colder. Despite the running and walking, Julia's teeth were chattering. All the while I glanced back, desperate to avoid any headlights coming from Ardfield or that strong torch beam again.

"Come on, Foley, where are you?" I said out loud. "Come on!"

I handed Julia the picture, edged out onto the driveway to look back, and saw nothing.

Waiting made the cold even worse. Part of me considered keeping going, trying to make the village a few miles away. But that would mean travelling the roads, leaving us vulnerable to anyone in a car. Cross-country didn't look on. I didn't know the lie of the land. And there had to be a limited amount of time we could stick this cold. Nevertheless even Julia was pondering aloud whether we should keep moving when a car pulled into the avenue. It was Foley. I ran out and waved him down.

"Jesus," he said, staring at us. "What's going on?"

"There are three of them at least – in the house!" I shouted.

We climbed into the car, Julia in the back. Foley turned around.

"Who are you?"

"This is Julia. She's a friend of mine. She knows what's going on."

"I wish to God I did," the policeman said, accelerating forward.

"Wait. There are three of them. And they'll have guns."

"How do you know that?" Foley demanded.

"He did before."

"Who?"

"The guy with the red hair that tried to shoot me."

I could almost hear Foley's brain whirring, trying to keep up with this barrage of information. It was easy to be sympathetic with him. Part of me still hardly believed all this was happening. But there was no need for pinching. The cold made sure of that.

"Keep the engine running – and keep the heater on," Foley said, pulling up just short of the house. "And don't move until I get back."

"You can't go in there on your own," I said. "I'll come with you."

"Stay put. You'd just be in the way. I want to examine this without having to worry about you too."

He walked ramrod straight to the front door. It was open, and Foley walked inside.

"I hate this," I muttered. "What if they're waiting somewhere else?"

Julia huddled in the back, desperately trying to get warm again, rubbing her bare arms. Simply sitting there was impossible.

"I'll be back," I said, and jumped out.

"Luke. He said to stay!"

That was the book. He was expected to say that, obliged almost. But sending a man in against three and sitting back was ridiculous, especially since I was the one who knew precisely how dangerous they could be.

The front door was wide open. There wasn't a sound, until a shout came from down the hall, downstairs in Michael's office. I paced down, trying to remain as silent as possible in bare feet. Where the hell was Foley?

The loudest voice was Red Hair's. I remembered the strong Dublin accent from before. There were only murmurs from the others.

"There's fucking nothing here. They must have it!" his harsh voice shouted.

Suddenly footsteps started coming up the stairs. I glanced down, trying to peer around the 180-degree turn in the spiral staircase. There was Red Hair. Just the sight of him made my insides dissolve a little. He was climbing slowly and looking back at the figure following him.

"Relax. They're not going anywhere," Foley said reassuringly. "Just let the lads make one more round in there, just to make sure. Then we go out and make them talk."

Having bare feet now paid off. I padded backwards, praying they wouldn't appear around the corner. And they didn't. And then a rogue floorboard gave me away.

"Hello?" Foley shouted.

I turned and ran. Noise didn't matter. I roared for Julia. It was nothing intelligible, just a primal need to cover fear with sound probably. There were no more than fifty yards between the front door and the car but in that time she jumped into the driver's seat and gunned the engine.

"*Go!*" I roared, and she spun the car around in an arc, spraying stones and creating a noise that even drowned out the sound of the men shouting.

"Foley is with them," I said. "He's bent."

Julia looked stunned. But that didn't stop her flinging the heavy car around corners on the way back to the gate. A radio phone was stuck to the dash, crackling into life every few seconds with traffic from other police units and their base. But apart from that there was little to identify the vehicle as belonging to the police.

"Just as well I didn't hang on to the picture, isn't it?" Julia said eventually.

"Jesus Christ."

In the midst of everything I'd forgotten about the picture. I must have looked stricken.

"Relax," Julia said, skidding to a stop as we came to the gate. "Get out and look behind that granite rock."

I did as I was told and there it was, just probably the

most valuable art object in the world, sitting on two rotten old branches and balanced against a rock, open to the elements.

Julia jammed the car into first gear and accelerated away.

"I figured if we were going back to Ardfield, it might be better to leave the prize possession somewhere safe," she said.

I could have kissed her. But she was accelerating around the tight country bends at such a speed, discretion seemed a better option. It was better to let her be.

"Head to the M50 and go south," I said, picking up a pen and getting to work on the frame.

"What are you doing?" Julia demanded.

"Trying to make myself useful," I said.

Getting the canvas off the frame would make concealing it a lot easier. It was something every painter knew how to do in their sleep, usually in frustration at having gone wrong. But as I started easing the nails out, every movement made me nervous, almost as nervous as when looking back for headlights. Julia couldn't help flinching every so often too. The idea of a tear was one both of us put to the back of our minds.

There was also the police radio to consider. Foley calling on his colleagues to track us down seemed unlikely but hardly impossible. What he could do, however, was use the resources available to him to keep tabs on a black Audi with two occupants who happened to have a stolen painting on their persons.

It didn't take long to get the canvas off. Michael couldn't have spent too long on the process. It was finely woven linen. It felt right for a Van Gogh. Whether it was

262

or not was another matter. But it wasn't hard to imagine the great man visiting Tanguy's arts supplies shop in Paris and paying for something like this, or not.

Traffic on the ring road around Dublin was light. We sped around to the south side of the city where I made Julia get off the motorway and make towards her apartment.

"You need to get home and stay put," I told her.

"Are you crazy," she retorted. "What will you do?"

"I have to get down to my mother and try to get her out of there. Foley obviously has any amount of ways to keep tabs on us. How else could those guys have got to Ardfield so quickly after I rang him first? I have to get to her."

"But then what?"

"I don't know. But I do know you're better off away from us. Foley doesn't know you. That means the further you stay away the better. Maybe you could go home to your family for a little bit."

"But I can help here," she argued.

"I know you could, and you've been brilliant. But I'd end up just worrying about you, and what might happen."

"You're going to have to do that some day, Luke," she said.

"I know. But not now. There's too much happening. Please, Julia."

She pulled in at a tram stop. We sat briefly, staring ahead. Then she leaned over, kissed me and jumped out. I wanted very much to follow, kiss her properly, take her away, just the two of us. Instead I got behind the wheel and accelerated.

Chapter 31

Dorothy was incredulous.

"But he's a policeman," she gasped.

"Which makes him even more dangerous," I replied. "God alone knows what information he has access to about stolen goods being brought into the country. Or turning a blind eye to what leaves, and where it goes."

It made more sense the more I thought about it. Nobody could ask for better cover. And there could hardly be a bigger threat, bar guns, and being dumped into a quarry to die. Christ, what have I got myself into, I thought. But I knew only too well. If they were willing to kill Michael for this, then his wife and a son-in-law he knew nothing about would be no impediment either.

"But, Luke, I don't understand. Did he kill Michael?"

"I don't know. Maybe he didn't physically do it himself, but he has to have known about it at least."

"Oh God. We can't do anything against this. It's impossible."

"I don't know. The fact he's police mightn't be such an

important thing now we know what his real agenda is. He can't want to let this get out."

On the short drive south, the police radio had crackled with information about everything from burglary to assault to drunks staggering out into traffic and what kind of burger the desk sergeant back at base wanted. But there'd been nothing about a stolen police car.

Dorothy had peered out the window before letting me in. She'd smiled as she opened the door. Her mood had clearly lifted, at least until I'd filled her in and unveiled the canvas, spreading it out on the sitting-room table.

"Michael had this?" she almost whispered. "How?"

"Michael was apparently involved with what were referred to me as 'old guys,' people who were involved with World War II material, usually stolen by the Nazis and which either disappeared or was stolen again. My guess is this arrived at Ardfield at the end of a long chain of people."

"Is it real?"

"I don't know. But if it isn't, it's a damn good fake. And they can be valuable too, to those who want to believe."

"So it could be real. This could actually be a Van Gogh."

I nodded.

"What on earth was Michael planning to do with it?"

"I don't know: sell it on probably. Or maybe he just wanted to keep it for himself."

"In a house crumbling around his ears?"

"People can do strange things around great art."

Which was true. Only one thing was certain. He knew its value all right: why else had he stashed it away?

"I don't suppose you've a pair of socks I could wear?"
I asked.

"Good Lord, in the heel of the hunt! I barely noticed –
you must be freezing. You might be in luck. There are clothes
in a press in one of the bedrooms. I'll make us some tea."

I knew where she was talking about. Sliderobes had
replaced the old timber doors from years before but the
smell when I opened them was the exact same: dust,
fading linen, a slight smell of my father's sweat from his
old suits and a touch of my mother's perfume. The pang
of nostalgia it generated caught me by surprise.

There was a suit that just about fitted me, and socks
that Dorothy threw in which at least managed to get
above my ankles. An old pair of black brogues fit okay
too. It felt weird, wearing his clothes, like a kid pretending
to be grown up. But they looked okay in the mirror.

I had just heard her shout "Tea!" from the sitting room
when the back door crashed open.

It was the three men from earlier. Red Hair was the
second of them through from the kitchen. A heavier,
bigger man was first. He met me head-on. Instinctively I
jumped towards him, using my head, making contact with
his nose. Even in the midst of the chaos, the sound of bone
breaking was unmistakable. He howled with pain just as
I fell forward with the momentum.

Red Hair didn't hesitate. His boot caught me on the
side of the head.

"The fucker's broken my nose!" the other one shouted
balefully. He stood up and approached. He started kicking
me too.

I curled up, protecting my face and letting my back and
kidneys to their fate. It didn't last long.

"Leave him alone," Red Hair ordered. "Where's the old bitch?"

Dorothy was unceremoniously dragged into the hall by the third man, and was protesting loudly about it in language that clearly nonplussed those not used to the little old lady with the colourful vocabulary. There were a few farcical seconds where everything seemed to stop. Even Red Hair appeared stunned.

"Bloody people looking for bloody attention!" she bellowed. "Why don't you fuck off and work for a living! Get fucking jobs!"

It was Foley who laughed. He sauntered in late, looking completely relaxed, and paused over me.

"You have some tough old bird for a mother, you know that?" he said. "You have to admire her."

He put the heel of his shoe on my outstretched hand and pressed down. I didn't want to moan but it escaped anyway.

"Leave him alone," Dorothy commanded.

"Of course: tell me where the painting is," Foley responded.

The last I'd seen it was on the sitting-room table, in full view. No one could miss it.

"Let me make this clear," Foley continued. "You will tell us. For your own sakes, just make it easy for everyone."

I turned my head. Dorothy's face was a picture of quietly furious indignation. She didn't look scared at all: but anger oozed from her tiny frame. Compared to her, I must have presented a deeply unimpressive figure, stretched on the ground, trying not to scream, even after Foley removed his foot.

The hope we would be okay if we just told them was too faint to be entertained for more than a moment. What use would we be? All we would represent was trouble, loose ends that required tying. I'd already experienced how such trouble was dispensed with, in the back of a car at the bottom of a quarry. Getting lucky once was incredible; twice was not on.

There was no way Foley could survive with us around. This racket hardly co-existed peaceably with police duty. Getting rid of us would be just an afterthought, something he could guarantee would be investigated very shoddily. The only value we had was the painting. It was vital to maintain at least the appearance of possession. I prayed Dorothy had worked out the same.

"Oh, please don't start this hero nonsense," Foley sighed. "Believe me, you want to talk. You do not want anyone else taking over here."

He walked over to Dorothy, smiled briefly and then lashed his hand across her face. The sound reverberated around the thin walls. I sat up quickly.

"You're the tough cop all right," I spluttered.

"Give it a rest. If either one of you is going to talk, it's her."

That's your first mistake, I thought. You really don't know who you're dealing with. The problem was I did. Dorothy would say nothing.

"Did he bring the painting here?" Foley demanded of her.

Her face was unreadable. He hit her again.

"I don't like doing this, love. It's like he says: hardly an honourable course of action. But I will hurt you if I have to."

Her thin face looked like it might crack. There was no way aging sick bones could put up with such treatment. But she said nothing, barely even changed expression. Dorothy was not going to say anything.

He hit her again.

"For fuck's sake, this could take all night!" Red Hair shouted.

"Shut up," Foley exploded. He wasn't as calm as he'd made out. The policeman was under pressure too. That wasn't good.

"I didn't bring it here," I shouted. "Just leave her alone."

"So, where the fuck is it?" Foley demanded.

Dorothy's expression didn't alter but I swore there was pleading in her eyes. It didn't matter. This couldn't continue. And for everyone's sake, I had to make it sound right.

"If I get it for you, she gets let go," I said, getting to my feet. "Nothing happens to her."

"If you fuck us around, then the opposite, right?"

"And if we play ball, you let the two of us alone," I said. "We won't say anything to anyone. All we want is to be left alone, and forget about you and the stupid painting. We just want to go home."

"Fair enough," Foley said, believing it as much as I did. "Let's go."

It was a last throw of the dice. If there was a plan at all, it was to try and escape and come back to get Dorothy. Red Hair said he could take care of the little old dear on his own, and said it in a way that hardly calmed my fears. The other two went either side of me with Foley ahead as we went out the front door. A car sped towards us on the road, lights on full. In the darkness they were very bright. The driver must have had the beam on higher than recommended. As it swept past the gate, the glare was blinding. I ducked, tucked and rolled to the right, getting to my feet in a flash, and started sprinting.

In the dark, I tripped over a child's bike left lying to rust at the side of the house, and stumbled over a discarded concrete block. But once I met the high dunes it was remarkable how memory returned to help. The sand was as powdery as over twenty years previously, the sharp grass stalks as sharp. The solution to moving through it was to get down on all fours and crawl.

There were shouts and curses behind but I didn't look back. The dunes had got bigger with time. But an increasingly salty tang told me I was nearing the top. Staggering back to shifting but relatively level ground, I chanced a look back. Another beam of light blinded me. They still had their torch. I turned and half-fell, half-jumped down the soft sand.

Running baldly across the strand was a risk. It was wide open, almost two miles long. The tide was out, so the sand by the water would be pretty hard and good for running. But where would I run to? The nearest towns were miles away. The main Dublin road was a mile away but would mean going the other way. And leaving Dorothy was not an option.

There was nothing for it but to get back into the dunes. In places they were like mini-mountains, with dips and rises, even plateaus. The going was hard though with powdery fine sand making every step treacherous, especially when trying to remain silent. At times my heart sounded in my ears like it was on stereo.

I stopped and lay down exhausted after twenty minutes, listening intently for any alien sound over the echoes of the wind and surf. But it also gave me time to think. I needed help. Even with three of them outside, there was no guarantee of being able to overpower Red Hair. Instead I had to get to a phone. All the holiday homes were empty for the winter. There was a pub over a mile away. And the main road was there too. That was the best option: the only option really.

Moonlight intermittently emerged from behind the clouds and acted like a flare. Trying to judge the wind and its impact on the cover of darkness became as important as quietly trekking back over the dunes. But I ran into nobody. Even chancing a narrow lane down to the road worn through the grass by summer holiday makers didn't result in shouts. In a second I was across the road and hiding behind a timber chalet on the other side.

There were five lines of such buildings, swaying and creaking in the wind. After that it would be mainly bare fields. At least bare feet weren't an issue any more. I forced myself to stop and listen, and not to think about Dorothy. There was nothing out there I could hear or see. Small fences divided each site, designed probably to generate an open, friendly atmosphere and more likely a cause of territorial dispute. Their advantage was ease of movement. In less than a minute I was past them, and over a ditch into open country.

A few miserable-looking sheep tugging morosely at poor winter grass got the fright of their lives at the sight of the strange human running past them. Apart from them there was nothing else to stop me. Even gates conveniently appeared to save me scrambling over thorny ditches. The moon was back out now, bathing the countryside in light, and it was very cold again.

It didn't take long before roaring night-time traffic interrupted the idyll. The racket of the cars and trucks sounded unnaturally loud but they offered potential sanctuary. I broke cover, ran through the car park and flung myself against the pub's front door. It stayed resolutely closed. There weren't any cars parked. I didn't have my watch, had no clue how late it was, but it was clearly well past closing time.

"Help me! Help me!" I roared, banging on the door. "Open up! Open up!"

Noise came from upstairs. Then a light came on, and a window opened.

"Who is it?" a man demanded.

He looked middle-aged, tired and angry.

"Please, let me in. I'm in trouble and –"

"We're closed for fuck's sake. Get away from there or I'll call the cops!" he shouted, slamming the window closed.

There wasn't time to argue. A temporary lull in traffic allowed me sprint into the middle of the road, run down the wide striped middle island and pray drivers were awake enough to spot the arm-waving obstacle before mowing me down.

All I got were beeping horns, dramatic swerves and a couple of shouts to get the fuck off the road. It was while the reverberations of the last bout of swearing faded away into the distance that I saw the flashing blue light approaching from the north. The beach was east. It had to be a police car, or an ambulance, something official anyway.

"*Stop!*" I roared, veering out into the middle of the road.

There was a single light flashing I noticed – not an ambulance then or a police or fire engine car. Maybe a private vehicle then, like a tractor, although it looked a bit low for that.

"*Stop!*"

It didn't veer away suddenly at the unlikely obstacle. Instead it accelerated towards me. At the last second I recognised Foley's car, just before jumping onto the speeding bonnet to avoid being run over. Bouncing on to the roof, I fell to the side, thankfully landing onto the hard tarmac on my side. It was enough to wind me though.

"You're a slippery one, I'll give you that," Foley said, standing over me a couple of seconds later. "But if you're going to start banging on pub doors in the middle of the night, it's probably best not to do it with a landlord who likes ringing the guards."

In the car, I could hear the familiar sound of the radio crackling.

"Now," he said to one of the heavies, who hoisted me up. "Let's get the suspicious character out of here before uniforms show up."

Chapter 32

Julia was bleeding from a cut over her eye. As she wept, blood streamed down her cheek. A little spilled on to the hard lino floor. It pooled slightly before draining into an invisible hollow. My eyes followed it rather than look at someone so plainly terrified.

"Luke!" she sobbed, and staggered towards me.

I tried to move, to stand up from the chair, but it was impossible. Hands tied behind my back, there was no way of doing anything.

"Sit down," Red Hair scoffed, pushing me back and almost sending the chair over. "Tie this one up over there."

He pointed to a couch underneath the front window where Dorothy was already sitting. Her back remained straight, eyes barely flickering from a spot on the opposite wall. Julia was dressed the same as when I'd left her. That seemed like an eternity ago.

Two more large men arrived. One of them grabbed Julia's arms, pulled them behind her back and quickly tied them up with the same thick nylon cable-ties used on us as handcuffs. Trying to break them was useless. I'd tried. All it did was make them dig harder into the skin.

"What are you doing here?" I asked Julia. Foley didn't know who she was. That had been the whole point.

"She's here because I saw you making cow-eyes at her in the Ormond. Once Foley told me about a good-looking bird with dark hair and a great arse, it didn't require a genius to figure it out."

Gerard O'Donoghue strode through the front door, in jeans and a tweed sports jacket rather than the usual suit, but still exuding power and authority. Absent though was the usual bonhomie. Instead the flabby face was hard and unyielding.

He barely acknowledged everyone, preferring instead to look around the tiny house that had been torn apart in a fruitless search for the canvas. Everything that could be turned over or torn apart had been. Tempers flared and a couple of times Red Hair slapped me around a bit, purely it seemed to work off some steam. Even if I had known where it was, I wouldn't have told him. But I didn't. What worried me was what would happen when the search stopped. It had, but nothing had happened – until now.

Even in the midst of everything, having one of the country's richest businessmen standing in the middle of such a situation was baffling. Even Dorothy's face registered surprise. Julia just looked scared as hell.

"We couldn't find anything at this one's flat," O'Donoghue said, nodding at Julia. "And there's nothing here. So Luke, where is it?"

I said nothing.

"Believe me, Luke, you don't want to start being a

hero. For one thing, it's so fucking boring. But the other thing is, you're going to be a hero on the back of someone else's pain."

I stayed silent but my stomach heaved.

"No? Okay, then. Mick!"

The second of the new arrivals stepped out. He was huge, both tall and heavy, with a big dark beard and a smile that revealed good teeth but which didn't extend to his eyes. He was wearing all black: boots, jeans, and a padded anorak. Red Hair, I noticed, was sniggering. One or two of the others started shifting their feet.

"Mick here has a talent," O'Donoghue said. "Show him, Mick."

A terrible silence was interrupted by Red Hair's nasty laugh as the big man unbuckled his belt and let his jeans fall to the floor. He pulled his underpants down too. I looked away.

"You really should watch this, Luke," O'Donoghue continued. "It's amazing. Doesn't matter where he is, or what the circumstances, not even how pissed he is: Mick can get it up in just a few seconds."

Behind him Red Hair hallooed and whistled. Foley, I noticed, was looking uncomfortable. O'Donoghue looked excited, all trace of suavity gone, just enjoying the horror on our faces.

"I've told him he's wasting his time beating people up," he said. "He should be in pornos, screwing for a living. But I guess he's loyal. To me. Isn't that right, Mick?"

Mick nodded.

O'Donoghue walked up and grabbed my head, jamming his fingers painfully into my skull.

"Look at it!" he roared. "Want to guess where that's going unless you play ball?"

The pressure of his hands produced involuntarily tears, the effort of trying to control them produced snot and noises that obviously only added to the terror on the couch opposite. Red Hair's laugh sounded ever uglier than before.

"Where is it?" O'Donoghue demanded, tightening his grip even more.

"I don't know," I gasped. "It was here. But it isn't any more."

"Do you expect me to believe that shit?" he whispered, the tone becoming even more menacing with the volume turned down. "It just fucking vanished?"

"There were others here before you," I said, my voice sounding like someone else's.

The pressure eased slightly. He was clearly considering this. Foley looked over at us.

"Don't listen to that. He's spoofing," he said. "Trying to divide us."

"It better be like that, smart boy," the voice said close to my ear. "I'm not paying you to be stabbing me in the back."

"Gerard, no one is stabbing you in the back. It's not here. We've looked everywhere," Foley argued. "But don't do this. Get that moron away."

"The moron does what he's told," O'Donoghue responded. "At least that I can be sure of."

There was a breathlessness to his voice that was new. He wasn't as much in control as he might seem, or as he might like us to think. And that made things even more unstable.

"Get over there," O'Donoghue commanded the big man who had pulled up his trousers but now went over in front of the couch where the women were.

"Leave them alone," I spluttered before fingers dug tightly back in. "Leave them, please."

There were laughs from some of the men looking on. My eyes caught Foley's. He looked very uneasy with this. If we had a hope it was with him.

"Go on, Mick, shoot on the old bitch!" Red Hair roared, accompanied by laughs.

I couldn't see Dorothy but Julia's face was suddenly stony, glancing sideways, giving nothing away, completely different to before. Being a reporter she must at least have an idea of what rape and sexual assault entailed. Maybe she was steeling herself, preparing to partition off the dreadfulness of what was happening and what was about to happen.

Straining on the ties didn't achieve anything but I did it anyway. And trying to move my head was similarly futile. But this was too much: for a damn painting, I thought despairingly, a stupid piece of cloth and paint.

"No!" I bellowed and received a punch in the back of the head.

"Go on, Mick!" Red Hair roared. "Slap it off her again. Go on!"

I got another punch to the back of head, harder this time, propelling me forward. The chair rocked and I leaned deliberately. It collapsed sideways.

"Leave them alone!" I pleaded again, scrambling around helplessly. "I don't know where it is. Believe me, I don't know!"

The obscenity of what was happening was terrible,

making my stomach heave. Scrambling around on the floor produced nothing but noise and more laughter.

"Gerard, enough is enough," I heard Foley say. "This is madness. Get him away from her."

I could hear him, but I was all but helpless on the ground. I couldn't see what was going on. There was the sound of a brief scuffle. And then the air was shattered by the sound of a gunshot.

Chapter 33

The impact was primal. Despite being bound up, the urge to burrow into the ground was overwhelming. So was the instinct to not look, as if by pretending not to see made it less real. I wasn't the only one. A couple of O'Donoghue's men dropped to the ground too. Even Red Hair had dropped to one knee, in a reflex move to make himself smaller. The acrid stench of fresh urine made itself known. It could have been mine. I didn't care.

The room seemed to be swirling in slow motion. Remaining still, with ears ringing, and not fully conscious of what was going on, briefly felt preferable to moving. Having to look at the impact of that noise was appalling. But there was nothing for it. It took every ounce of will I had to turn over and half sit up. Julia and Dorothy were half-lying on each other, scrunched down into the sofa, their eyes wide and terrified.

Foley sat a couple of feet in front of me. He looked dazed. And then my eyes went to his shoulder and a gaping wound of blood, shattered bone and hideously exposed tissue.

"Oh, Jesus, no," he whispered.

The stricken policeman moved a hand to where his mangled limb heaved and convulsed hideously. He looked down for a moment and then stared back at me. "Oh Jesus."

Just behind him Julia's composure wavered. Tears poured silently down her face. But she was unharmed.

"Help him!" Dorothy's voice was unwavering. The obscene spectacle in front of her was forgotten.

Mick rushed to the front door and barely made it outside to vomit, his famous ardour forgotten.

O'Donoghue looked at the gun he'd just used with detachment, like he'd just fired at a plastic target, weighing the weapon in his hand.

"Cut these things," I shouted to another of the heavies, who, remarkably, obeyed.

I crawled over and put my hands on Foley's unharmed shoulder and chest. He stared pleadingly at me, his body starting to shiver with shock and reaction.

"Check to see if there are exit wounds," Dorothy ordered.

She knew about guns, had figured out about Myles and his weapon. All those years working with animals meant she had some expertise. I scampered behind him. There didn't seem to be anything, certainly nothing obvious. I tried to move his jacket but that provoked a terrible groan.

"Never mind that. We have to stop any bleeding. Is there a massive pool of blood, anything arterial?" Dorothy continued.

It looked terrible but there was no huge pool of dark

red. I told her so. She nodded.

"You'll have to put some pressure on the wound – try and get it to clot."

I took off my father's jacket and pressed it gently against the wound.

"Press firmly," Dorothy said. "Make it hurt him."

Foley groaned and his breathing started to get more strangled and desperate. But he could still speak.

"Please, don't let me die," he pleaded to me, eyes boring into me. "Please, don't let me die. Please."

"You're not going to die," I told him, trying hard not to be sick myself. I turned to O'Donoghue. "Call an ambulance."

The big man looked pityingly, a response not even required.

"No one fucks with me," he said simply.

"Please, please," Foley sobbed, his hand grabbing mine with an intensity born out of desperate fear.

I'd seen Michael dead. That had been terrible enough. But watching a man grievously hurt in front of me was horrifying. It was raw terror, eyes boring into a reality that was frightening and awful.

"Oh Jesus, help me, please!"

The image of the cool, collected big policeman had disappeared in a minute, all front reduced to frantic terror. He must have seen something in my face because his sobs became hysterical.

"No, I don't want to die – *I have kids*!" he screamed hoarsely. "They don't deserve this. They need a father. Who's going to look after them? They need me."

"You're going to be fine," I said.

"He's going shocky," Dorothy shouted. "There are

some blankets in those sliderobes too. Get them."

I looked at O'Donoghue. The chance he might shoot me in the back if I moved without his say-so was real enough. He motioned to one of the goons to get them.

"Boil a kettle too, will you?" he shouted after him. "It's bloody freezing in here. Close the front door on that bollocks throwing up outside."

When the goon came back with the blankets I lay Foley down on the floor, put a cushion under his head and covered him. The motion seemed to awaken some primal fears in the man, like the position meant a repose before death.

"Fuck you! No!" he cried, switching his gaze to O'Donoghue. "Gerard, do something. Please. My kids."

The big man stared stonily back, and said and did nothing.

"Fuck you, you bastard . . ." A strangled noise from the back of his throat produced a trickle of blood from his mouth.

Dorothy said to keep him warm. That's all we could do for him – until he got proper medical help.

O'Donoghue came and stood over us.

"Hurry up and die," he said.

Tears rolled down Foley's face. But he stayed quiet, and then his eyes closed. I desperately fumbled around, trying to find a pulse, a reaction to years of watching stupid television shows. But it worked. Behind his neck, there was a pulse. He wasn't dead yet. But he desperately needed help.

I should have tried to attack O'Donoghue there and then. I was free. There would be a second before anyone could react. But the thought never occurred to me. Too stunned and too sore, it was all I could do not to break down myself. And that would achieve nothing. If there was to be any hope, some sort of cool head was required.

The goon came into the room again and bizarrely presented O'Donoghue with a mug of tea.

"I take it I have everyone's attention now," O'Donoghue said, as casual as if addressing a boardroom. He sipped his tea.

Even Red Hair and the others looked shocked by the brutality of what had happened. The only sound was of the man outside, still hacking. Judging by some of the faces around the room, he could have company. Everyone appeared devastated. Everyone but Dorothy. There was a small smile playing on her lips. And O'Donoghue spotted it before everyone.

"What are you grinning at?" he spat.

"I always knew you were cheap," she said. "Despite all the money, you were always a guttersnipe. All the money in the world, and no class."

It was a remarkable display of bravado. One man lay badly wounded at her feet and she was still able to insult the other man who'd shot him. Even in the midst of everything, it was impossible not to admire the woman, and to silently plead for her to shut up. Everyone waited for an eruption.

"That's right. All the money in the world, and no class," he said. "And you're the opposite, of course. All class and no money. And that class makes it all right the look down your nose at everyone, even though you don't have a pot to piss in. And it's all right to be married to a thief. And of course, to let your child be brought up by someone else."

Dorothy flinched at that, but maintained enough composure to pounce on the interesting part of his statement.

"What do you mean 'married to a thief'?" she piped up, voice still steady.

"Oh, that husband of yours was no thief? Let's face it, Dorothy, we all know he was a glorified fence – just that instead of tellies and jewellery it was art. Which means it can't be anything as vulgar as plain thieving, right?"

"My husband was an honourable man," Dorothy replied. "Did you kill him?"

"I wish I had," O'Donoghue said with a sudden ferocity. "I really do. But he went and died on the lads. The fucking eejits hit his head too fucking hard. And before he squawked too, which is the important part."

He paused, taking a sip out of the mug of tea.

"I'll tell you how honourable he was," he continued. "He'd been selling stuff on for years. I knew. Because it's my business to know. Why do you think I dealt with that bent bastard there?" he said, nodding at Foley. "I mainly knew because it's important to know what's on the market. Even the small-time stuff that your husband handled. If I'm shelling out big money on art, avoiding the crap can be difficult. And I've put out a lot of money over the years. And for one simple reason: I love it. There's very little out there I can't see something admirable in. Even this guy," he added, pointing a toe at me.

The door opened slightly and O'Donoghue roared for it to be shut, complaining of the cold again. What was a nightmarish situation for the rest of us seemed to be entirely normal to him. I began to think he was psychotic. No one could view this as normal. But there he stood, sipping contentedly at tea.

"I'd have left Michael alone to do what he was doing: might as well be him as anyone else. But then I heard the *Tarascon* was floating around – remarkable really, after all these years – and by some fluke of nature was residing in Meath. You understand the significance of that?" He looked at me. "A Van Gogh, believed lost forever, turning up out of nowhere. Apparently some German had the thing in his attic for decades, afraid to try and sell it. And then it gets nicked and ends up here. This piece of history, right on my doorstep. Absolute greatness within touching distance: a thing of beauty that will live forever, because of me."

He said it matter of factly. What was Michael thinking of, trying to stem this remorseless wave of self-belief? Easier, I reckoned, to turn back the tide.

"Except the bollocks wouldn't play ball, would he? Said the thing was priceless, and then tried to play me off against some other potential buyer, if in fact he ever existed. I offered millions, and then he comes up with how he doesn't want to sell: says he can't sell. And how it's the most beautiful thing in the world, and that he can't swap it for mere money. Actually I could understand that – a bit. But I can afford to indulge in that sort of sentiment. He couldn't. He owed a fortune on that blasted house. I offered to buy that too. He said he couldn't sell it. What he did let slip though was that the painting was stashed there. He thought he was being clever, taunting me, saying he got it out every night just to gaze at it. I had Foley check the place out. He never left the estate, never even left the house. So it was in there all right. And that's where things went wrong."

He looked scornfully over at Red Hair. The hard man seemed to physically shrink, cowering under his boss's disapproval.

"I was assured the information would be got out of your husband with a little bit of pressure. They were even given a lesson in my own favourite tongue-loosener. All it needed was a little bit of heat strategically applied. Even an ordinary cigarette lighter does the job, if applied in the right place. But they couldn't even do that."

I remembered the stench of Michael's burning flesh and felt my stomach heave again. Dorothy didn't even blink. Despite herself, I could see Julia looked fascinated and appalled at this man she'd previously only known as an avuncular benefactor-figure. What had she got dragged into – by me?

"And your fucking children are about as useful as a third tit. All they had to do was persuade you to face reality," he said, turning to Dorothy. "You don't give a fuck about art. From what I hear, you didn't give too much of a fuck about your husband either. And you clearly don't give a fuck about your kids. That older one, married to the loudmouth, is on her uppers, as far as I can see. But no. That upper-class spine of yours just can't bear the thought of having to bend a little to the guttersnipe."

Even Dorothy's resolve couldn't prevent her face betraying hurt at such a sustained assault. Even if the words were from the mouth of a madman, they couldn't fail to sting. No one was impervious to barbs about their loved ones.

"So they're not working with you?" she asked.

"Those morons? Christ, I wouldn't rely on those hoorays to find their own arse-holes on a consistent basis.

No, they're just looking after their own corners, trying to squeeze as much out of me, and you, as they can. They still think I'm Santa Claus. And they are going to get a present. Because it really is true you have to do something yourself if you want it done properly. You," he said to Red Hair. "Get a fire lighting and I'll show you how to properly persuade someone to sing."

His tone never changed. Our attention never wavered. Everyone knew he was going to burn us. And after he got what he wanted, there would probably be a bullet, just like Foley got. I looked at Julia again. She gave me a slight grin. Christ, what a girl! She knew it as well. How could she smile?

Foley moaned a little, opened his eyes a little and then closed them again. I'd read once about how resilient the body could be once no vital organs were assaulted, even if a bullet and its fragments were still inside. But how long anyone could survive in these circumstances was unknowable.

Red Hair rolled up some old newspaper, found some kindling by the side of the fireplace and checked there was coal in the bucket before lighting a match. Almost immediately some smoke billowed back down the chimney.

"Christ," he muttered, jumping to his feet and coughing.

"Draught the damn thing," O'Donoghue commanded.

Spreading a big sheet of newspaper in front produced a surge of flame which in turn produced another blow-back of smoke and ash. Outside the wind wasn't blowing too much. And then I looked at Dorothy, and realised. As Red Hair kept the paper in front of the rapidly rising flames, I realised completely. She caught my eye and held my stare. And O'Donoghue saw it.

"What's going on with you two and . . ."

Leaning down, he peered at some of the ash that had settled on the floor. Then he felt it with his fingers.

"No! *No!*" he roared. "Put it out. Get some water!"

Red Hair looked blankly around and got a kick into the ribs.

"Put it *out!*"

A bucket of water and the kettle got flung in and the fire sizzled out. Red Hair stayed with us, but O'Donoghue rushed outside. Through a crack in the curtains, it was easy to see him staring into the sky. He ran back in, knelt at the fire and stared up the chimney.

"Get the torch!"

He shone the light up, coughing at the fumes. But there was nothing there. Slowly I began inching towards the couch.

"Stay still," Red Hair roared, and kicked me hard in the back. I fell down over Foley. He didn't even flinch, still unconscious.

"You fucking bitch," O'Donoghue said, standing over Dorothy.

I waited for the gun to emerge again. This time, I would have to do something, no matter how desperate.

"You've destroyed something more valuable than anything we will ever see again," he continued. "How could you do that? How? To something so beautiful? Have you any idea what you've done, you crazy cunt?"

He appeared genuinely outraged. Springing at him would be futile. I wouldn't last a second. But he couldn't be just let extinguish our lives just like that. He continued staring at Dorothy, hatred oozing out of him. It took some time for him to speak again.

"Well, now I'm going to destroy the most valuable thing in your life."

The last thing I remembered was a boot slamming into my face.

Chapter 34

It seemed every part of me was too sore to move. Better not to, I reckoned; just stay put, eyes closed, detached.

And then my sense of smell returned.

There was smoke, just like when it all blew back down the chimney, but different. And there was heat. Unsettling, I reckoned, ominous. Much better to stay still, and not face it.

Carpet nestled against my cheek, a rough texture, different to the old lino in the summer house. We were somewhere else. I opened my eyes.

Orange flame dazzled me. It looked beautiful and dangerous. They were curtains, on fire, producing smoke. Out of sight, I could hear coughing. Much better, I told myself half-heartedly, to shut my eyes again.

"*Luke!*"

It was Dorothy again. Why couldn't she leave me in peace, I thought petulantly. And then my brain clicked back into gear.

"*Luke, wake up!*"

And I did. Suddenly and clearly, I was all too aware. We were in the drawing room at Ardfield. And it was on fire.

I tried to get up, and couldn't. My hands were tied together again, with the thick cable ties from before. Except this time, they were in front of me, not tied behind my back. My legs were tied too. No amount of straining could budge them.

"*Luke!*"

It was Julia, from behind me as well. Foley was lying on the ground to the left, a few yards away, obviously dumped there. I shuffled around desperately, muscles protesting at the effort. I saw Dorothy and Julia by the door, bound up like me. Julia had manoeuvred herself to lean, sitting up, against the door. But they were detail against a backdrop of fire and flame. The whole room was ablaze. We were going to burn.

"Luke," Dorothy spluttered, the fumes of acrid black smoke making her hack. "Help!"

They were helpless. So was I: what could she expect me to do? It was asking too much. There were no super-heroes, no dramatic ability to leap from burning buildings. Except this building really was burning. And so would we.

"Where's Donoghue?" I coughed, spluttering on smoke.

It was Julia who answered.

"Gone. He flung petrol around the place, and then lit it. He was laughing as he walked out of here, Luke."

Further explanation was impossible. It felt hellish. The smoke was starting to thicken and become more dense, deadlier even than the flames.

I forced myself to think. "Lie on the floor!" I yelled at Julia. Panic was easy, but wouldn't achieve anything. Doing something for the sake of it was futile. I had to think – and quickly.

Somehow an old physics lesson came into my head, about friction and tension, and old Mr Hickey's incantations about tribology. His tired, careworn words came back to me, and so did the experiment he'd so embarrassingly made me do twenty years before.

Scrunching up into the foetal position, even with the ties pulled tightly together around my wrists, it was straightforward to get fingers to the thick laces on my father's shoes. Getting them untied was harder but eventually I pulled them free.

I left one end of a lace in the last hole and tied the end of it into a knot so it wouldn't escape. Then I got to work doing the same on the other shoe, so that the lace joined both of them. I prayed it would be strong enough to hold.

"Help me."

It was Foley. He stared at me. The wound was horribly exposed, and he looked desperately pale.

"Just hang on!" I shouted.

"I have kids," he said simply.

The smoke was even thicker now, and the sound of the fire gathering more strength was terrifying. O'Donoghue had told Dorothy he was going to destroy the most valuable thing in her life. And Ardfield was burning around us.

Lying back flat on the ground, and pushing my legs in the air, I put my bound hands one on top of the other and manoeuvred the lace between them. Then I started moving my legs as if cycling. Pulling against the ties would be useless. What was required was persistent friction. It was our only hope, if enough strain could be put on the ties.

I cursed them vehemently. More than once I reckoned I was wasting my time and energy. More than once I expected the lace to snap, extinguishing whatever chance we might have had.

"Come on, you cow!" I roared, trying to boost flagging energy and morale.

A beam from the ceiling suddenly loosened, hung momentarily, and then crashed down to the floor, sending sparks of flame shooting everywhere. The noise of it was terrifying.

"Is anyone hurt?" I screamed.

"No!" both women shouted.

"We're not going to die," I said out loud to myself in between coughs, forcing my exhausted legs to move even faster. "We're not going to die. We're not going to die."

The idea of being dumped like garbage was awful, but it also made me angry. And we needed that anger now, more than anything. O'Donoghue was not going to treat us like nothing. I wouldn't allow it.

"Come on, you cow!"

It snapped out of the blue, like this inanimate piece of plastic decided enough was enough in the face of kinetic inevitability. It happened so suddenly, I lay there looking, hardly daring to move my wrists apart. And then I sat up.

With all the movement, a glass had fallen off a nearby table and shattered. I picked it up and cut at the cable keeping my legs together.

It took a couple of goes to get upright, circulation slowly coming back into cramped limbs, but a paroxysm of coughing had me quickly dropping to the floor again. It was the only chance against such evil-tasting smoke. Julia had her eyes closed and when I appeared in front of her almost jumped with shock. Then she cried with relief. I cut quickly at the cables, sawing frantically, ignoring the blood that started oozing from my cut hands.

"Well done, boy," Dorothy croaked as I cut her free.

Foley barely seemed to notice me cutting at the ties. But his eyes were open. He knew what was going on.

"Listen to me!" I shouted. "You've got to try and move. Think of your children."

He looked at me, and moved a leg.

I knelt up, put my arm around him and took the strain of his considerable weight. He groaned piteously with pain.

"I know, I know. But we've got to move," I said, straining with the effort.

Dorothy and Julia were ahead of us, at the door, coughing and urging me to go faster. The smoke didn't seem as thick in the hall, but it was only a matter of time before everything spread.

"Get something to tie over your faces!" I roared.

Julia took off her jacket and held it over her mouth, helping Dorothy do the same. I ripped at my shirt and a bit came off. Whatever effect it would have against the smoke would be minimal but it was better than nothing. Foley would have to take his chances. He wasn't able to hold anything over his mouth, and I couldn't do it for him. But most of all I had to think.

"Turn left and crawl!" I shouted.

"Left?" Dorothy shouted. "But the main door is right."

"And we don't know who's out there. Go left!"

She looked at me. Even in the midst of everything, I could see her weighing it up. But she pushed Julia ahead of her down the hall, away from open air and possible salvation.

Foley had to be dragged, pushed and pulled. He tried to help, but couldn't do much, and the effort had me gulping in great lungfuls of smoke that provoked paroxysms of coughing.

"Just let me go," he said at one stage.

"Fuck the heroics," I gasped.

Trying to keep my bearings was the main task. If I hadn't got to know the hall so well, we would have wound up hopelessly disorientated. But there was an inch-wide thread through the wallpaper that lined the long walls and, like floor-lights on a plane, or centre-lines on a road in thick fog, I focussed on that.

The two women stuck close, pushing and helping Foley as best they could. Crashing sounds reverberated around us, terrifying in their intensity. All the public-service advice about how quickly fire could envelop a room or a building couldn't even begin to capture the reality. But the one part that helped us was the instruction to stay low.

"Come on," I said, turning round, standing up to heave Foley's heavy body onto my shoulder. My knees buckled with the pressure and the policeman groaned with the pain of this unexpected manoeuvre.

Julia smiled encouragingly: remarkable.

Taking deep breaths, we went down the stairs and into Michael's office in one burst. The smoke wasn't as bad there yet. But I had to drop to the floor again to get my bearings. Fear was a remarkable disorientater.

"Stay close," I shouted, dropping Foley.

The heat got more intense. Suddenly the glass panels from the office shattered above our heads, raining shards of glass on top of us. There was a moan of pain behind me. The back of Dorothy's head was sliced open. Blood trickled down her neck. She reached around to touch it.

"Keep going," she ordered. "Wherever it is you're going."

"He knows what he's doing," Julia shouted back. "Just keep moving along the wall."

Bit of plaster began falling off the ceiling. The floor was covered in all sorts of glass and debris. None of it mattered. All that counted was getting to that tiny bit of hope created by a dead man.

It was getting harder to see more than a couple of feet in front and for a horrible moment, I feared the worst. There was no sign of the opening. If it had been sealed up, we were dead. If it was still there and I couldn't find it, we were dead too. My hands frantically pawed around the wall, searching frantically for the loose plasterboard I'd casually put back. I moved along the wall and found it. I'd miscalculated by a potentially lethal couple of feet.

Fresh air gusted in, tasting like nothing else in the world. But there was hardly time to sit there and relish it. I pushed Julia and Dorothy through.

"Just crawl, fast!" I shouted.

And pray we'll be able to get out, I thought. What Julia didn't know was that I hadn't made it to the end of this tunnel. The end would be as much of a mystery to me as everyone else. The volume of fresh air coming in suggested it could hardly be some tiny ventilation space. But that wasn't certain. Neither was it certain we'd find out. Foley was all but unconscious. Even pulling his head towards the shaft didn't revive him.

"You've gotta help me here!" I screamed at him. "You've gotta try!"

His eyes opened again, took in the screaming face in front of his and tried to reach for one last ounce of energy. I dragged him through, and stared down the dark, claustrophobic space.

"There's no room. You're going to have to help yourself," I told him. "Lie on your back, legs away from you. Push yourself backwards. You've got to try."

And he did. From somewhere, reserves of strength propelled him slowly backwards. It was inch by inch but he did it, facing back towards where we'd come from, he didn't have to stare into the black darkness either. I could hear the women ahead of me, but couldn't see them. The smothering fear returned with a vengeance but couldn't compete with the alternative behind us.

"Luke!"

It was Julia. I plunged faster into the dark, and then it got a little lighter, and the air felt fresher and stronger. Turning a corner, I crawled into Dorothy's back. There was a thick wall in front of us. But above, pale winter-morning light poured in through what looked like an old-fashioned circular iron grate. I pushed up against it and there was a faint budge. It was enough. Another frantic heave and it moved.

"Get up!" I shouted.

Julia was up and out like a cat. She leaned down and grabbed Dorothy's hands.

"You're a great girl," she said gratefully.

I peered back around the corner. Foley's shape was

indistinct but definitely still moving. He had only about a dozen feet to go. I started down towards him, planning to pull him as much as possible. But there was sudden '*whoosh*' sound. Suddenly it got a lot less dark. I stopped. And then it came.

Flame spurted into view. Foley screamed. There was nothing I could do. The fire had found oxygen. It was following its course, through the shaft. Scrambling backwards, the last thing I heard was a piercing cry of terror.

Chapter 35

Fire spurted out the drain like a flame-thrower venting its anger at the sky, shooting up metres, and sending me spinning to the ground. Julia and Dorothy stood above me, looking shocked, hardly daring to ask.

"Is he . . .?" Julia eventually said.

"Yes," I replied breathlessly.

Nothing could have survived that. It was an inferno. And no one should have to look in there. I certainly wasn't going to.

It would have been lovely to lie back on the cold cobblestones, close my eyes and try to banish the memory of Foley's scream, another sound to plague my dreams.

We were at the back corner of the house, almost at the edge of the stables. The cobbles extended into the yard. There would still be straw in the boxes there, I thought: perfect to simply lie down on and sleep.

"We have to phone the fire brigade," Dorothy said.

"I'll go to the nearest house and ring from there," I said, staggering to my feet. "You two go into the yard and stay put – those bastards might still be around somewhere."

"They're miles away by now," Dorothy said.

"You never know," I replied.

"The whole place is ablaze," Julia said as we walked away from the house and stared back. "Someone has to see it."

She wasn't wrong. The sounds of the old house creaking and groaning inside were alarming. Windows were starting to blow open with the heat, sending black smoke billowing out. Ardfield was being gutted. It was only a matter of time before the roof was destroyed. So much history razed due to one man's obsession.

"I'll see you later," I said, and kissed Julia. "Be careful."

My legs protested at having to break into a slow jog. The rest of me was battered and bruised too. Maybe it was that which made me ignore my own advice.

O'Donoghue stood a hundred yards from the front of the house, staring up at the devastation he'd caused. His expression was blank. The brazenness of remaining to appreciate his handiwork was instinctive, an arrogance refined by time. He was on his own. A massive black Mercedes was parked to the side. No one was in it. No one else appeared to be around. He wanted to appreciate this alone.

I was rooted to the spot. Even after everything, there was an unreality to seeing him there. It looked the same for him. The shock of seeing me there, when I should have been burning inside, meant there was a ridiculous pause: him pondering the implications of me still being alive, and me cursing my stupidity. You never know, I'd said.

He moved with surprising speed, running towards me and at the same time reaching into his jacket pocket. The gun, I suddenly remembered.

It was too late to turn and duck out of sight anywhere. The only option was back where I'd come from, and that meant heading back towards Julia and Dorothy. There was nothing else for it. Only by sprinting towards him could there be any hope of preventing him getting a clear shot.

I clattered into him just as he was lining up to fire. The weapon fired and the noise was deafening. As we collapsed onto the stones, a memory stirred about the never hearing the shot that hits you. Nevertheless, I scrambled onto all fours, desperately running my hands over myself. There was nothing, at least nothing obvious. Any relief was banished by an overwhelming impact that knocked the wind out of me and sent my face into the stones.

"You're a tough fucker to kill," O'Donoghue breathed into my ear, his weight crushing me into the ground. "But don't worry – I'm the man to do it."

He was too heavy. Even if I was fully healthy he would have been impossible to budge. A few brief heaves proved that. But panic can be an improviser. Dreading the smell and feel of the heavy weapon, I forced myself to relax momentarily, stopped struggling. Despite himself, O'Donoghue did the same, and leaned nearer to my ear.

"I'm going to enjoy this," he said.

Whatever force was left I concentrated into driving the back of my head into his face. There was a sound of bone crunching. He groaned. I threw my head back again. His grip loosened just enough. Turning quickly, I drove my forehead into his face, shuddering his head back enough for me to slide out from underneath him.

But he was tough. Blood poured out of his nose. It was obviously broken, the bone twisted into an ugly shape. Far from hurting him though, it made him even more angry. His hand shot out and caught my ankle, pulling me back. I punched him and I might as well have punched the sky for the effect it had. He didn't break step in getting to his feet. I did the same, a lot more shakily.

"You'd want to take better care of your hands, Luke," he cackled, blood trickling between his teeth. "They are your fortune."

"Why don't you just give it up?" I gasped. "It's over for you."

I scanned the ground around us for the gun. But there was no sign of it. Did he still have it on him? But if he had, he wouldn't be standing there jawing. There would be a bullet in me faster than he could blink. Where was it?

"Over for me," he laughed. "Jesus, don't be so naïve. What are you going to do? Call the police?"

The idea didn't perturb him at all. And why should it, I thought. This was someone who had a Detective Inspector in his pocket. Who and what else had extreme wealth bought him? I hadn't been out of Ireland long enough to forget how small everything was. My father always warned us as kids to be careful of what we said about anyone. You never know who you're talking to, he'd intone. Better to say nothing. A man of O'Donoghue's power and influence didn't have to hunt down anyone: they came to him.

I thought of running. Battered as I was, there was a good chance I could keep out of the way of a man a good twenty years older and far from peak fitness. But I delayed, trying to catch my breath. And then he rushed again. Like a lot of big men, he was surprisingly light on his feet. And his power was overwhelming. He flung me to the ground again and this time pinned me down, knees on chest, hands around my throat.

He tightened his grip. The sensation was terrifying. Hungry for air, I began tearing at his hands, digging fingers into my own throat to try and loosen his grip. It was useless. He was too big. The weight on my chest was oppressive. The life was being strangled out of me. Pain shot through my arched body, desperately trying to find a way to breathe. And it was useless. His hands gripped even tighter around the larynx. I began to drift out of consciousness, the brain beginning to shut off. What a stupid way to die, I thought bitterly.

I was unconscious when the shot went off, out cold in the few seconds it took for Dorothy to retrieve the gun from near his car and move quickly to where O'Donoghue lay on top of me. Julia said later she didn't hesitate, pointing it expertly just inches from the big man's head. He glanced briefly at her and gave a slight grin, apparently not believing the older woman capable of using the weapon. It was the last miscalculation of his life.

The dead weight was the first thing I became aware of: and then exhilaration at being able to feel anything. Jesus, I wasn't dead. It was air going into my lungs, wind blowing against me. Nothing ever felt better. Julia's face was what I first muzzily made out.

"His eyes are open!"

Trying to speak was impossible. The worst of the excruciating pain from where his fingers had pressed was gone but a throb remained that made even breathing sore.

"Don't do anything," Julia added.

She tried to move the vast weight from off me but might as well have been trying to move a mountain. Time, I felt, to make an effort. Bringing my hands up to his chest, I pushed and the impact of a bullet on the human brain was all too obvious. Gore went all over one side of my face. I vomited to the side and thanked God I was alive to do it.

"Dorothy shot him," Julia said.

She was shouting, but I couldn't hear properly. The impact of the gunshot on my eardrums was significant. It didn't matter. They would recover. Nothing mattered if you were alive and able to move.

Between us we managed to let O'Donoghue's body slip the ground. Dorothy was a few yards away, walking slowly towards the house and examining its destruction. The wind blew gusts of hot air towards us. Clambering shakily to my feet, I hugged Julia, said and did nothing except relish the feel of this remarkable girl. She eventually nodded towards Dorothy and I walked to where she stood.

"I'm glad he's dead," she said after a little while. "And I'm glad I killed him."

"I'm glad you did too."

"He was an evil man. Because of him, Michael's dead," she continued. "And he was going to kill you too."

"But he didn't, thanks to you."

I grabbed her hand and squeezed. It shook violently. I squeezed tighter and still it shook.

"I couldn't have lived if you'd died too," she whispered, suddenly looking directly at me. "You're a wonderful man, and I'm very proud of you."

She put her hand on my face and I put mine on hers. There was plenty I wanted to say. But there would be time enough for that.

"Will they put me in jail?" she asked.

"No."

"He was a very important man: a very influential man."

"Me and Julia know what happened. And we know what the others look like. They'll talk, or at least some of them will. That will be more than enough."

Julia joined us and I took her hand.

"This is Julia," I smiled. "Isn't she brilliant?"

Dorothy smiled sadly.

"I noticed all right," she said.

"Julia, this is my mother, Dorothy."

"I noticed too," she said. "I'm sorry about your house."

"Bricks and mortar, my dear, that's all," Dorothy said. "I forgot about that, to my eternal shame. Just bricks and mortar."

"Bricks and mortar can be replaced," I told her.

"Let's think about that another time," she replied. "We have work to do now."

Chapter 36

Newmarket was at its most winter bleak. The skinning wind whistling across the heath seemed to come direct from Siberia, picking up speed over the North Sea. Even the sun appeared to have given up trying. A harsh white frost meant even stepping deliberately on the frozen grass barely made it budge. There was no chance of galloping horses on it, and hadn't been for some time. Instead the town's thousands of residents kept on the move on the all-weather gallops that snaked through the white landscape and which were kept open by all-night harrowing.

Only scarves wrapped around the bottom half of our faces kept us riders from being frozen as we cantered up the brown-coloured strips, the horses' breaths clouding the atmosphere and contributing even further to the eerie early-morning silence. A few of the other lads around me grumbled through the material about the cold. Even that made me smile. Anyone who ever worked with horses knew it was always either too cold or too hot.

Right then it was just about perfect for me: back on

familiar ground, doing what I knew, where the only rogues trying to do harm had just teeth and legs to call upon. The joy at feeling all the muscular power beneath me was amplified by muscles and joints that now ached through exertion and not pain. We pulled up at the end of the mile workout, horse and rider warmed up and happy to have proved our wellbeing.

Normally the string walked back slowly, allowing limbs to ease out. But in such weather, and with no trainer about, the other lads elected for a leisurely trot. I let them off. They knew I wouldn't rat on them, and they were only halfway through their morning's work. It wasn't like I'd never pulled short-cuts in my time. But right then, I wanted to appreciate everything around, the calm of it.

We'd spent a comparatively small amount of time dealing with the official fallout of that awful morning. But it had felt like forever.

The police had been decent. A short, squat superintendent called Johnson was in charge, clearly could have done without having such a high-profile body on his hands as O'Donoghue but managed to resonate an understated efficiency.

He'd been an acquaintance of Foley's, not a friend. Before the police and fire brigade had descended on Ardfield, I'd said to Julia and Dorothy it might be best not to highlight Foley's role. That didn't mean lying exactly, just remembering that he had kids. They were missing out on their father. They didn't need to be aware of other stuff they had no control of anyway. So we pleaded ignorance of why Foley was present at Ardfield, and in Brittas – not exonerating him, but not implicating him either.

I remembered Johnson looking at me and suspecting he

knew a lot more than he was willing to admit. But he didn't press it. Maybe that was self-interest in holding the police line, or maybe it was he couldn't contradict direct statements. More likely it was that all the attention was on O'Donoghue.

It was a story made in media heaven. One of the most recognisable men in the country revealed as a psychopathic gangster and shot dead by a granny. It wrote itself, but was no less distasteful for that: both the living and the dead reduced to cartoon figures, motivations and characters reduced to tabloid-sized portions for easy consumption by a public eager to console itself with the misery of others. Or maybe that was too harsh. It just seemed corrosive being in the middle, rather than outside staring in.

Remarkably Julia's name never featured. It seemed the police, who were feeding their tame reporters lines throughout, didn't twig the beautiful art critic's role in everything that had happened. And she wasn't going to tell. Despite being a reporter herself, she didn't volunteer anything, didn't indulge in any "My Hell" posture. I mentioned it to Dorothy at one stage and she told me not to be so ridiculous: of course Miss O'Neill wouldn't stoop to anything like that – she was a genuine person that should be snapped up immediately by any right thinking, red-blooded man. And she was right.

It was exhausting to feel like everyone was watching you every minute of the day, but after a week the intense focus eased a little. And in another week it eased a lot. The media found another story and the police concluded their investigation. Dorothy was told she would have to make herself available to the police investigation, but there was no rush to slap her in handcuffs. Harry Cross said the legals would be lengthy and complex but wouldn't involve charges.

He was a lot more relieved than he made out though. The scale of the coverage meant there was always a danger of officialdom taking longer than normal to make its mind up. And O'Donoghue had been very well connected. However those connections appeared to be more than happy to disassociate themselves from the memory of someone they'd once queued up to be seen with. Behind all the bonhomie, there were plenty it appeared who'd seen at least some of the brutal reality. Nevertheless it was prudent to keep Dorothy out of the limelight for a while. And it was Harry who came to the rescue. He lived in Dublin city centre.

"The best place to hide out is usually right in the middle of the chaos," he declared, and insisted on Dorothy staying with him. "There's loads of room. And as long as you don't try and boss me around too much, it might be fun."

There was something about the two of them that made me suspect there might be something going on. Or there had been at one stage. Harry was devoted to her. And she was uncommonly relaxed and girly around him.

"How do you feel about a step-dad?" Julia had said as we watched them disappear into a large and extremely expensive Georgian townhouse. "I'm not kidding. They're perfect for each other."

"Not like us then," I smiled.

"No, not like us. All we do is get into trouble."

"I kinda like getting into trouble with you."

"Do you now?" she smirked. "Well, I guess it can't be

314

said that you're boring. But can you not be quite so troublesome in the future?"

That seemed reasonable enough, I reckoned. It was certainly a happier thought than some I'd been having: not so much thoughts as nightmares. More than once since that morning, I'd woken up soaked in sweat and hopelessly disorientated, breathing deeply in relief at realising it was just a nightmare. Foley's scream wouldn't go away: neither would the memory of the hot glow and the noise of death powering through that shaft. And there was the sound of the gun failing to go off. Maybe time would lessen their impact; maybe.

Indulging in straightforward physical exertion was a happy contrast. Slipping off the horse and beginning the routine of cleaning him off brought back the memory of when Peter Miller showed up. It felt like a long time ago. In many ways it was. There was a reassurance about being able to get back to normality.

"Back to basics again," a voice said behind me.

John Greening was not one to indulge in too much idle chit-chat. But O'Donoghue's reputation within racing had been Anglo-Irish. The story had been splashed all over the racing pages in Britain too, complete with reports of the ex-jockey's involvement: plenty there for Newmarket's notorious gossip-peddlers to get stuck into.

"Yeah, something like that," I said. "I might take a break from riding out here for a while, John, if that's okay?"

"Hey, you're your own boss. I'm just glad you put up with me for so long."

We chatted for another while, surface stuff, nothing important, comfortable. I gave Rhinestone a rub, fed and watered him, and the climbed into the car and returned to the cottage. Jerry phoned on the way.

"You're not going to believe this," he said. "Apparently there is a *Road to Tarascon* in a shed in Texas – been sitting there for years. The galleries in the States are going crazy."

"The real one?" I said.

"Hey, it's probably as real as the one you sent up in smoke!"

"I didn't put –"

"I know, I know," he interrupted. "God, you're easy to wind up. But you know what I mean. If enough people say it is, then it is, right?"

"Maybe."

"Maybe is enough when you want to believe bad enough," he said. "How're you doing anyway. Sold anything recently?"

"As a matter of fact, yes," I said. "But it won't be any good to you."

"So little is," he sighed theatrically. "Best of luck with it anyway."

"Thanks."

I drove into the driveway of my beloved little cottage and got out of the car. The sign on the front fence was gaudily blue and shiny. Stuck jauntily across it was a bright red sticker: *SOLD*.

Chapter 37

The gloom outside reflected the atmosphere in Harry's office. Myles and Elizabeth and George and Alicia sat rigidly towards one half of the lawyer's desk; Dorothy and I on the other. It felt like sides facing off in some Napoleonic battle, waiting for the first shot to be fired. Harry dolefully pulled the trigger.

"Cut away the legal flannel and the bottom line is that Ardfield was uninsured," he said, gazing intently at a sheet of paper he could probably have recited off by heart.

There was a stunned silence across the invisible border. Dorothy was still staying with Harry and knew a few days before. She'd told me because I had money involved. But her daughters had years of history and were hearing this news fresh.

"That just about puts the cherry on top of this pile of shit, wouldn't you say?" George announced, standing up and clearly preparing to go on a rant.

"Sit down," his wife said, wearily. "We know what it is. There's no need to make things worse."

The Dennings looked resigned. A small smile even played briefly on Myles's lips, like a man whose dark expectations had been met. Overall, the fireworks weren't as bad as feared.

Harry took his opportunity and ploughed on with some more legal jargon about contents and site value. It was all very matter-of-fact and businesslike, unlike the detritus of centuries of family life that stood gutted and grey out in Meath.

The fire-brigade's efforts had been primarily to stop the blaze spreading to the stables. It was too far gone to save the house. Everything had gone. A week later, I'd driven Dorothy out to inspect. We only stayed five minutes. There was nothing to see and too much to remember.

"You'll never be short of a place to live," I said to her, driving away.

"That's very kind of you, Luke, but the last thing you need is an old woman under your feet."

"It's nothing like that."

"I think Julia might have something to say on the matter," she smiled.

"It might have escaped your attention but Julia thinks you're pretty brilliant," I said.

"The feeling is reciprocal. But young lovers need space to discover each other."

It sounded both quaint and formal the way she said it. And also right. Without anything being said, I'd started to stay in Julia's apartment for longer and longer until it couldn't be ignored we were starting to live together. That felt right too. So much didn't have to be articulated. That was the best part, or nearly the best part.

"Don't worry," Dorothy continued. "I'll never be short of a roof."

It seemed better to leave it at that, for the time being anyway.

"The question remains, what do you want to do now?" Harry announced.

There was a pause before anyone spoke. And it was Elizabeth who took the initiative.

"That is something to ponder for us all. And I think it best if we ponder together. The holidays are coming up, Mum. Myles and I would love if you could join us. Maybe stay for a while, until you get sorted out accommodation-wise – give Harry a break!"

Whatever I'd expected out of this meeting, it wasn't that. As a gesture between parent and child it was hardly anything out of the ordinary. In the Maxwell-Williams context, though, it was hands-across-the-water stuff.

"That's very kind of you, Elizabeth," Dorothy replied. "And Myles."

"Of course, you're invited too, Luke," Elizabeth added. "And you can bring whoever you like."

I looked at Myles. He shrugged slightly, contented himself with another little smile and nodded.

"That's great," I said, and meant it.

"In fact," Elizabeth continued. "Why don't we make it a family affair?"

She glanced to her sister.

For once, Alicia's expression was impossible to read. She was clearly tired and drawn. Maybe that was having to keep George's combustible tendencies under control; maybe not. Or the money problems that had propelled their earlier desperation had deepened even further.

Whatever it was, she sounded as tired as she looked.

"I can't believe you thought we were in cahoots with that horrible man," she said quietly, staring straight ahead, and then looking directly at her mother. "I am so hurt by that."

Whatever about the logic of what she said, there was no denying the emotion behind her words. Alicia was so similar to her mother, I noticed. The thin face lived and breathed defiance.

"Alicia, you're my daughter and I love you dearly," Dorothy said. "And I apologise for having hurt you like that."

Not I noticed for believing she might have been involved with O'Donoghue. But if Alicia noticed the distinction, she chose not to acknowledge it. There was a sketchy nod and she stood up. Dorothy did the same and they hugged in the middle of Harry's no-man's-land office. I noticed the older woman whisper something into her daughter's ear.

When they separated, Alicia looked at me.

"I'm not going to lie to you and pretend everything is sweetness and light between us. That would be insulting," she said. "The fact is I don't know you. And you don't know me. And first impressions probably haven't been great – on either side. But the reality is we share a mother. We are siblings. And while the start has been less than ideal, I would like it if we could start to be more cordial to each other, nicer, if you like."

It was quite a brave little speech in its way. I could see even more of my mother in her. There'd been no hesitation in saying what had to be said. And she'd maintained her dignity, not come out with platitudes that would have rung hollow to everyone. There was something there to work on. And in the circumstances that was more than enough.

I stood up and kissed her cheek. She froze momentarily.

"I think you're great," I said.

She looked for irony in my face and decided there wasn't any there. There was a nod, a toss of the hair and she sat back down next to her puzzled-looking husband.

"These are things you have to deal with when your mother has a racy past."

Harry's words hung there for a second, no one quite believing them, until Dorothy burst out laughing. The rest of us joined in, as much through released tension as anything else. Even George managed a smile.

"And I can still manage a bit of a gallop now," Dorothy laughed, although to my ears it suddenly sounded forced. She suddenly found something very interesting on the floor. Maybe Harry's joke was a little too close to the bone for her.

"Actually, I think it's important to point one more thing out," Harry continued hurriedly. Maybe he'd sensed the same thing. "I realise the James Norton offer is still a possibility, and that some of you may be keen to go down the selling road. But the investment company who wanted to use Ardfield aren't walking away. I know it's only a shell now, and you probably can't even think about the future. But if it can be rebuilt, which is possible now that that injunction is no more, then the opportunity to make it viable still exists."

"And what do you propose it is rebuilt with?" Alicia said.

"Your mother may have the answer," Harry responded.

Chapter 38

It was a foul afternoon, freezing rain lashing down, and only a handful of hardy devotees around the parade ring. Most of the sparse crowd had given up by the last race, retreating to their cars and the drive home after a tough day even by the standards of winter jump racing in Ireland.

But the hardy souls that remained were purposeful. Punters mostly, interested in betting on the last race, the bumper, those two-mile flat races for prospective young jumpers, designed to give inexperienced horses some racecourse experience but which in reality were school exams designed to establish a quick pecking order of potential talent. And gamblers liked them because there were no jumps to send their money crashing out at the last, and because bookmakers were mostly in the dark about horses that had never raced before.

Standing in the middle of Navan's long parade ring, it wasn't punters that caught my eye. In a corner by the weighroom were two men in green wax jackets, staring intently at the twenty runners plodding around for pre-race inspection.

"The one on the right is Jennings, buys a lot for the top trainer in Britain," Dorothy explained. "The other one's name is Beresford. He's the racing manager for Sir Matthew Cryer. They're always on the lookout for good prospects."

"Rich?" I asked.

"Filthy," she replied. "Ideally, you'd love to have the two of those competing against each other."

"So if we win this, what sort of money are we talking about?"

"Good young horses going to England can make up to half a million," she said.

"No pressure then," I laughed, a little nervously.

"Just get yourself and the horse back safely. That's all that counts," she urged.

Spirit of Michael plodded around looking disinterested. The young girl leading him leaned forward into the wind and rain, no doubt grateful for her waterproof gear. He gave the impression a quick detour back to the warmth of his stable might suit him. The impulsive energy of his racecourse gallop looked to be gone.

That was a relief. This was the first time in over a decade for me to venture onto to a racecourse competitively. Gallops were one thing. This was a different world: everyone for themselves. Any weakness would be pounced upon and taken advantage of. That last thing I needed was to spend my time fighting a horse wanting to go too fast on ground that was too slow and testing for extravagance.

"He's actually bred to go on the heavy going," Dorothy said. "His sister loved it – won a couple of races on the very soft."

I nodded, feeling damp soak into the thin riding boots, and turning my back on the wind. Light enough to make the twelve-stone weight requirement not an issue, I had a couple of T-shirts on underneath the back-protector and silks, yet still felt very cold. How much of that was due to nerves was something best not to ponder too deeply.

It felt both strange and familiar to be standing in silks, going through the old routine of checking out the opposition, which of them looked fit and which didn't, chatting about nothing, trying to picture the various permutations of the race ahead. That felt instantly familiar. What didn't was not feeling hungry. And having an emotional rather than professional interest in the outcome was different too. But White Nose – I would always call him that – did look well.

"He's been doing good. I think he might be very decent."

Colm McDonald joined us and launched into a pep-talk, designed I guessed to boost his rider, not his own expectations. He'd wanted his usual stable amateur to ride, argued he'd done most of the day-to-day work with Spirit of Michael. I had no problem with that. He was right. Taking the kid off after putting the work in was unfair, especially for a thirty-five-year-old ex-flat jockey who might fall off with exhaustion trying to push a big, strapping gelding through glue-like muck. But Dorothy had insisted. And McDonald conceded to the inevitable.

The trainer gave me a leg up and retreated back to his owner who delivered a thumbs-up. We did a circuit of the ring, the stable-girl resolutely walking ahead and barely acknowledging me. I wondered if McDonald's keenness to have his own man on board might have something to do with wanting to get a bet on. Dorothy had told me he liked a flutter on his own horses. Maybe the girl was the same. After all, she knew Spirit of Michael better than anyone, dealt with him every day. Was my presence putting her off having a few quid on?

The red-lights on the bookies electronic boards shone through the gloom. I glanced over at the prices. Spirit of Michael – number 17 – was a 16-1 outsider, unusual for a McDonald horse in a bumper. No doubt it was due to the unfamiliar jockey who'd been granted a licence just days before. The old competitive urge started to pump again. We'll just have to show a few people, I thought, patting the horse on the neck.

I'd lowered the irons a few notches compared to when riding professionally. It would be a little easier on my out-of-practice leg muscles and also allow me fit in a little better among my colleagues. Most were youngsters starting out and hoping to become the next big thing in the pro ranks. But there were a few professional amateurs too. Mark Maguire was among them, on the favourite, and conspicuously staying out of my way.

McDonald had kept instructions to a minimum, just said the horse was fit and ride him as I found him. When the tape was released I took a deep breath and a good hold of White Nose's mouth. The last thing I needed was him carting me away. He had to settle if he was to last out the two-mile trip.

And he did. There was a brief fifty yards of head-tossing anxiety to get on with things but he then took my lead and dropped the bit. I felt worse for the stable amateur who'd taught him so well and even happier for myself.

The pace was a crawl but understandably so. I steered White Nose to the outside to avoid any traffic problems and also to try and get him on some ground that hadn't been chewed to ribbons in the earlier races. Even with daylight in front him, he didn't take off. We settled into a comfortable rhythm as we passed the post the first time, lying seventh and going easy.

Maguire was on the inside in fourth and I used him as my touchstone. He knew the pace to go. We were a few lengths off him and travelling really well. Down the back stretch, I found out again why riding a racehorse could be so intoxicating. White Nose was under control, but only just. There was a wildness and an extravagance to him that let me know he could take charge anytime he damn well pleased. If he'd been good in the gallop, he was even better now.

Dorothy was right. The ground was no trouble. After just a mile, half of the field were finished, finding the pace and the conditions too much. White Nose glided over it as if on a carpet. It was no effort to him. If McDonald was right and fitness was assured, then we had a chance.

Maguire went to the front just after the turn in to the long near-half-mile final straight. I noticed he peeped over his shoulder at me just beforehand. No doubt he remembered the outsider from that gallop at Fairyhouse and reckoned the way to beat him was to stretch out early.

But this time White Nose was fit. And his rider gratefully found out he wasn't entirely unfit either. A squeeze of the calves, a click of the tongue, and a gathering of the reins signalled it was time to get serious and the horse leapt into the bit, relishing the chance to go faster. It was remarkable. Plenty horses when asked to move from cruising into work-mode decided cruising was easier. This one relished the job. I knew the talent was there. Now the attitude to match it emerged.

Maguire's whip was up when we reached him at the two-furlong pole. I hadn't asked White Nose for anything serious. And I didn't want to. Avoiding the whip was important, a last resort. I was out of practice. There was a good chance all it would achieve was to get the horse unbalanced.

But his remorseless gallop overrode everything. Curling up behind the mane as much as possible, I concentrated on not getting in the way. White Nose was more than up to the job. For the last hundred yards we were clear. My legs gave up but it didn't matter. We passed the post with me standing up in the irons to the sound of silence from the stands. Outsiders were never popular.

He slowed to a walk. I tried to catch my breath and patted him repeatedly on the neck, telling him he was a great guy. Taking it all as his due, he even pricked his ears as Maguire's horse trotted wearily past him. White Nose didn't like being passed like that. The instinct to get to the front of the herd was deep within him. This horse was going to be very good.

The stable-girl was a lot happier running out to meet us, plenty of smiles and slaps on the horse's neck. I even got a quick "Well done!" myself. If anything the rain came down even harder but nothing could impinge on the moment for everyone concerned. McDonald appeared beside us, his hand on the bottom of my boot.

"By Christ, boy, that was great. Well done. The two of ye looked great," he grinned.

"He's a lot better than very decent," I said, leaning down. "He's got bags of talent – and he likes the game – wants to win."

"Yeah?" McDonald said.

He knew so much of racing came down to attitude. There was nothing more frustrating than talent that wouldn't try. To find out so early a horse was sound on that score was important.

"If he can jump, he'll be some horse for you," I added.

"Oh, he can jump," the trainer said. "I've schooled him already. Don't worry. He can jump all right."

There was a tiny smattering of applause as we stopped in the No. 1 spot. Dorothy stood there, looking tiny, and cold, and quietly ecstatic. She delivered a thumbs-up to me, and to a photographer snatching pictures of the winners. I knew a little how she felt. It was all I could do not to laugh out loud. But it was still only a little of what a woman who bred such a horse could experience. The satisfaction was written all over her. Slipping out of the saddle, it was impossible to resist: I gave her a hug and a big kiss on the cheek.

"Oh, that was wonderful," she said to McDonald. "Isn't he wonderful?"

"He's something else," I agreed.

"And the horse isn't bad either," Dorothy smiled.

We posed for more photos, I passed questions from the few reporters present on to the finest trainer in Ireland and walked back to weigh in much the same way White Nose had travelled over the wet turf – hardly feeling the ground.

An official asked me to join the winning party for a trophy ceremony and I followed him out. A bulky figure got into step beside me.

"Aren't you the Delamere that rode on the flat?" a rich English accent said.

"That's me."

"John Beresford," he said, holding out his hand. "That's a damn nice horse you rode there. Is he for sale?"

"Anything's for sale at the right price," I responded. "But you'll have to talk to my mother who owns him."

Fifty yards away Dorothy was chatting amiably to a figure I recognised as Jennings.

"Looks like you might have a little competition," I said.

"Lucky you," Beresford replied.

"Lucky me."

The End

Leabharlanna Poibli Chathair Bhaile Átha Cliath
Dublin City Public Libraries

Now that you're hooked, why not try
Threaten to Win Chapter One, also by
Brian O'Connor, as a taster

Threaten to Win

Brian O'Connor
Threaten to Win

Chapter 1

After a couple of hours he emerged. The stocky figure briefly stood outside his red-brick house on the expensive South Dublin road and inhaled deeply. Despite it being close to summer he was heavily wrapped up in a coat and scarf. Long grey hair swept untidily out from underneath a tweed cap. One more appreciative breath and he skipped down the steps and walked towards where I was sitting in my car.

There were barely fifty metres between us but it felt like an age as he approached. I got out and stood on the footpath. I still wasn't sure what I was going to do, or what I wanted to do. It was a new experience. How are you supposed to behave with someone who has torn your life apart?

His stride shortened when he saw me but he didn't stop. Pulling iPlayer leads out of his ears, he pulled the strap of his laptop case higher over his shoulder and thrust his hands into his coat pockets. But that deeply tanned face that had plagued my sleep looked anxious. I stood there, still trying to decide what to do.

Logically, I found it hard to be outraged. It was a male thing after all, making the most of an opportunity. What man hadn't at some stage been at least tempted? Logic, though, doesn't apply when that opportunity is your wife.

Other gender generalisations had been swirling in my head too, like how sex is always the woman's choice. No doubt there were any number of exceptions to that rule but Cammie was not the sort to be cajoled or intimidated into anything she didn't want to do.

There had certainly been nothing indecisive about the way she had run to Thorpe outside the city-centre hotel just a week earlier. The pair of them had kissed intensely in full view before going inside. I'd stayed in the car then.

They actually made sense as a couple: both musicians, both artistic, both much more in thrall to the cerebral than a broken-up ex-steeplechase jockey. Camilla's passion for music was rivalled only by her passion for our child: Max, a tiny two-year-old bundle of energy that had transformed everything. But there wasn't a time Cammie could remember when her musical love didn't exist and even motherhood couldn't shake it.

The biggest regret of her life was not being able to play it well enough. I looked in awe at her hands sweeping over the piano keys, but she dismissed her playing as merely competent. There was regret in her voice when she said that, but not pain. Years of practice had got her so far, but no further. She likened it to being able to ride a horse but not being good enough to compete. Since I'd spent much of my adult life competing, she'd often said she envied me the proficiency I'd developed.

It was that open-hearted enthusiasm that had first

attracted me to the terribly well-bred daughter of an old and still tolerably rich Anglo-Irish family. That, and a smile saved from perfection by a little gap between her front teeth, which could drive me insane with desire when combined with a look from dark eyes that never attempted to hide their owner's open and hearty attitude to love. The fact Cammie also possessed tawny skin, long almost jet-black hair and a leanly magnificent body only deepened my despair at the idea of this man enjoying it.

Thorpe had slowed almost to a standstill. He was forty-nine, a decade older than me, Australian, and a piano virtuoso married to an Irishwoman. An internet search had revealed the details. The idea of contacting his wife and telling her how our respective partners had been having an affair had briefly flashed across my mind and then disappeared. It wouldn't achieve anything and nothing would change. Better to spare the woman that.

He was shorter than my six feet but heavier. A never-ending battle with weight when I was riding hadn't resulted in any ballooning when I stopped: still tall, still thin. But with ten years on my side and still reasonable fitness, there was little doubt in my mind I would be able to hurt this man.

It had been an afterthought to come here. The spirit-sapping domestic dramatics had consumed the last week. What did it matter who Cammie had gone off with? She'd gone, that was all that mattered. She'd risked everything we had to furtively meet this older guy who probably couldn't believe his luck to be pursued by her. She really was too old for hero-worship, too classy and stylish to be some groupie. And yet she'd still gone with him.

I wanted very much to hate this guy, and hurt him,

indulge in a violent physical release that would make this abstract pain disappear, however briefly. Who cared how stupidly macho it might seem? Some things needed to be done. Parse it down any which way and he was still fucking my wife.

There was a tic under Thorpe's eye. It flickered again and he touched it with a finger to make it stop. I could see him glancing sideways, maybe wondering if there was anybody to shout to for help. But if he was worried it didn't stop him walking straight towards me.

He was close enough for me to smell his aftershave, just a couple of metres away and aiming to walk straight past me. Our eyes were locked on each other. I balled my fists and willed myself to hit him, to smash that stubbled, ruddy face into a pulp, to make him and her suffer.

But I didn't. He walked past, and I did nothing. Just let him by. My arms felt like they belonged to someone else. I could hear Thorpe striding away quickly. Then I heard him shout "Taxi!"

He smiled at me as the car pulled away.

Also by published by Poolbeg

Brian O'Connor
Bloodline

Liam Dee's world is turned upside down when a young
foreign groom is murdered at Bailey McFarlane's stables
on the Curragh. Liam, a champion steeplechase jockey, is
initially both witness and suspect. However, shrewd police
detective Diarmuid Yeats takes a gamble on his innocence
and enlists his help in the hunt for the killer.

This nightmare experience exacerbates the tensions in
Liam's life. He has been falling out of love with his job, his
joy in racing relentlessly worn away by the struggle to keep
the weight down on his six-foot frame. Is it time to quit?
But McFarlane's stables houses the brilliant Patrician, a
potential Cheltenham Gold Cup winner, and Liam wants
to be the jockey to get him first past the finish post in the
race that matters most.

With emotions at pressure point, Liam falls in love with
the exotic blonde Ukrainian stable girl, Lara, leaving him
in an even more vulnerable position than before.
Then the killer strikes again and the race to the finish post
is replaced by a race for survival . . . and there is no second
place.

ISBN 978-184223-4860

POOLBEG WISHES TO

THANK YOU

for buying a Poolbeg book.

If you enjoyed this why not
visit our website:

www.poolbeg.com

and get another book delivered straight
to your home or to a friend's home!

All books despatched within 24 hours.

POOLBEG

WHY NOT JOIN OUR MAILING LIST
@ www.poolbeg.com and get some
fantastic offers on Poolbeg books

@PoolbegBooks